SMALL TOWN LAWYER

Defending Innocence

Influencing Justice

Interpreting Guilt

Peter Kirkland is a pen name created by Relay Publishing for co-authored Legal Thriller projects. Relay Publishing works with incredible teams of writers and editors to collaboratively create the very best stories for our readers.

www.relaypub.com

SMALL TOWN LAWYER - BOOK ONE

DEFENDING INNOCENCE

PETER KIRKLAND

BLURB

An innocent client harbors dark secrets...

Defense attorney Leland Monroe lost it all: his big-city job, his reputation and, worst of all, his loving wife. Now he's back in his hometown to hit restart and repair the relationship with his troubled son. But the past is always present in a small town.

Leland returns to find his high school sweetheart hasn't had the easiest of lives—especially now that her son faces a death sentence for murdering his father. Yet what appears to be an open and shut case is anything but. As Leland digs deeper to uncover a truth even his client is determined to keep buried, a tangled web of corruption weaves its way throughout his once tranquil hometown.

Leland soon realizes it's not just his innocent young client's life that's at stake—powerful forces surface to threaten the precious few loved ones he has left.

CONTENTS

1

MONDAY, JUNE 10, 2019

The Ocean View Diner, where I was waiting for my fried shrimp basket, was a dump with a view of nothing but the courthouse parking lot. It was already shabby when I was in high school, living on fries and coffee while I brainstormed the college application essays that were my ticket out. Much to the surprise of folks in my home-town, I'd made it to law school and beyond. I owned more than a dozen suits. I had tan for summers in the office, navy for opening statements to the jury, charcoal for talking to the media on the Charleston courthouse steps. My kid had admired me at an age when it was almost unnatural to think your dad was anything but a loser. I was a law-and-order guy trying to make the world safer. I'd thought I might run for office.

I nodded to the bailiff who walked through the door giving him a cordial "howdy", but he looked right through me, as he walked past. We'd certainly seen enough of each other in the courthouse, and I tried not to take offense at the slight, but there's only so much a man can put up with when it comes to small town judgment.

They say pride goeth before a fall.

I'd seen enough, in my past life representing the great state of South Carolina, to know a man could have it a lot worse. The amount of depravity and human misery that had flowed across my desk reminded me that I ought to be grateful for what I still had left. My son, in other words, and my license to practice. I'd nearly lost both. The accident that took my wife had nearly killed him too, and even if he still hadn't entirely recovered from it, he'd come farther than anyone expected at the time. But Noah was incredibly angry all the time. Mostly at me but I tried not to let it get to me.

Like water off a duck's back, the little things ought not to have bothered me at all. It shouldn't have mattered that the locals at the next table had stopped talking when I walked in, apparently suspicious of anyone who wasn't a regular. Which I wasn't yet, since it'd been barely six months since I dragged my sorry ass back from the big city. Getting to be a regular took years.

A better man would not have been annoyed by the smell of rancid grease or the creak of ancient ceiling fans. It was even hotter in here than in the June glare outside, and a good man would've sympathized with my waitress, who was stuck here all day and probably never even got to sit down.

But I was not that man. I did say "Thank you kindly" when she dropped my order on the table and sloshed another dose of coffee in my cup, but I was irrationally annoyed that no one had ever fixed the menu sign on the wall between the cash register and the kitchen. The word "cheeseburger" was still missing its first R. When my friends and I were sixteen-year-old jackasses, we thought it was hilarious to order a "cheese booger." Now it was just pathetic that I was back. Especially since the reason I wasn't in the new '50s-style diner on the next corner—the popular lunch place for judges, local politicians, and successful attorneys—was that I couldn't afford it. Here, in exchange for tolerating the broken AC and worn-out furniture, I ate decent shrimp at prices that were fifteen or twenty years behind the times.

The folks at the next table had gotten back to jawing, though at a lower volume on account of me being unfamiliar, I supposed. Between crunches of my dinner, I caught the gist: a body had washed ashore a little ways down the coast, where tourists rented beach houses. Maybe I shouldn't have eavesdropped, but although I wasn't a prosecutor anymore, I was probably never going to lose the habit of keeping a close eye on every local crime.

"Bunch of rich tourists were playing volleyball on the beach," the man said. "You know, girls in their bikinis, one of them thousand-dollar gas grills fired up on the deck." His voice held a mix of humor and scorn. "They were having themselves just a perfect vacation. And then this *corpse* washes up! This, I swear to you, a decomposing *corpse* crashed the party!"

The table erupted with guffaws.

"So what'd they do?" a man said. "Hop in their Subarus and hightail it back to New York or wherever?"

"No, the thing is—and I heard this from my cousin, you know, the one working for the sheriff? The thing is, they thought a gator got him! Thought they had a gator in the water! And I'll be damned if they weren't pissing themselves like little girls, trying to get everybody back out of the water. Couple of them were so scared they started puking!"

They all lost it. One of them was so entertained he slammed a hand on the table, rattling the silverware. As the laughter started fading, one of them wondered aloud who the dead man might be.

"Aw, don't matter none," the storyteller said. "We ain't missing nobody."

I felt a sourness in my gut. I couldn't go a day here without being reminded why I'd left. In Basking Rock, compassion for your fellow man was strictly circumscribed. Tourists got none. The wrong kind of people, whatever that meant, got none. Your family and lifelong friends could do no wrong, and everybody else could go straight to hell.

I signaled the waitress and asked for a doggie bag. Might as well finish eating at home, away from present company. She scowled, probably thinking I was switching to takeout to avoid leaving a tip. I scrounged through my wallet, sure I'd had a few ones in there and grudgingly set down a five knowing I was leaving more than necessary. Making any kind of enemy was not my style. You never knew who might help you out one day, if you'd taken care not to get on their bad side. More to the point, I knew from friends who worked in health code enforcement that there were few things stupider than making enemies of the folks who make your food.

I'd parked my Chevy outside. It used to be the beater, until the nice car was totaled in the accident. When I fired it up, the engine light came on again. I kept right on ignoring it. I'd yet to find a local mechanic I could trust. The one I knew of had been a bully back in high school, and from what I'd heard, age had only refined his techniques. If he thought you'd gotten too big for your britches—which I certainly had, what with my law degree and my former big-city career —he took his rage out on your wallet.

The Chevy heroically made it home once again. I parked beside the clump of fan palms that were starting to block the driveway. I needed to get them pruned, and to fix the wobbly porch railing that would've been a lawsuit waiting to happen if we ever had visitors. I needed a haircut. My geriatric Yorkie, Squatter, who limped to the door to greet me, needed a trip to the vet. The to-do list never stopped growing, and checking anything off it required money I no longer had.

I tossed the mail on the table and scratched the dog on the head. He'd come with the house—the landlord said he'd been abandoned by the previous tenants, and I couldn't bring myself to dump him at the pound. As he wagged his tail, I called out to my son. "Noah?"

All I could hear was the breeze outside and Squatter's nails scrabbling on the tile. I was no scientist—my major, long ago when I thought I was smart, was US history—but I knew physics did not allow a house to be that quiet if it contained a teenage boy. It looked like I'd be eating another dinner alone. I'd texted Noah when I got to the diner, to see if he wanted anything, but he hadn't answered. I never knew where he was lately, unless he was at a doctor's appointment I'd driven him to myself.

After feeding Squatter I pulled up a chair, took a bite of now-cold shrimp, and flipped through the mail. The monthly health insurance bill—nearly thirteen hundred bucks just for the two of us—went into the small pile of things I couldn't get out of paying. Noah's physical therapy bills did too; as long as he still needed PT, I couldn't risk getting blacklisted there.

And he was going to need it for a good while yet, to have a shot at something like the life he'd been hoping for. We were both still hanging on to the thread of hope that he could get back into the shape that had earned him a baseball scholarship to USC in Columbia. The accident had cost him that, but he was determined to try again.

Or so he'd said at first. Lately he'd gotten depressed with how long it was taking, and how much fun he saw his high-school buddies having on Instagram. They'd gone to college and moved on with their lives. He'd started making new friends here, but to my dismay, they were not what you'd call college bound. College didn't seem to have occurred to them. One worked in a fast-food joint, and another didn't seem to work much at all.

I heard gravel crunching in the driveway. Even without the odd rhythm his limp gave him, I knew it had to be Noah; our little bungalow was an okay place to eat and sleep but too small to be much of a gathering place. I stuffed the bills into my battered briefcase. He didn't need to know we were struggling.

Squatter raced to the door to celebrate Noah's return and accompanied him back to the kitchen in a state of high canine excitement. Noah looked a little glum, or bored, as usual. Without bothering to say hi, he poured himself some tea from the fridge, sat down in the chair next to mine, and took one of my shrimp.

"I would've brought you some," I said. "I texted you from the diner."

He shrugged. "I didn't see it in time," he said, feeding the crispy tail to Squatter.

"That's a shame," I said. "What were you so busy doing?"

He glared at me. That look was a one-two punch every time. He had his mother's eyes, so it felt like the hostility was coming from both of them.

I knew I should back off, but I was never good at drawing the line in the right place. "Hanging out with Jackson again?"

He took another shrimp, got up, and went into the living room. At fourteen, Noah had perfected the art of sullen teenager. Now at nineteen, he'd turned it into a lost art as he immersed himself in the depression and apathy that comes with having your life turned completely upside down.

I was a big believer in surrounding yourself with people who had similar goals. Or at least not with people who'd just drag you down. Jackson wouldn't have been my first, second, or twelfth choice of friends for Noah. He was a troubled kid. Maybe it was time for me to admit that Noah was too, and not because of Jackson. We'd gone downhill as a family. It was as much my own fault as anyone's; although most days, I felt as though Noah blamed me for all of it. Many of those days, I was sick and tired of being on the receiving end of my son's anger. For a man who made his living talking, I couldn't seem to make any headway with my son.

In my head I apologized to Elise. She'd been dead nearly a year and I still talked to her, sometimes out loud. She would've wanted me to make peace with our son.

So I tried: "Y'all have fun, at least? I hope it was a pretty good day."

"We hung out on his porch," he said, digging in the couch cushions for the TV remote. "If that counts as fun." From his tone of voice, it didn't.

He found the remote and turned the TV on.

Later that night, when Noah had gone to his room to do whatever he did there, I parked in front of the TV to catch the local news. The big story was the body that had washed up. Unlike the guys at the diner, the newscaster displayed suitable respect for human life. "The condition of the man's body," as she put it, made identification difficult, but police were treating it as a homicide. She asked the public for assistance. A toll-free number scrolled across the screen.

Then she went from murder to town council elections, and I was glad to have the mental image of a decomposing corpse replaced with the perfectly healthy, smiling face of a man I remembered from high school. Henry Carrell was seeking another term. I didn't know how he had time, what with running the yacht charter company he'd inherited from his dad. He'd brought the company back from the brink of ruin, bringing a much-needed influx of tourists and jobs, and the town regularly rewarded him with reelection.

It was strange to see a guy I knew from high school on TV. It was strange to be back here and recognize so many people and see they hadn't really changed.

If the man whose body had washed up was from around here, I thought, chances are I'd known him too. I hoped not.

2

TUESDAY, JUNE 11, MORNING

The next morning, Noah was gone before I got up. I wrestled down the urge to text him. At nineteen, he had the right to start living his own life. As I mixed my coffee, I reminded myself that worrying about him wasn't helping my concentration any. I had to keep my eyes on the prize: building my fledgling practice into something that could keep us afloat. I'd gone straight from law school to the solicitor's office—what most states call the prosecutor's office—and had never learned the first thing about landing clients or running a business. It turned out all that was at least as important as legal acumen.

I was working for one of Basking Rock's only prominent lawyers, Roy Hearst. "Of counsel": a nice title on paper, but at Roy's firm it didn't come with a salary or benefits. Roy paid me hourly when I did work for him, and I was free to bring in my own clients if I could land them. I got a free office, and he got a bonus for his business clients: whenever some friend or relative of theirs ran into trouble—the usual DUIs or their kids' frat-boy drunk and disorderlies—he had a former prosecutor right there in his office to help them get out of it. A one-stop shop.

And I should've gone straight there—it was past eight—but when I opened the cabinet, I noticed Mazie's casserole dish. Jackson's mom had taken to dropping off home-cooked food once in a while. I didn't know if it was out of sympathy or if Noah had complained to her about my cooking skills. Either way, I had to return the dish at some point, and her house wasn't that far out of the way. Dropping by would let me see if that's where Noah had gone.

I wrapped the dish in a towel and drove over. Mazie lived on the far edge of town, right on the marsh, with a distant ocean view obscured by clouds of mosquitoes. She'd come down in life since high school, when we had dated. I'd gone off to college, and she'd followed the same sad path so many did: pregnant by some loser, a mother before she was twenty, and it never got better from there. I couldn't blame Jackson for being troubled.

I parked on the dirt road out front. Their rental was vinyl-sided hurricane bait, hardly more than a trailer. I made a mental note that if we had any big storms this season, I'd invite them to stay on an air mattress in our living room. At least we were a little ways inland.

She answered the door in a flurry, distracted, tying on her waitress apron.

"You just go on through to the kitchen," she said, heading back into what must've been her bedroom. "I'm running late. There's coffee on the counter. Help yourself."

From the room down the hall I heard thrash metal, muffled only slightly by the closed door. Jackson was evidently home. His taste in music didn't blend well with the modern country playing on the kitchen radio. I reached out to turn the radio off, thinking that even muffled metal might be better than the clash of both songs playing at once, but stopped before touching the dial. It wasn't my house; I should mind my own business.

Mazie walked in as I was putting her casserole dish away. Seeing her gave me déjà vu. She'd waitressed during high school too, and even though that place no longer existed, there was only so much variety in waitress uniforms.

As I closed the cabinet door, she said, "Aw, you didn't have to do that."

"Looks like you're in a hurry," I said. "Didn't want you to take the time. It was delicious, by the way. Thank you for thinking of us."

"You're very welcome." With a little smile she added, "That boy of yours is too dang skinny anyway."

"Well, you sure are helping him fill out." I saw her glance at the clock; her hectic face got slightly calmer, so I figured she must have a little time. "Why don't you sit here for a moment? I can pour you a cup."

"That'd be nice," she said. "Especially since I'll be pouring other people's coffee all day long."

When she got close enough, sitting down on the other side of the Formica counter, I could see she looked exhausted. The kitchen faced the ocean, and the morning light wasn't kind.

"Everything okay?" I asked. "I know my boy comes around a lot. Please let me know if it's too much."

She waved that off. "No, it's fine," she said. "He was here this morning, if that's what you're wondering."

I must've looked a little embarrassed, because she added, "I'm a mother. We worry. Good parents, I mean, not just mothers. I know what it's like."

I shook my head at the strangeness of parenthood, wishing for about the millionth time that Elise was still here. When she was sober, she was one of the best mothers I'd ever seen. That line of thought wasn't anything I'd share with Mazie, so I said, "Yeah, by the time you start getting the hang of whatever phase they're in, it's over and they're in a new one."

A flick of her eyebrows said, "Isn't that the truth."

"So what phase is yours in now?"

She exhaled, a sound of pure frustration. "When his bike was in the shop, that boy racked up so many parking tickets I'm still paying them off. Had to take extra shifts to keep the car from getting impounded."

"Surely he doesn't make you pay them all?"

"No, he pays what he can. Thank the Lord he's got that job at the hardware store."

"Oh, I thought—wasn't he at the burger place on the beach?"

"Last summer, yeah. When winter came he got in with the hardware store, and it just worked out better. But, you know, to get there on time he'll drop me off and then park wherever and run on in. He ain't working today, otherwise we would've had to leave ten minutes ago."

"Any chance Karl could help out with the tickets?" Karl was the loser who'd gotten her pregnant way back when.

She gave a bitter laugh. "You kidding me? Him?"

"I mean, even if it isn't his car, it's still his son. And, I thought, he owes you big time for raising Jackson." I wasn't privy to details, but Karl didn't seem like the kind who'd pay regular child support.

"Forget it," she said. There was anger in her voice that I'd never heard before. "I ain't seen him since last week, and he was about as bad as he's ever been. I'd do double shifts the rest of my life before I'd ask for money from him."

I figured that meant Karl had fallen off the wagon again. I was trying to think of something to say when Jackson came out of his room. Or so I inferred from the fact the thrash metal stopped and I heard a door slam.

As heavy steps shook the cheap flooring, Mazie called out, "Baby? Don't leave without breakfast. Come on in here. I got a few minutes to make you something."

Jackson loomed in the doorway. He was tall, and nearly as skinny as Noah. He wasn't a bad-looking kid, although the black eye he was sporting didn't enhance things any. I'd seen enough crime-scene photos to know the greenish color meant the injury was at least a few days old. I wondered what had happened. Noah hadn't mentioned anything, but then I wasn't exactly his confidant.

Jackson grunted hello, went to the cabinet, and grabbed two packs of Pop-Tarts from a box. He was wearing what I assumed was a band T-shirt. It was covered with skulls and said, if I was reading the spiky font correctly, "HateSphere." I couldn't help but notice scabs on his knuckles and scrapes on the back of his hands. A whole catalog of photos popped up in my brain: impact injuries, possible defensive wounds. I remembered the fights young men around here got into. When I was his age, sometimes it seemed like we'd fight just for the lack of anything better to do.

As Jackson left, kissing his mom on the top of her head but ignoring her insistence that he should eat something real, he trailed a faint stink of cigarettes.

The door slammed. Mazie looked a little ashamed. I got the feeling something was up. She tossed the last of her coffee down and got up without meeting my eye.

We went out. As she locked the front door behind us, I said, "You know, if Jackson's ever in trouble, I'd gladly talk to him. I know sometimes kids his age talk easier with folks who aren't their parents."

"We're fine," she said. "Or, I mean, as good as we can be." She headed down the steps, still talking as I walked with her to her rusted-out car. "When Karl came by last week, things got a little rough. He'd been drinking." She rammed her car keys into the lock and pulled the door open. "Jackson had to defend himself. And me, a little bit."

"I'm sorry," I said. "No boy should be getting a black eye from his own father."

She turned and looked up at me. "I know you're sorry," she said softly. The sunlight caught her eyes, which in high school had been a brighter shade of blue. Life had worn every part of her down. She looked away. "I gotta go. Another day, another parking ticket paid off."

She got in and slammed the door. I waited until the engine turned over —it sounded like I wasn't the only one with car trouble—and then walked back to my Chevy.

As I put my seat belt on, I realized she hadn't used hers. Maybe she was past caring, or maybe it was just broken. I wished I could toss some money her way to help out. But it's true what they say about putting on your own oxygen mask first.

Before I shifted into drive, my phone rang. It was Roy.

"Hey there," I said. "I'm on my way. I read those depositions last night, and I think we got what we need to bring the insurer to the table. Have you and the client talked settlement numbers yet?"

"Oh," he said, like he had completely forgotten about the insurance case. "Yeah, thanks. Sounds good. Hey, you won't believe what I heard this morning."

"What's that?"

"I stopped by the sheriff's," he said. "To see about that fundraiser for his reelection campaign. He told me Karl Warton's boat was found on St. Helena Island, run aground. No sign of Karl."

"Huh," I said. I was glad Mazie was already gone.

"You a gambling man? Fifty bucks says Karl's the floater that washed up yesterday."

I said, "Wouldn't that be something." Some people have a poker face; I have a poker voice. I didn't want him to hear anything from me but semi-interested politeness. "Well, anyway, I'll be in shortly."

I hung up, wondering about Jackson's injuries and the anger in Mazie's voice.

3

TUESDAY, JUNE 11, LATER THAT MORNING

I passed through our tiny historic downtown, which had more charm than I could afford, and headed out Sea Island Causeway with my windows down. The smell of the tidal marsh was a constant, so strong with salt and muck and life that you'd catch a whiff as soon as you exited the airport in Charleston. Back when we could afford to travel sometimes, that smell was how I knew I was home.

I tried not to think about Karl. With his motorboat being found on the island, the way the currents ran made it more than reasonable to think the washed-up body was his. I figured he must've gone out boating and fallen. Liquor and boats weren't a good combination.

I knew what it was like to lose people. If the father of her child was dead, I didn't want Mazie to get the news from anyone but a friend. That pretty much left me. I reached for my phone. As hers rang, though, I reminded myself there wasn't any actual news yet. Her phone went to voicemail, and I hung up.

Seagulls squawked as I turned into the little six-car parking lot that showed, along with a sign, that the gray bungalow beyond it was a lawyer's office and not some old-timer's home. The sign didn't have my name on it and never would. This was Roy's territory. If the sign didn't make that clear enough, the point was repeated by the "ROY 1" vanity plates on the steel-blue BMW 760 parked out front.

This morning a silver Mercedes was parked beside it. A client, I supposed. I hoped the day would come soon when I'd have clients who drove cars like that.

Roy had mentored me when I was in law school, back when older partners like him wrote briefs longhand on yellow legal pads or dictated them to their secretaries. He'd just made name partner at that point, making the firm's name Benton & Hearst. Now old Mr. Benton had died, and Roy reigned supreme. Our long-ago connection was the official reason he'd taken me on: a desire to help someone he still saw as a kid, despite my thinning hair flecked with gray.

The unofficial reason, which was as tangible as the humidity but not something he'd ever admit, was that witnessing my daily humiliation —my ancient Chevy, my phone that never rang—made him feel all the more successful himself. Sixteen years in Charleston, appearing on the news to announce wins against major criminals, and I was still his underling.

As I walked in, I smelled coffee. Roy's secretary, Laura, always made a fresh pot when clients were expected. From his office I heard laughter of the back-slapping type—this client must be a long-standing one, or an old friend—and then a man I recognized came out, followed by Roy. It was councilman Henry Carrell, dressed for his reelection campaign in navy pinstripes. I couldn't imagine he wore suits like that when he was down at the marina renting out yachts, or whatever his day-to-day activities were.

"Morning, Leland!" Roy said. "Let me introduce you two. This is my old friend Henry Carrell. He operates Blue Seas Yacht Charter."

"Morning, Henry," I said, heading over for the obligatory handshake. I told Roy, "Everyone knows Henry. We went to high school together, although we were a couple years apart."

"Oh yeah!" Henry was doing a kind of double-pistol thing with his hands, a *Hey, buddy* gesture, although he didn't actually look like he remembered me.

"Oh," I said, "best of luck in your council race. Not that you need it."

They laughed, though I wasn't sure what the joke was.

"I tell you what, Leland," Roy said. "You want people to take you seriously around here? You got to either get rich or get yourself elected to something. Henry here did both."

Henry smiled and said, "No, but—you interested in politics? Give me a call if you are. Now, if you'll excuse me."

"Well, Leland sure isn't interested in business," Roy said. "Don't get me wrong, he's a damn-good lawyer or he wouldn't be under my roof, but he's got all the business skills of a French poodle. A client shows up, he just sits there in his basket, shivering."

Another round of laughter. Then Henry asked, "You're the ex-prosecutor, right? Handling criminal defense now for Roy?" I didn't know whether he meant to salvage my dignity or if he just wanted my vote. "I hope I don't need you," he went on, "but I might. I employ some sailors, obviously, and sometimes they do stupid shit ashore."

Roy laughed.

"And not just sailors," Henry said. "Roy got one of my Warton brothers off on a careless driving charge a year or two ago. I take it that's your bailiwick now? Or one of them?"

"Glad to help with anything," I said.

"Oh," said Roy. "Speaking of Wartons, you wouldn't have heard yet, but they found Karl's boat run aground on St. Helena Island, no one on board. I hope he just got drunk and forgot to tie it up, because otherwise, I have to wonder about that body they found."

"My God," Henry said. He looked horrified.

Roy seemed to catch the look on Henry's face, and he changed tack. "I'm sure Karl's fine," he said. "I watch too many cop shows, that's all. He still work for you?"

"Not since he fell off the wagon again. I still got his brothers doing their thing. Those boys are like idiot savants with woodworking and anything mechanical." His phone rang. "Oh," he said, looking at the screen. "Sorry, I have to take this. Great seeing y'all." He did his hand-pistol thing again, to both of us, and answered his phone on his way out the door.

I'd barely settled into my office when Roy appeared in the doorway. He was still in a sociable mood. Anyone else would've taken the hint from the Redweld folder I was setting on my desk next to the open laptop, but he didn't do hints. I knew from the way he slouched against the doorframe that he was here to shoot the breeze.

"You know what I heard about Karl's body?" he said. "Or I guess we're still saying 'the' body? His head was so bashed in, some kid thought it was a half-deflated ball washing to shore. Like a volleyball, you know? Even swam out to get it, but had to stop on account of the smell."

I cleared my throat.

"They said it isn't clear yet what happened," he continued. "So that's the Basking Rock mystery: Did some killer rip his face off, or did the fish have it for dinner? I don't know how his brothers are going to identify him. They're supposed to go in and do that this morning. And I'm not sure Karl had enough teeth left for them to use dental records. You know how the Wartons are. More arrests than teeth."

"You know, Roy, I actually—"

"Aw, don't tell me you're busy. You won't be busy for real until you start spending time getting to know folks. Good folks, I mean." Something in the look he gave me made me think he meant people unlike Mazie.

"I do mean to get to that fundraiser," I said.

"Well, good. But I still haven't seen you at church. People got to see you as part of the community if you want them to think of you when they need a lawyer."

"Yeah, that's a fair point." He was masterful at the social side of business, but I wasn't getting much of a chance to learn from him. I did most of the legal work while he was out glad-handing people. It being his firm, he pocketed 75 percent of what he billed clients for my time.

"Speaking of socializing," he said, "have you seen that Grant woman lately?"

"Oh, now and again. Her son's friends with mine, so, you know."

"I saw your car outside the diner yesterday," he said. "You talk to her? She hear about the body yet?"

"She wasn't working, I don't think." My shrimp place was one of her two jobs. "I was just picking up dinner."

"Classy joint," he said, in a tone that meant the opposite.

"Yeah. Anyway, is there something you need? I actually do have a couple things I'd like to get off my desk."

He looked irritated that I wasn't joining in his lurid speculation, but he wasn't one to hold a grudge. He moved right on. "You have time to do a bit of research for me? Insurance question. Henry's got some liability concerns about sailing to the Caribbean. He's had some clients ask him what he's covered for. You know, if a business gives a cruise as a bonus for employees and something happens. He didn't say it straight out, but I think he might be concerned about that drug cartel stuff—there've been some news stories about that out of the Dominican Republic, visitors getting caught up in the violence and whatnot, and Blue Seas sails there."

"Sure," I said. "What's the ETA?"

"Oh, end of the week. Excuse me." He leaned out the door and said, "Laura, can you pull Blue Seas' current liability policies and give them to Leland? Thanks." He leaned back in and explained, "I'd do it, but I have a client waiting to beat me over on Kiawah Island, so I have to run."

I nodded. He headed off to his golf date. There were half a dozen courses on Kiawah Island, and he was so skilled at the game that he could dial back his performance just enough to make every client believe he'd played his best and just barely lost. It was, he'd told me several times, what all clients want: a lawyer good enough to challenge them, but not be better than them.

That silky ability to make every client feel how they wanted to feel was not something I'd ever learned. It just wasn't relevant as a prosecutor. Without it, I questioned how I was ever going to get my practice off the ground.

I checked my email on the off chance someone had sent an inquiry through my new website. They hadn't. Instead I had notices that made my gut twist up in knots. Back when keeping on top of finances was just an item on my to-do list instead of the double-barreled hell it had become, I'd opted in to automatic emails from our health insurance every time a new medical bill came in. This morning there were three of them, all for Noah's recent care. Together they added up to more than $6,200.

Two years earlier I could not have imagined being in this hole. I had everything on autopay and enough coming in every month to cover it. Things were going so well that I was bored and considering a switch into politics. My son was getting high on stolen Vicodin with his friends, but I didn't know that. My wife was an alcoholic, and that I did know.

The way I was trying to help her deal with that was called enabling, and it didn't help anyone. But I didn't face that fact until after she passed away. Her accident, Noah's care, and the lawsuit from the other guy she hurt took everything we had.

That, and some mistakes I'd made in trying to look out for her. There was an investigation. It was suggested I should resign in order to avoid being fired.

Getting out of town was my idea. When Noah was out of rehab and down to two PT visits a week, putting some distance between us and our old life became possible. But I'd been overly optimistic about the career options for suddenly retired former prosecutors. The normal path would have been criminal defense, but the life of a small-town criminal defender, helping good ole boys get away with DUIs and domestic violence, wasn't something I could stomach. I was shooting for business law, for better money and less-unsavory clients.

So I was starting from scratch.

I logged into my accounts to see where things stood. The savings account that was supposed to carry us through building my new practice would barely cover two more months' worth of expenses—or less, if I counted Noah's medical bills. The only account that wasn't running on fumes was his college fund. If I tapped that, he might not be able to afford college. If I didn't, he might have to stop PT and accept his diminished state as just how things were.

Work was the only solution. I started working on the papers for Roy.

The phone rang, startling me out of my work trance. The sunlight was coming in the other side of the office; hours must've passed.

I looked at the number. Local, but I didn't recognize it. I felt a blast of hope: an opportunity, maybe? A new client? I let it ring twice, not wanting to seem desperate, and then said, "Hello?"

"Leland! Please help me. Oh my God, I don't know what to do!" It was Mazie. I'd never heard her so upset.

"What's wrong?"

"Karl's dead! He's dead, and the police came by, and Jackson's run off!"

"Now, whatever's wrong," I said, "I have you, Mazie. I have you." My crisis voice kicked in, the one I'd developed over years of dealing with crime victims and their families. A little deeper than my normal voice, and slow enough to soothe. I was damned if I was going to let a friend of mine go over the edge. "Just tell me where you are."

"The police took me down to the station."

I didn't like the sound of that.

I said, "I'll be right there."

4

TUESDAY, JUNE 11, EVENING

A s I drove over, I kicked myself for getting so deep in Roy's work that I'd forgotten to keep an ear out for news. I should've found a way to tell Mazie about Karl's death myself. Hearing it from the local cops, who weren't exactly friendly toward her kin, had to be about the worst way to find out. And to have Jackson run when the cops came did not look good. I could've spared the two of them a lot of trouble today if I hadn't fallen into my old tunnel vision, seeing nothing in the world beyond the work on my desk.

The police station's tiny lobby was more crowded than I'd ever seen it. Back in Charleston we counted murders per year, but Basking Rock was so small you could count the years between murders. Karl's death was big news. I recognized some faces—a detective I knew, and a couple local losers trading gossip about the condition of the corpse—but didn't see Mazie. The sullen cop at the desk stopped chewing his tobacco long enough to tell me she'd gone into the ladies'. I started making my way through the gossipers to check-in with Detective Blount, maybe get some sense of what the news was and why Mazie had been brought here, but when he glanced my way and I gave him a nod hello, he glared, turned his back, and headed down the hall.

When I was a prosecutor, no cop would've done that. I was still getting used to being persona non grata by virtue of my new sideline in defending people accused of petty crimes. And if that weren't enough to dent my reputation, any connection to the Warton clan knocked a man down a notch or two around here. I'd never thought of Mazie that way, but I was realizing she was considered basically a Warton despite never having married Jackson's father.

It occurred to me she'd probably taken refuge in the restroom just to get away from the gossip and the nasty looks. I wondered if she'd called me from there. I stepped out of the fray and leaned against a wall to shoot her a text saying I was here.

She came right out. She had the masklike expression I'd seen countless times. The mothers of murderers and murder victims, the wives of dead men and of perps, they nearly always had this look on their faces when they had to wade through crowds of reporters, cops, and curious onlookers. She was barely holding it together.

I stepped over to her and offered her a ride home.

As we drove, windows down because my AC was on the blink, she didn't speak. I didn't either; I didn't want to upset her, especially not when we were still in stop-and-go traffic near the courthouse and the jail. She didn't need some gawker snapping photos of her crying in my car.

When we turned onto the causeway, the long view over the water seemed to relax her. Since there was nobody around—the causeway only had two lanes, with nothing but rocks and palm trees on either side—I asked, "So, what all happened there?"

The floodgates opened. She started sobbing.

"It was Karl they found," she said. Again, I wanted to kick myself for letting her find out from someone else. "It's so awful. I hated that man, but nobody deserves that. His *face* was gone, Leland! His brothers had to identify him by his tattoos!"

I dug a pack of Kleenex out of my center console and handed it to her.

She took it and said, "And they kept asking me about Jackson. I don't know where he went. I'm just glad they didn't need *him* to identify the—"

She started crying again. When she'd blown her nose a couple times and started calming down, I said, "So... tell me, Mazie. Walk me through it. How'd you end up at the police station?"

"Well, I got home around six-thirty," she said. "With the grease, I always take a shower after work. I was just drying off when the doorbell rang. When Jackson didn't get the door, I yelled for him a couple times. They just leaned on the bell and started hammering, louder even than Karl when he's drunk."

I guess that made her nostalgic, because she went quiet and looked out at the water. The sun was getting low, and the palm trees were casting long shadows on the waves.

To get her talking again, I said gently, "What happened then?"

"Oh, I went and answered the door. And that Detective Blount, you know, he just blurted it out about Karl, like you'd expect him to."

He was blunt, she meant. That was the joke in high school, on account of his last name. It was a nicer way of saying he lacked basic courtesy, to the point that I questioned his Southernness.

"I'm sorry," I said.

"Oh, it ain't nothing. Remember, I stayed here. I never had occasion to forget how he was. But Leland, the thing is, he kept asking about Jackson. Where he was, where he'd been the past few days. I went to get him, so he could set Blount straight, but he was gone. His window faces the back, and I guess he just jumped out. That's going to give them the wrong idea, isn't it?"

It was the kind of thing that would've gotten pride of place in my opening statement, back when I was a prosecutor: *Ladies and gentlemen, when the police arrived to inform the family of Mr. Warton's death, the defendant didn't answer the door. Instead, he jumped out the back window and fled.*

There was no point telling her that. I asked, "Do you have any idea where he might be?"

"Might want to ask your Noah. But no, I don't. I didn't even know he'd left until we looked in his room. But that Blount, he right out accused me of stalling so Jackson could run! I was in a robe, my hair was all wet, and I still had to take him in the bathroom and show him the fogged-up mirror before he'd believe I really was in the shower when they got there."

I didn't like how aggressive Blount was being. I didn't know if he was bluffing or just making assumptions, or, God forbid, if he had hard evidence.

That wasn't a question that could be answered yet. "So how'd you end up down at the station?"

"They asked me to come. We got nothing to hide, and I didn't want them thinking I wasn't cooperating."

"Oh, uh-huh." I kept my voice casual. What she did was the opposite of what I would've recommended, but there was no sense making her feel bad now. "So what did they want to know?"

"Oh, everything. Where was I on this day or that? Where was Jackson? They already knew he and Karl had fought, so they wanted to hear all about that. I told them it was Karl who started it. He came over drunk and raring for a fight. They wanted to know every single thing that happened after that."

"Mm-hmm." That did not sound good, and it was my fault. If I hadn't been so focused on getting Roy's research done, I could've told both her and Jackson to sit tight. I knew even good cops could be overzealous sometimes, so the first rule of not getting railroaded was to not talk to them.

I eased off the causeway into the little business district on her side of town. Gun shop, gas station, dollar store. I asked her, "Any idea why Jackson went out the window?"

She sighed. I could tell she was embarrassed.

"Now, Mazie," I said, "you know I'm not going to judge him. Not only do you and I go way back, but compared to what I saw in Charleston, nothing in this town is going to shock me."

"Yeah, I know. It's just, he's gotten in a few scrapes. Like possession of marijuana. I know it's wrong, but—"

I sighed. "It's about as low on the totem pole of wrong as a crime can be. Hell, I wish my Noah'd just been doing that. He had a problem with painkillers, and then with the accident it got even worse."

"Leland, I am so sorry. I didn't know."

"Hardly anyone does. He's come out of it now, I think, but I almost lost him. Smoking a joint is a cakewalk compared to that."

"Well, still," she said. "He shouldn't be doing it. But I think he must've had some stashed someplace, and he ran to dump it in case they searched his room."

"Okay," I said. "That's not great, but it's understandable."

28

As I reached an intersection and stopped at the light, I could feel her looking at me from the passenger seat. She said, "I probably shouldn't have talked to them, huh?"

Before I could answer, a car shot past and something exploded across my windshield.

"What the hell!" I veered to the shoulder, my heart hammering. The glass was covered with what looked like a chocolate milkshake. I leaned out the window to see what I could of the other car. Its taillights were disappearing in the distance.

"What *was* that?" I said. "Some new YouTube prank or something?"

She gave a bitter laugh. "Oh, no. Leland, you've been gone a long time."

"How do you mean?" I turned the wipers on. They didn't help much.

"That's what you get for mixing with the Wartons. Somebody must've spotted me in your car."

I hit the windshield-washer button, trying to think of another explanation.

"More likely just some stupid prank," I said. "The speed they were going, I don't know how they could've gotten a good look at you. They weren't even on the passenger side."

"Maybe," she said after a moment. "It's just hard. After a while, I mean, you get to expect the insults and being the butt of every joke."

I sighed. "I'm sorry things went this way for you," I said. "You should've had a better life."

She shrugged. She didn't say anything, but as she exhaled I heard a catch in her throat that made me think she might start crying again.

"Listen," I said, "let's get you home. Don't let those punks distract us from what's going on. Jackson's got to be scared. He's not thinking straight, but he's just a kid." I pulled out into the road again. "We're the grown-ups. We got to think this through."

"You're right."

"So, what do you think might've made the police want to talk to him?"

"The fight, probably. Half the neighborhood saw it. And all of them heard it."

"But they also saw Karl leave, right?"

"Yeah. And he was alone. Jackson came back inside."

"Well, okay then." It sounded to me like if Karl fell in the water after that, the killer was probably Jack Daniels, not Jackson.

I parked in front of her house. As we went up the rickety porch, I saw the next-door neighbor's curtain twitching and made a mental note to keep my voice down even when we got inside.

Jackson still wasn't home. As Mazie turned on the lights, I asked if I could make her something: coffee, maybe a sandwich?

"I'm not hungry," she said. She was planted right in front of me, staring up into my eyes, desperation in her voice. "All I care about is whether my boy is going to be okay."

That was exactly how I'd felt at the hospital after Noah's accident. Her pale, tired face had the same vulnerability she used to have in high school. She'd always have that, I thought; if life hadn't hardened her by now, it never would. But motherhood had made her fierce, and I understood that down to my bones.

"Mazie," I said, "you can help him. Let's figure this out. Hang on one second."

I didn't want any nosy neighbors to overhear, but it was too hot to shut the windows. I turned the TV on loud and signaled that we should talk quietly. "So," I said, "everyone saw Karl show up drunk, right? What happened then?"

"He just stood in the front yard hollering. He was saying horrible things about me. Nothing new, but still. Jackson was mad. I tried to stop him, but he went out on the porch and told Karl he was a loser and needed to go home and never come back. And, Leland, everybody heard that. Anybody who could see anything must've seen that Karl came charging up the porch, yelling that Jackson had no right to talk like that to his own father, and hit him right in the face."

"That's the black eye," I said.

"Yes. I ran out and got between them. I don't think Jackson even landed a punch at all. He just went out to defend me, and then he had to fend off his dad. He didn't get Karl's mean streak, thank the Lord."

"Well, he's your son too," I said. "And you raised him right. What happened then? He come on back in and, what, eat and go to bed?"

"He came in, and I put him in the shower and cleaned his face up after. He needed a Band-Aid." She touched her cheek as if remembering. "And we watched TV a while. But then he went back out. I told him not to, but he wouldn't listen."

"Sounds like Noah," I said. "You tell a boy that age the right thing to do, he'll do the opposite just to mess with you. About what time was that, when he left?"

"Right after *Law & Order* came on," she said. "I remember because I hate that show. He got up when it came on, and we argued a little. When he left, I switched over to *Magnum, P.I.* It can't have been more than a few minutes past nine."

"How long did he stay out, do you know?"

"Well, I finished my show," she said. "But I just didn't feel right. He'd gone off on his bike, and I was worried. I drove around a little while, here and there, keeping an eye out. Went down to the marina, because he's like me—likes to look at the waves. They're relaxing."

I remembered that about her. It was how she'd met Karl, unfortunately. He'd always had some shabby little boat to tool around in.

"You see Jackson there?"

"No. And I looked for Karl's boat, but it wasn't there either. Which I thought was a little strange—what is there to do out on the water in the dark? But then, Karl never did make much sense."

She sighed and stepped over to the kitchenette. She got instant coffee from the cabinet, offered me some, and put the first cup of water in the microwave to boil. I could tell something was troubling her. When our coffees were fixed up how we liked them, she gestured to me to join her at the counter.

"Leland," she said, "Jackson's never set foot outside the Lowcountry. He can't have gone far. But they're looking for him, and they're taking this real serious. We're going to need help, and I don't know any other lawyers but you."

"Well," I said, "I think they're just doing their due diligence. He had a fight with Karl on the night Karl died. They're going to want to talk to him, that's all."

"You sure?" she said. "What if that's not all? What if they arrest him?"

"I mean, they can't just do that without evidence." Even as I said it, I knew I sounded like a fool. Some cops liked to pin crimes on whoever the local scapegoats were. It made their jobs easier and left everyone's assumptions comfortably intact.

She was staring at me. We both knew that in this town, anyone associated with the Warton clan was fair game.

I switched gears. There was a simple answer to her question, so I rattled it off. "Okay, if they did, for a major felony they could hold him for between thirty-six and ninety-six hours without charge. That's when they'd try to question him, but he's entitled to have a lawyer present. He just needs to know not to talk without one."

"So you'll be there with him?"

"Well," I said, and paused. If there did turn out to be evidence, if this went to trial, it could take a solid year of work. Months at the minimum. I was trying to get my business litigation practice off the ground, not do murder trials. Not even for pay, much less for nothing. I could barely float another month or two on what I had left, and she didn't have anything.

"Leland," she said. Her voice was trembling. "He's just a kid. *My* kid."

"I know, Mazie, but what I was saying is, there's public defenders who do nothing but this type of work. The court would appoint—"

"But I don't know them! Where do those folks work, Charleston? They don't know this town. And they don't know me."

A tear ran down her face. In all my life I'd never seen her cry until today.

"Mazie," I said, "you can call me anytime you need, but I think this is going to blow over. Karl fell off his boat and drowned. Jackson can't get in trouble for that."

"Then why'd the cops come for him?" she asked. "What's going on?"

5

WEDNESDAY, JUNE 19, EVENING

Walking into the Ocean View Diner, I was surprised to see it packed with locals and tourists alike, all of them rubbernecking to get a look at Mazie. A lot had come out about Karl's murder—not least, that it looked like a murder. People were gossiping about autopsy results, but I knew how that worked; the police probably wouldn't get the full report for another four or five weeks. Still, the word on the street was that Karl had been brutally beaten and then tossed overboard to drown.

It was possible the rumor mill had amplified bits of information beyond all recognition. It was also possible the coroner's office had sprung a leak.

From the way the customers were treating Mazie, they liked scandal whether it was true or not. With Jackson still gone and the whole town knowing about his fight with Karl, she'd been branded the killer's mother.

She was handling it as well as a person could. I'd come to get coffee and give moral support, but she was run off her feet with all the gawkers getting early dinners. Apart from when she poured my coffee, she hadn't even looked at me.

When the place closed, I headed out to wait while she cleaned up. I'd dropped her off at work and told her I'd get her home, so she wouldn't spend her shift worrying about her tires getting slashed or someone tossing a rock through her windshield.

I drove over to the diner's back door so she wouldn't have to go far. At twilight, when she came out and slid into the passenger seat, she looked more exhausted than I'd ever seen her. As I pulled onto the street, I asked, "You okay?" It was a stupid question, but I didn't know what else to say.

"You tell me," she said. "My son's gone, the whole town thinks he's a murderer, and on top of that, old Mr. Graham just asked me not to come back to work tomorrow. Or ever."

"Aw, dang." It was a lousy job, but I knew she needed the money.

There was a hint of humor in her voice when she added, "I can't believe he didn't appreciate all the business I was bringing in."

I smiled. Finding humor where she could had always been her way. Maybe that was why a hard life hadn't hardened her. "Someone else will see the business opportunity," I said. "You'll find something."

"Yeah, if I want every shift to be a freak show," she said, sounding very tired. "Jackson's boss told me he hasn't shown up to work. I've texted him, but I have no idea where he is. This can't go on long, or we'll lose the house. The landlord doesn't take kindly to unpaid rent."

"Maybe Roy has something," I said. "Some work where you wouldn't have to deal with the public. He's got a secretary, but I don't know, cleaning, maybe? He could ask around if he doesn't have anything himself."

She gave a laugh that was past hope. "Even before all this," she said, "Roy wouldn't have hired a Warton. He runs a respectable firm."

"Maybe things have changed," I said. "I mean, he's got Blue Seas for a client, and they had Karl and his brothers on the payroll."

"They did?"

We were on the causeway now, and I kept my eyes on the road, but I could feel her looking at me in surprise. "You didn't know?"

"Oh, Karl never wanted me to know anything about his money. According to everything he ever told me or filed in court, he had none, especially not for child support. I guess I was supposed to think that boat of his ran on seawater and thin air."

"He said that in court filings?"

"On the stand, once. But it was a long time ago."

"Dang. I wish I'd known. Maybe we could've put some pressure on him to help you out. Doesn't matter how long ago it was. There's no statute of limitations on crimes in South Carolina, and perjury's a crime."

She didn't say anything. I put the window down for a breeze. The palm trees alongside the road were so close that each one made a whooshing noise as we passed, a rhythmic punctuation. Streetlights were few and far between, but in the light of one I caught sight of more tears on her face.

"Mazie, if there's anything I can do to help you feel better..."

She wiped her face roughly, seeming annoyed that I'd caught her crying, and said, "It's not about how I feel. It's about Jackson. He needs help. I need you to save my son."

"Mazie, I know he's running scared, but I don't see a case here. I know the gossip is pretty horrifying, but it's got to blow over sometime, and—"

She slammed her hand down on the dashboard. "Leland, no! This kind of thing doesn't blow over for people like us. Haven't you heard, or do you just not listen? They have a witness now. Some cop who docks at the marina says he saw Jackson there that night."

I tried not to let her see me wince. A defendant who fled out his back window, and now a police officer who placed him at the scene. She had reason to be scared.

"Mazie, gossip isn't evidence. I want to help, but…" I signaled a turn and checked traffic, taking the opportunity to stop talking. I didn't want to get into my finances with her.

Of course, compared to seeing your only child imprisoned for murder, worrying that mine might have to take out big loans in order to afford college felt ridiculous.

"But what?" she said. "My boy didn't do this. I know him. Maybe if Karl had attacked me, Jackson might do him harm fighting him off. I could see that. But he would never have chased his father down and murdered him. I need a lawyer who understands that. And who understands that this town has always thought the worst of us."

I nodded, still looking at the road. "I do understand that," I said.

"Then help us!"

"Let's shut the car windows," I said, hitting the button to close them. We were getting into the built-up part of her edge-of-nowhere neighborhood. "I don't want anybody to hear us talk."

When we pulled up outside her house, I put the car in park, turned to her, and said, "Look, for a lot of reasons, I don't know if I could take this case—if it turns into a case, which it still might not."

She laughed like I was foolish to think there was any hope of that.

"If you hear from Jackson," I said, "you tell him to call me. And tell him he's not to say anything to the police without me there, no matter what. Easier said than done, for a kid his age, but it's critical."

"Okay," she said, nodding. "I'll tell him just that. Can I tell him in a text, in case I don't hear from him?"

I hesitated. I didn't want her creating any evidence that might look bad to the cops or a jury. "Okay," I said, "here's what you do. Tell him exactly this: 'Jackson, don't worry.'"

"Hang on a second," she said. She pulled her phone out and started typing.

"So, 'Don't worry. You have the right to a lawyer, and we'll get you one. But don't talk to the police without one. I'm not sure I trust them.' Just say that, and then sign off however you normally do."

When she'd finished writing, I said, "If you hear from him, or if he's arrested, call me right away. In the meantime, I'll do some digging. I'll see if I can find out what the police have. There's a decent chance they don't have anything at all."

"But how? Old Mr. Graham said he had it straight from a cop he knows that they got another cop who saw Jackson there."

"Mazie, the police are allowed to distort things, make them sound worse than they are. It flushes out witnesses, gets people to tell them what really happened, gets one crook to turn state's evidence against another. They do it all the time."

"But that's terrible! It's immoral!"

"Well, it's a legit investigative technique. Or at least, it can be. I'm just letting you know it can be misused, and also, once rumors get going, they take on a life of their own. It doesn't mean the police actually have anything. It doesn't mean your boy's really in danger."

The streetlight at the corner let me see her well enough to know I'd lost her there. Her expression closed off like I was moving back into the "stranger" category.

"My son *is* in danger," she said. "You know who we are. We're the kind who get the consequences. He's no worse than those summer kids who smash mailboxes and smoke weed on the docks, but then those boys all go off to college and nobody ever holds them accountable. Maybe that's how it was supposed to be for Noah too, before the accident. You know, just floating through life whichever way he wanted, and nobody stopping him, nobody blaming him for anything that went wrong. But it was never going to be that way for Jackson."

She opened the door and got out before I could think of anything to say. I called out, "Evening," and watched to make sure she got in safely, but she didn't say another word.

She was right. If Jackson had gone through what Noah had—if he'd been arrested for stealing prescription drugs, if he'd been in an accident that nearly killed him and would've left him disabled if not for all that rehab and PT—well, he wouldn't have gotten a second chance. He might've done time for the pills, instead of getting off with a stint in juvenile rehab. And he would've been left disabled, because there was no way Mazie could pay for all the care it took to bring a boy in that condition almost all the way back.

I'd given Noah that second chance. It had cost almost everything I had, but wasn't that what money was for?

Surely Jackson deserved the same.

6

WEDNESDAY, JUNE 19, EVENING

I left Mazie's and drove back up the causeway, but I didn't go straight home. I hated to leave Noah waiting, but half the time he wasn't there anyway. And, I told myself, at least now I wasn't ignoring him to focus on my work. I was trying to help his friend.

If Detective Blount was still on duty—it was only a little bit past six —I might be able to find out some things from him. And if he wasn't, I could find out when his next shift was. He'd been pretty rude in the crowd the other day, but then he never had any social graces to begin with. I pulled into a spot outside the police station.

As I went up the steps, the door at the top opened and Terri Washington came out. We'd been friends in high school, two outcast nerds who shared an interest in the law, but I'd only seen her maybe twice since returning to Basking Rock.

"My goodness, Terri," I said. "For half a second I thought Oprah Winfrey was coming down these steps. I was about to look for a TV camera." She really did look like Oprah, and she'd loved the comparison back in high school.

"Uh-huh," she said, with a glint of humor. "Wish I had her money instead of her looks. How you been?"

We stopped to chat, her standing two steps above me on account of how petite she was. I asked, "What you doing at the cop shop? You back on the force?"

With a look that clearly said I had lost my mind, she asked, "You suffer some kind of brain injury, Leland? You here to report some mugger hit you upside the head? I quit about thirty seconds after my pension vested. It'd take an act of God to bring me back."

A breeze came up as we chatted. Evening was one of the few pleasant times to be outdoors in the summer. Terri told me she was working as a private investigator while studying part-time for a degree in social work. "People are always underestimating me," she said. "When you're a cop that's a bad thing, but as a PI, it's good. I don't get noticed. And even if I do, people still do any damn fool thing in front of me."

"What, do they just think you don't carry no consequences?"

"That's exactly it. Like, what harm could *I* do?"

"Well, you could put 'em on your TV show, make 'em have some kind of embarrassing heart-to-heart with Dr. Phil."

She laughed.

"That why you're here?" I asked. "Some PI thing?"

"Uh-uh." She explained that she volunteered for Jumpstart, a local halfway house for women in recovery. I felt a pang of guilt. What if I'd done more to push Elise into something like that?

"You okay?" she asked.

"Oh, yeah. It's just, you know, it's a sad thing."

"Addiction? Yeah. Especially when they relapse. We had two of those in the past week, and one of them got picked up. I was just in there talking to her. Going to need a public defender."

"I know some good ones up in Charleston County," I said. "They might have some intel on whoever you get down here."

"Well, thank you." She looked at her watch. "I should let you go take care of whatever you're here for."

"Yeah, hoping to talk with Detective Blount."

In her eyes I saw her put two and two together. She said, "The Warton thing?" When I nodded, she said, "He was already gone when I got here."

Without moving her head one iota, her eyes flicked around like she was checking that the coast was clear. Then she looked at me quite pointedly and said, in a tone much more casual than the look in her eyes, "I do have time for a quick drink. Unless you want to keep standing here on these steps?"

I took that as the strong recommendation it was and suggested a nearby restaurant. We headed over. Of the two we could walk to, it was noisier; whatever she had to say would be harder for anyone else to overhear.

We took a seat at the corner of the bar and ordered beers.

"You mind if we split some wings and fries?" she said. "I never got around to having lunch today, and the smell just, you know, hit me. I didn't realize how hungry I was."

I mentally reviewed what was in my wallet: a little cash, and I did have the one card of mine that still worked. I hoped whatever intel she had would be worth my eating cereal for lunch tomorrow.

"No problem," I said. I called the bartender over and ordered the food.

She took a sip of her beer, set it down, and said, "Okay. So, you can cross Blount off your friends list right now. The boys have themselves a witness, and he's it. He's got a speedboat he keeps down at the marina, and he's saying he went fishing that day and saw Jackson coming into the marina around ten at night, when he was heading out."

That wasn't great, but it didn't seem like the bombshell Mazie was afraid of. It didn't even place Jackson with Karl.

I said, "They're going to need more than that."

"Yeah."

"Motive, for one thing."

"Mm-hmm. Everybody knows Karl wasn't the best father in town, but they also know he was pretty damn far from the worst."

That rang true. And she would know. Even in high school, I remembered, she'd had a sixth sense about that kind of thing. Whose bruises really were accidental and whose weren't. Which girl wore long sleeves because she was cutting, and sometimes even why she was doing it. I'd told her in our junior year she ought to be a detective.

The bartender set down our fries and wings. While she started in on them, I took a swig of beer. "I suppose that's what's got them so aggressive," I said. "They feel like they got a little bite, and they're itching to haul it all the way in."

"Mm-hmm. Easier than throwing the whole net out and seeing if they catch anything." She set what was left of a wing on her napkin. "One of the reasons I left is, there wasn't a whole lot of investigating going on. They'd always rather bust the obvious suspect in under a week, instead of taking the time to look deep. And, I mean, it's a small-town police force. This isn't where the great investigative minds end up."

I nodded. "I can't say I met a whole lot of Sherlock Holmes types up in Charleston either."

"Few and far between," she agreed. She dabbed a fry in ketchup and added, "They had Karl's brothers in again today."

"Huh," I said. "Wonder if they're trying to exclude them. I doubt those two can say much about Jackson. I don't get the impression he ever was close to that side of the family."

"You sure seem interested," she said gently. "Is it purely professional, or you worried about Mazie?"

"Oh, of course I'm worried about her."

"So folks have been saying," she said. "That, and more."

I looked at her and said, "Sometimes I hate this damn town."

"Aw, but you know how it works. People see you driving her around, dropping by her restaurant, they're going to talk." She smiled and said, "Don't let it bother you. If there's still something there, there's still something there."

"Well, but what about you and that guy?" I said. "Can't remember his name, but the one with the Dennis Rodman hair? Tall as Big Bird?" I was referring to her high-school boyfriend, who'd left town even before I did.

She laughed. "Okay, point taken."

We'd always enjoyed teasing each other. To keep it fair, I turned it on myself: "There's no truer guide to life than how you felt when you were seventeen, is there. Keep that flame alive! Hell, at that age I thought I might end up on the Supreme Court."

She cracked up. I did too. The distance between how the future had looked then and how things looked now was so great that laughing was about all you could do.

She finished off another wing and said, "Speaking of teenagers, how's yours?"

"Oh," I said, checking my watch. It was almost seven-thirty. "He's okay. I hate to run out on you, but I did tell him I'd be home for dinner tonight." I called the bartender over for a doggie bag and reached for my wallet.

She reached for hers and pulled out a ten. "My half," she explained. I must have looked puzzled, because she added, "You ain't paying for me. You want the whole town to think we're on a date?" We both laughed.

"That is the last damn thing either of us needs," I said, laying my own ten on the bar.

"Well, I don't know," she said. "I can think of a few diseases and some crimes that might be lower on the list."

"Why thank you," I said, "for the compliment."

We strolled out and went our separate ways.

When I got home, Noah was at the kitchen table just closing his laptop. Seeing him with it gave me a chill. The remains of a TV dinner sat nearby.

I headed for the kitchen. "What you up to?" I said, in what I meant to be a cheerful tone.

He glared at me. "Nothing."

It had been a few months since he'd earned back the right to use his laptop, in public parts of the house only. I'd taken it from him after seeing some messages between him and a friend in Charleston. They'd both been high on stolen Vicodin.

I sat down across from him and reached for the laptop. He jerked it away and asked, "You going to keep on thinking the worst of me? Like, always?"

"Well, when you act like you got something to hide," I said, "it makes it hard to think you don't." I sighed. "And there's a lot going on. If you know anything at all about Jackson, about where he is, you tell me, okay? Or if, God forbid, you're having any trouble staying clean?"

He gave a shake of his head like he could not believe I was thinking either of those things.

"How long did I spend," I asked, "thinking everything was fine with you? And where did *that* get us?"

He shoved his laptop over to me and folded his arms across his chest.

I opened it and typed his password—sharing it with me was part of our deal—and the website he'd been on appeared. It was some veterinarian's page about how to tell if your dog has arthritis. The other tabs were home remedies for arthritic dogs and how to make your pup more comfortable.

I felt like such a heel.

He took the laptop back without a word, opened it up, and hunched over it. It reminded me of how as a kid he'd made forts around his breakfast bowl with cereal boxes.

"Noah, I'm sorry," I said. "Jackson's in trouble, and it's making me worry about both of you."

"Worrying's one thing," he said, tapping away, not looking at me. "Big Brother's another. I refuse to live under a microscope. Either you start trusting me or I move out."

That made all the fight go out of me. I tried to think of a way to ask him not to, but the words wouldn't come out of my mouth. Before I could get them to, Squatter tottered into the room. I picked him up and set him on my lap.

Noah said, still not looking at me, "That site said to massage his hips."

It felt like a ridiculous thing to do, but I gave it a try. Squatter seemed happy about it.

After a while, Noah said, "What'll happen if Jackson gets arrested? You'll help him, right?"

I still didn't have it in me to explain the financials. We'd lost our house in Charleston, lost just about everything, and helping his friend would mean struggling through probably another year before I could even begin trying to put the fires out.

Instead I stuck with the facts. "I just came from the police station," I told him. "I was looking into it."

He glanced at me, gave me a nod, and looked back at his screen.

That glance stuck with me. It'd been a long time since I'd seen any kind of approval in his eyes.

7

THURSDAY, JUNE 20, EVENING

The next day, with Roy's work finished by lunch, I tried to read up on marketing my law practice. Jackson's predicament kept me from concentrating, so I called a friend in Charleston to see what he could tell me about getting a public defender and whether he knew anything about the PDs down in my county. I'd hoped to be able to give Mazie and Terri some intel on that, but what I learned wasn't exactly encouraging.

I decided to leave early and stop by the trailer park Karl's brothers lived at to see if I could find out what they'd told the police. It was on the other side of the same marsh Mazie's place looked over. As I drove past the beat-up wooden sign reading "Sheep's Lodge"—for reasons lost to time, that's what this park was called—I had flash-backs to drunken high-school parties I'd attended here. The place did not look to have come up in the world since then.

An older woman using a walker was shuffling down the side of the only paved road. I pulled alongside to ask her if she could remind me where the Warton brothers lived.

She glared at me. "Who's asking?" A stray breeze tossed her gray hair, and I noticed, above her right ear, a single pink curler that she seemed to have forgotten.

"Uh, it's Leland Munroe, ma'am," I said. "Pleased to meet you. I seem to recall they're off to the left up there, but I can't remember which street exactly and didn't want to intrude."

My politeness, and maybe also the beater I was driving, seemed to convince her I wasn't a process server or the tax man or whoever she wanted to keep out. She pointed the way.

When I turned up the third dirt road to the left, I spotted Tim Warton in a lawn chair nursing what looked like a forty-ounce bottle of beer. He had on a dirty white tank top. His brother Pat was setting on the top step of their porch. When I got out and slammed my car door, Pat hauled himself to his feet and went inside without a word. Tim just took another draw on his beer.

As I trudged across the gravel between me and him, Tim pulled a phone out of the pocket of his shorts and held it up. "I'm Livebookin' you!" he called out. "You're on camera, and I know my rights!"

"Yessir," I said. "Afternoon, Mr. Warton. I'm not here to interfere with your rights whatsoever."

"You law enforcement?"

"No, sir. Name's Leland Munroe. I'm a local attorney. I heard about your brother Karl, and it's a damn shame. My condolences."

"Uh-huh," he said. I waited for the flash of brotherly grief across his face, but none appeared. When he took another drink and then shifted to set the bottle on the ground, I noticed he wasn't sitting in a lawn chair after all. It was wood, and handsomely carved. I thought I saw a mermaid twining around one of the rails behind him.

He settled back against the mermaid and asked, looking downright cheerful, "You think we got somebody we could sue? You one of them lawyers that don't charge nothing unless you win, like on the TV?"

"Well, sir," I said, "there's cases where I can do a contingency, yes. But let's not get ahead of ourselves. By the way, that's a mighty unusual chair you got there. I don't believe I ever seen one like it."

"Made it myself. Carved every detail." He looked proud, and rightly so.

I gave a low whistle and said, "My goodness. You have a God-given skill." He nodded in acknowledgment. The red glow of the wood made me ask, "Is that teak?"

"It sure is," he said. "And teakwood ain't easy to carve. It's hard. You need a mallet and chisel. You can't even cut it with a regular blade. Got to be carbide."

"Oh, yeah?" I whistled again. As he reached for his forty on the ground, I saw the muscle and sinew shift under his skin. He was tanned as only a man who all but lived outdoors can be. I took him for about a decade older than me, but he still looked like he could take just about any man in a fight.

After another gulp of beer, or malt liquor, as I realized when I saw the label, he asked, "So what all you come down here for? We don't get a lot of lawyers round here."

From inside the trailer, I heard his brother laugh. Tim turned and hollered over his shoulder, "We don't, though, do we? Hey, when you come out, bring me my T-shirt with the, uh, the tuxedo printed on it. We got a fancy guest, and I want to dress appropriate."

Inside, his brother cracked up.

"You dress how you want," I said. "This is your property. I just came by to see what I could figure out about the situation."

He squinted at me, hesitant. "You from the insurance?"

"No, sir. I don't have a dog in this race as of yet. I'm just trying to understand what happened. If there was a wrongful death situation, if there was insurance, we can get there in due time, and I can refer you to somebody, but first I need to understand how your poor brother lost his life."

"Huh." He went to set his liquor down on the arm of his chair, then paused to flick a fly out of the way. It was so hot even the flies didn't move unless they had to. When it had crept off around the side of the armrest, he turned to yell back at the trailer, "This here lawyer don't even know how Karl died!"

Pat yelled, "What? That's crazy." He stuck his head out the window and told me, "Whole town already knows Jackson killed him."

With a slow nod, Tim said, "He sure did."

"Huh," I said. "Now, you're sure about that? How come?"

"Well," he said, and took a swig of liquor. "He said he was going to kill him, and now Karl's dead. It don't get much more case-closed than that."

"Huh," I said. "Now, when exactly did he say that?"

"What was it, now," he said. "Thanksgiving?"

"Christmas," Pat said from inside. "Hang on." The flimsy trailer shook as he walked. He pulled the door open, leaned against the frame, and said, "There was an ornament on the Christmas tree shaped like a red Mustang, and Karl said he'd always wanted one. I remembered that after he got the car."

"Oh, yeah," said Tim. He asked me, "Speaking of which, who gets a man's car, if his normal heir is who killed him?"

"Well, that would depend on a whole lot of things," I said. Brothers like these two made me happy Noah was an only child.

Tim was still staring, waiting for an answer.

I said, "Sir, I can't tell you for sure without seeing the title and so forth."

Pat, whose knuckles were rapping a rhythm on the doorframe, said, "Aw, he probably left the convertible with that stripper he was banging. And you know possession is nine-tenths of the law."

"Huh," I said. "Well, I could look into that, if you'd point me to her."

Tim said, "Ain't she a waitress?"

"Might be," said Pat. "Works at the Broke Spoke, anyway. A waitress there might as well be a stripper."

"Jackson didn't like her none either," Tim said. "No, sir. Said something about her too, that same night when he told Karl he wanted him dead."

"Speaking of which, what was it exactly he said?" I asked.

"Let me think," Tim said. "We were all up at Mazie's. And Karl was drunk as shit. Drunk when he got there and just kept on going. Every drink he had, you could see Jackson looking at him meaner."

"I don't blame him," Pat said. "It's a hard thing for a boy to see."

"But I mean," said Tim, "if he ain't used to it by now, when's he going to? You can't change what you can't change."

"Well, sure," Pat said.

"Anyhow, Mazie had made a pecan pie," said Tim. "She makes a hell of a pie. And Karl stuffed it in his craw, and he got to choking. I mean, like he was gonna die, turning blue, bent over the table…"

"I thought that was it," Pat said.

"We all did. But Jackson did that thing from the TV, where he grabs him—it's like a punch to the stomach, but you punch from behind. And it worked! Damned if that pie didn't come right back up!"

Pat said, "He saved his life."

"He did. But drunk as Karl was, and eating like he had, getting punched brought everything back up. He barfed all over himself, and on the table too. He was too drunk to even know Jackson had saved his life. He just popped him one right in the lip."

"That kid bled everywhere."

"Yeah, he's a bleeder. Always has been. But he said right there, in front of everyone, that he shouldn't have saved him, and matter of fact he'd put him six feet under if he ever got the chance."

"He did," Pat said. "Can't blame him, though."

I said, "I guess anybody might get hotheaded in a situation like that."

Pat shook his head. "He wasn't hotheaded at all. He was just… dead calm. Like he meant it, you know?"

"And that wasn't the only time," Tim said. "I recall Jackson saying more than once that he'd like to see his daddy dead. Whenever Karl fell off the wagon, which was a lot, he said something like that."

Pat agreed. "Christmas was just the, you know, that's the one that sticks in your memory."

"Uh-huh," I said. "Well, I can understand why."

"You know," said Tim, "you ought to check Jackson's Facebook or whatever that is. Instagram? I don't know. But I bet he's even put that down in writing."

His brother said, "That sure would be dumb."

"Yeah," he said. "But how dumb you got to be, to tell a man in front of everybody that you'd like to see him dead, and then go killing him?"

When I got home I took Squatter for a walk in the dog park, hoping to clear my head. Talking to the Warton brothers had brought home how hard it was going to be for Jackson to get an unbiased jury. I'd seen jurors believe the damnedest things, but to see even his own kin thinking that way was alarming.

At his age, Squatter wore out quick, so he soon curled up in a sunbeam to nap. I sat on a bench with my phone, scrolling through Jackson's social media. Apart from some surprisingly biting commentary on life in Basking Rock, which I mostly agreed with, it was mind-numbing. How many times, I wondered, did a person have to let the world know he supported legalized marijuana? I would've thought one meme stating that opinion ought to be enough, but Jackson apparently did not share my view. I scrolled through page after page, feeling like an old man as I shook my head at kids today.

When my phone rang it was a welcome interruption, and all the more so because it was Terri calling.

"Hey there, Oprah," I said. "How you been? You solved the crime for me yet?"

She laughed. "Naw, I actually wasn't calling about that at all. I just wanted to apologize for sticking my nose in your business last night. I don't know why I listened to those rumors about you and Mazie."

"I know how it is, though," I said, as Squatter, curled up beside my foot, gave a muffled bark in his sleep. "In this town, rumors can all but replace reality."

"They sure can."

"Speaking of things replacing reality," I said, "I've been doing a deep dive on, uh, his social media." I looked around. There was hardly anyone in the dog park, but I didn't want to say Jackson's name out loud. "And I have to say, if social media's more exciting than reality, then reality is even more boring than I thought."

She laughed. "I can tell you how to search if you want. So you don't have to scroll through all the memes and whatnot."

"Could you? That would be—"

Another call was coming in. It was Mazie.

"Hey," I said. "I have a call I need to take. Hang on one second, if you don't mind."

I switched over. She interrupted my friendly hello with a frantic, "Oh my God, oh my God!"

"What is it, Mazie?" I said, trying to calm her down, though I had a pretty good idea what was coming next.

"They found him, Leland! They arrested my boy! They're charging him with murder!"

8

THURSDAY, JUNE 20, EVENING

I headed for my car. Mazie had said she and Jackson were at the county jail. My phone was buzzing with text alerts. I glanced at it, but the sun was so bright I couldn't see anything until I shadowed it with my hand. Noah's name popped up. His message said, *Cops dragged him out of some shed in cuffs! Help!*

I wrote back, *I'm on it.*

Then one from Terri popped up. I'd completely forgotten we'd been on the phone. She'd heard the news, she said, and would find out what she could.

I had the feeling I'd forgotten something else. I stopped on the sidewalk, trying to think what it was. Then I realized the dog purse slung over my shoulder, this ridiculous accessory Noah had gotten to keep Squatter from having to walk too much, was empty. I looked back. My poor old dog was still curled up beside the bench.

I went back and scooped him up. He was full of doggy joy at the sight of me. Unlike Noah, he had no clue I ever neglected him—or if he did, he had total faith I'd rescue him in the end.

．　．　．

I parked by the jail and headed in with Squatter in his bag. The guard manning the X-ray machine perused my ID and bar card for a good while, like he wished there was some problem with them so he could harass me. When they passed his heightened scrutiny, he zeroed in on the dog purse.

"Can't bring that in," he said. "I can't put a live animal through this here machine."

I held the bag out. "You want to take a look? I can't leave him in the car. It's almost 90 degrees."

He peered at the sleeping Yorkie. "I take it that's not a service dog," he said. "He your emotional support animal?"

"Course not," I said. I was getting a little annoyed.

"Well, then," he said in triumph, "you can't bring him in."

There was no convincing him. I stepped aside to text Mazie. She came out of the waiting room to babysit Squatter, and the way she fussed over him made me glad I'd brought her the distraction. I pointed out the pockets with his treats and his leash, explained that I'd be incommunicado for a while because the cops would take my phone before letting me talk to Jackson, and left them to it.

I knew the cops wouldn't let me see Jackson unless I called myself his lawyer, so I did. They said he'd been booked on suspicion of murder. One of them walked me to the interview room. Through the window I could see him looking like what he was: a sullen teenage kid who'd clearly got on the wrong side of somebody. The cop unlocked the door. Jackson looked up, part defiant, part scared. He was still in his street clothes, about as filthy as you'd expect someone who'd been sleeping in a shed to be. When I sat down at the table, I realized he stank. I also made a mental note to never let him pick his own clothes for court. His black T-shirt had a picture on it of bodies hanging in some sort of dungeon, and it said "Supreme Carnage" in letters made of bones.

The cop left, locking the door behind him.

Jackson still had his hackles up, but I could tell he was relieved to see me.

"How you doing?" I asked. "They treating you okay?"

"Not exactly. Look how hard they cuffed me." He held up his wrists. They were bruised.

That wouldn't get him anywhere, but I sympathized. Sitting down across from him, I asked, "You tell them anything?"

"I told them to go fuck themselves," he said. "Told them I wished I killed Karl, but I didn't."

"Uh-huh," I said. "Son, you got the right to remain silent, and that's a right you ought to exercise. No more smart remarks, okay?"

"What are you," he said. "My lawyer?"

"Well, they'll tell you about getting a public defender tomorrow, in your Summary Court appearance. But I guess I am for now, if you want."

He crossed his arms, cocked his head at me, and said, "I guess you got some experience. Maybe you'll do." His pose made me remember how I'd been at his age: a know-nothing kid trying manhood on for size, and picking the most awkward kind. Manhood of the defiant jackass variety, demanding respect that hadn't been earned yet.

I decided to give it to him, to put him at ease. I smiled and said, "Well, I hope I satisfy. Let's pretend I don't know anything. Start from the beginning. What happened the night Karl died?"

"Aw, who the hell cares?" He shook his head, looking at the ceiling like he was mad at it, like this was all just a waste of time. He reminded me so much of Noah right then that I had to fight the urge to shake him by the shoulders and then give him a hug.

I said, "You got the chance to set the record straight."

"Yeah?" he said. "He was a drunk, and he fell off a boat. He lived and he died. So what?"

"I'm not asking because I care about Karl," I said. "I'm asking because nobody's heard your story yet, and I want to make sure they do."

"They ain't gonna care."

"Making them care is my job. All you have to do is tell me what happened."

He sighed and looked at the door we both knew was locked.

Then he said, "The stupid thing is, that day started out good."

"Oh yeah? How so?"

"I got a raise," he said. "At the hardware store. Ten cents more an hour. I never got a raise before and it came with a gift card and some cookies that Cyrus's wife baked for me."

Cyrus was his boss. "That was mighty nice of her," I said. "What kind?"

"Butter pecan."

"Damn. I bet they were good."

59

He nodded. "I ate a couple at work. Brought the rest home for my mom. I left them on the table and took a shower." He stopped, shaking his head. "You ever had that happen, where one minute everything's fine, but next thing you know, it's all gone to shit?"

I nodded. "That what happened?"

"Soon as I turned off the water," he said, "I heard them yelling. I know what he sounds like when he's drunk. Or sounded like. I barely dried off, just got dressed and went in. The cookies were all over the floor, and he was in her face, and—" A flash of pain crossed his face. "And he was *touching* her. He was all over her, and she was about crawling across the counter to get away."

The mental image disturbed me too, but not nearly as much as it did him. His eyes were wide and blank, like he couldn't stop seeing it.

"So what happened next?"

"I pulled him off her. And he took a swing at me, but he was drunk. It didn't even land."

"Was he saying anything?"

"Aw, just hollering that she owed him fifty bucks. Something about how he bought her a tank of gas. He ran around the counter and got ahold of her again. I pulled him off and shoved him outside. You know she doesn't have fifty bucks to spare. She's still paying off the hospital for the time he broke my arm, when I was sixteen."

I shook my head. "That's a damn shame. I'm sorry you had to deal with him."

"I'm sorry *she* did. She shouldn't have to work double shifts all the time just because he's a drunk. If he wants to spend money on drink, he should've sold that Mustang he was going around in. I saw him driving around with some woman."

To get him back on track, I asked, "So, what exactly happened after you got Karl out the door?"

"Well, he didn't leave. I didn't want him driving drunk and killing nobody, so I went after him to say I could drive him wherever he was going. He was just setting on the porch swing yelling at me to bring him a beer. Said he didn't need a ride, he'd walked from the marina and now he was thirsty."

I felt like punching Karl myself, so I wasn't surprised Jackson did. I asked, "You give him a drink?"

"Told him the hose was round the side of the house," he said. "And he could drag his thirsty ass over and get it." While I was laughing, he added, "That's what made him turn on me."

"That how you got the black eye?"

"No." He was shaking his head, eyes blank again, like he was reliving it. "He, uh, he told me I should ask my mom about something. About the night they were at the Broke Spoke together."

That was the local strip club.

"He said my mom got so drunk she crawled up on stage and showed her tits to half the men in town. And he said it wasn't the first time most of them had seen them, neither. I just lost it. I popped him right in the face, dragged him off the porch swing and kicked him down the steps."

I didn't like the way this was going. I said, "Oh. Uh, you're saying you hit him first?"

"Yeah. First, and second, and a couple more times after that." He looked proud.

This was not what Mazie had said. I wondered if he'd told her that Karl had struck the first blow or if she'd embroidered that detail herself.

To avoid leading him, I asked, "Okay, so then what happened?"

"He hit me back. We fought until Mom came out, and then he ran off."

"And then what'd you do?"

"I don't know. Listened to music, probably." He shrugged like the rest of that evening had totally slipped his mind.

"Okay. Uh, am I correct in thinking you went out again?"

"Oh, yeah," he said. "Not right away. A little later. I went... Look, is this confidential?"

"Absolutely."

"I went looking for him. I was going to have a come-to-Jesus with him, to warn him off. I went to the marina, but his boat was gone."

"About what time was that, would you say?"

"I don't know. Ten? I just kept walking after that. Down to the beach, because it's relaxing, you know, the waves. And I slept on the beach. End of story."

"Okay," I said. "Well..." My crisis voice was back, slow and soothing. I doubted he'd slept on the beach. This time of year it was full of partying tourists and regularly patrolled by the boys in blue, so it didn't seem likely. I shifted in my chair and leaned toward him, my forearms on the table. "Jackson, I want you to know you can tell me anything. I'm duty bound to keep your secrets. And the more you tell me, the better chance I have of helping straighten this out."

He looked at his hands, shaking his head. "I didn't kill him," he said. "When can I go home?"

Judges didn't normally grant bail to murder suspects. That had always made sense to me. But telling him was not easy.

He didn't take it well. He swore, stood up, and tossed his chair over.

I didn't blame him. I still hadn't seen any evidence that he'd killed Karl, and to my mind, even if he had, it could well be manslaughter on account of the provocation. Maybe even involuntary manslaughter, depending on what went down. But the cops were calling it murder.

"After the bond hearing," I said, "you do get another shot. Your lawyer can request a probable cause hearing, which would be ten days later. Then they get to cross-examine the lead detective, and if the judge thinks they don't have probable cause for a murder charge, it'll get knocked down to some lesser charge that the judge could grant bail on."

"What's the point? My mom can't bail me out anyway."

"Well, I'd still like to see the charge reduced."

"Yeah? And I'd like a blow job and a trip to Disneyland, but I ain't getting those anytime soon either." He turned his back and crossed his arms. To the wall he said, "Even when he's dead, my dad can't stop ruining my life."

I decided right then to step up where Karl had not. Somebody had to fight for this kid, not just at a bail hearing but all the way through trial. And an appeal, if that's what it took.

I made a mental note to find out when they were taking him to court tomorrow and be there to offer my services.

Stepping up might cost me what little I had left, but I knew Noah would forgive me for that far sooner than he'd forgive me for leaving his friend at the mercy of the criminal injustice system.

I told Jackson that, and we shook on it.

When I left and got my phone back from the cops, I saw texts from Noah and Mazie looking for updates, and one from her saying she was driving Squatter back to my place. I answered, suggesting I bring pizza we could share while I told them the plan.

By the time Mazie left that night, I was exhausted but too revved up about Jackson's case to sleep. Insomnia won. I flipped on the TV. The local news mentioned Jackson's arrest and then moved on to the arson from a couple of weeks earlier: the ice cream shop on the beach had burned, and now a friend of the owners had started a GoFundMe for repairs. I stared at the ceiling wondering if maybe I should start a GoFundMe: *Help impoverished local lawyer defend an unpopular murder suspect!* The whole situation was so appalling that I started laughing.

The news moved on to the opioid crisis—someone in town had over-dosed, the second in as many weeks—and finished on an upbeat note, with Henry Carrell in full campaign mode: holding a baby, attending church, striding across a construction site in pinstripes and a yellow hard hat. He'd always known how to win folks over. Even back in high school, he'd been class president. I fell asleep thinking I should've watched him and taken notes.

9

FRIDAY, JUNE 28, AFTERNOON

The beach was crowded, like it always was this time of year, but even so it was hard to beat the salt tang in the air and the long view. Mazie's lunch shift was over, and she was on her way. I'd suggested a beach walk, thinking it might help clear her head. Jackson was still in jail, and whichever side you were on, it was always hard getting families to understand that criminal proceedings are marathons, not sprints.

I saw her parking and went around back of some tourists' volleyball game to go meet her. I was still six or eight yards away when she slammed her door and yelled, "You found out yet when I can visit?"

"Hang on just a second," I said. When I got closer, I reminded her that we needed to talk a little quieter. "We have to pull ourselves together," I said. "For his sake."

In a frantic whisper, she said, "Leland, I can't stand this! They're still saying he can't see nobody but you until he's through reception and evaluation, which the Lord only knows when that'll be done. And even then, I still got to fill out some form and wait to get approved. My God, I am his *mother*."

"C'mon," I said. I took her elbow and led her onto the sand. Down the beach a ways, I could see the burned-out husk of the old ice cream shop. "Look at that," I said. "Now that's a damn shame."

"I don't care about that old place," she said. "I'd burn the whole town down to get him home."

"Look, we're in it for the long haul. You got to brace yourself for the fact that if he doesn't get bail, he's looking at six or even twelve months in jail, waiting for trial."

"Oh God," she said. She broke away from me and ran down to the water's edge. To the unfurling waves, she yelled, "Lord, don't do this! I can't do this!"

When I caught up to her, I said, "You can do it, Mazie. You've got to, for Jackson. And listen. He's been holding up pretty dang well, considering. I'll be seeing him again shortly, so if you got a message to pass on, you just tell me."

She didn't look at me. Watching the waves come in, she said, "Leland, I am so grateful for everything you're doing. But as a father you have to know that nothing is going to be right for me until he walks out of there a free man."

"I do understand that," I said. "Listen, you want a coffee? Or something to eat?"

"I ain't hungry," she said. "And besides, I got an interview up in Awendaw in a half hour. It's a nicer place; the tips should be better. I need to work more. I need money so I can help him."

"Well, best of luck with that," I said.

I walked her back to her car, then got myself a hot dog and watched the seagulls fighting over scraps.

Then it was time to head over to the jail. I'd gotten some initial discovery from the solicitor's office, and perhaps more importantly, I'd heard from Terri what the local cops were saying about the evidence against Jackson. His arrest report showed his conversation with the cops had been longer than the majestic "Fuck you" he'd mentioned when we spoke. The story he'd told them was consistent with what he'd told me, though—that he'd spent the night on the beach—so it didn't worry me.

What did worry me was Terri's intel. The word on the force was that Detective Blount had not only seen Jackson near the marina, but he'd also seen him carrying a crowbar and then trying to hide it when he spotted Blount's truck. That seemed not just bad news for Jackson, but awfully specific, considering the autopsy report wasn't due back for another few weeks. If Blount said he'd seen Jackson with a crowbar and then the autopsy came back saying Karl's injuries were consistent with being hit by exactly that, we were going to have a problem.

I needed to get Jackson's side of the story. And I wanted to drill down more into his sleeping-on-the-beach story. I'd been going to that beach since I was a kid, and I couldn't think of a spot on it where a person could sleep without being in full view of anybody who was there—which was normally a lot of people this time of year. It also occurred to me I should check the tide tables for that night.

As I was resigning myself to the fact there were no shaded parking spots near the jail, my phone rang. I was in the habit of answering whether I recognized the number or not, since you never knew where a tip or a new client was going to come from. This was neither. Aaron Ruiz was calling from the county solicitor's office. As we said hi, I eased into a spot in the blazing sun and rolled up the window. Despite the lack of AC, I couldn't risk letting some passerby overhear the conversation.

Ruiz said, "I'm just calling as a professional courtesy. I got the short straw on that murder case, so I guess you and I will be seeing a lot of each other, and I wanted to start out on the right foot."

"Well, thanks," I said. I could feel the sweat gathering on the back of my neck.

"You got a tough row to hoe," he said. "And it's way too early to talk about any kind of plea, but I did want you to know I favor them when it's appropriate."

"Good to know," I said. "Thanks. But I'm actually confident in our case. And I know you got to do whatever case you get assigned to, but I don't envy you."

He chuckled. He knew what I meant. "Yeah, the tragedies are easier," he said. "The pillars of the community, the innocent kids—if it keeps me up at night, it'll keep the jury up too."

"Exactly," I said, wiping the sweat off my forehead with the back of my hand. "I imagine you been sleeping well."

"Well, but a man is dead here."

"And a kid's in jail. A kid you can't even place at the scene." I was fishing to see what he had.

"About that kid," he said. "He just your client, or is it Benton & Hearst we're dealing with?"

"Oh, just me. I'm of counsel for Roy, but I maintain my own practice." I liked the fact he'd pivoted to a different subject and his voice had stayed light. It was a good sign.

"Well, good for you," he said, and he sounded like he meant it. "Good for you. I know you and the kid's mom go way back, but still, it's a lot of work for what they pay you."

68

After we signed off and I went into the jail, I took a second to refresh my overheated self in the restroom. When Ruiz mentioned the pay, it reminded me of the financial nightmare I was about to walk into. I'd reached out to the county public defender's office, telling them I thought they had a conflict on account of how often they'd represented Karl in his various scrapes with the law, including child abuse against Jackson. They were more than willing to agree—they had more cases than they could handle already—so at Summary Court, I'd gotten the magistrate to appoint me Jackson's lawyer. That meant the state would pay me—at most—the princely sum of $3,500 to spend probably the next year of my life trying to bust him out of jail. If this went all the way to trial, I'd be lucky if it worked out to five bucks an hour.

When I came into where Jackson was waiting for me, he cracked a weak smile and asked, "You here to tell me it's all been a mistake? I can go home tonight?"

It was a joke, but it just felt sad. I sat down and looked at him squarely. "Look, Jackson, I wish I could. Going back in time a few weeks would be nice too. But we got to deal with what we got."

He nodded and looked at his lap.

I said, "Now, I need you to answer some questions. Like they say, with nothing but the truth, and the *whole* truth. All the details."

He shrugged.

I decided to spring it on him like a prosecutor would, just to see his response. "So what were you doing carrying a crowbar around that night?"

He looked up at me, confused. He truly did look confused.

I said, "Word is Detective Blount saw you walking by the marina with a crowbar in your hand."

"That is *bullshit.*"

"Which part?"

"All of it! I don't even own a goddamn crowbar. And I know Blount, or I've seen him around, but I didn't see him that night. I didn't see no cars on that road, nobody."

I sat back and sighed. "Do you have any idea why he might say that?"

"Because he's a dick."

"Fair point, but you're going to have to do better than that. The world's full of dicks, but most of them don't go around committing perjury."

"Do most of them tell a kid whose dad broke his arm that he deserved it?"

"Jesus. He said that to you?"

"He said all kinds of shit. He's had it in for me since, I don't know, ninth grade. He busted up a party I was at, and a bunch of us had weed." He looked off at the corner, shaking his head. Whatever he was thinking about, I had the sense he wasn't going to share it. He went back to joking. "Ruined a great party. Maybe he's just jealous of anyone having fun."

"Jackson, dang it, this is your life on the line here. It's not a joke. I can't help you if you don't take this seriously and really think about what might be going on."

"You don't get to tell *me* this is serious," he said. He was looking at me with barely concealed rage. "You ain't the one who's in jail and who got strip-searched yesterday."

"Oh, goddammit," I said. "I'm sorry. What the hell did they think they were going to find?"

"Drugs, they said. You know me: I'm pot dealer number one in Blount's book. He arrested me and threatened me with hellfire after that party, but I was fourteen years old. I got off with community service. I'm no dealer. I just smoke."

I shook my head, looking at him, letting him know I knew this wasn't right. I wanted to kick the shit out of whichever guards had strip-searched him—and whoever had set him up for it. But I had to set the small battles aside and focus everything on getting him out of here.

"Listen," I said. "Were you smoking that night? Is that why you can't remember too much detail or don't want to tell me?"

"What the hell's the point?" he said. "You wouldn't believe me anyway."

"I'm trying to help you," I said. "You just let me know when you're ready to give me the means to do it."

Back home, I went over what I had. The only way I could even confirm whether the solicitor's office was going to put Blount or anyone else on to testify that Jackson was near the murder scene was if I filed a notice of alibi. But unless Jackson gave me something better than him sleeping on the beach in a state of apparent invisibility, I couldn't do that.

When Noah popped in looking for something to eat, I asked if he'd seen Jackson at all, the day Karl was killed. He checked his phone, scrolled a bit, and showed me their texts: *Park tonight?* Jackson had said. Noah had answered, *Dunno maybe.*

Pretty useless. He shrugged an apology and went back out with a bowl of cereal.

His quick search for evidence on his phone reminded me that Terri had said something about social media, and that got me wondering how I could get her involved in this. What I needed was detective work to find anything that could throw doubt on Jackson's involvement, and that was her skill set, not mine. Maybe the $3,500 the state was paying me could finance my hiring her. Hell, hiring her might free me up to try to make some real money.

I gave her a call. I thanked her for the tip on Blount's statement and told her I'd realized I needed an investigator and the job was hers if she wanted it. "I'm playing catch-up as it is," I said, "and researching this social media stuff is not my thing. I had other people doing that for me at the solicitor's office."

"Must be tough," she said, "being David when you used to be Goliath."

"Heck yes. I don't know how those career public defenders do it. They've got fifty of these cases going at the same time."

"I've helped some of them too. Once in a while they need an investigator."

"I know you got a lot going on," I said, "working and getting your degree. So go ahead and sleep on it, but if you could let me know tomorrow—"

"I don't need to sleep on it," she said. "I need the work. And internet detective work is what I like best." I could already hear her tapping away on her keyboard. "It's unbelievable what some people put up there. I once had to tell a PD that his car-theft client had posted a video of himself stealing the car."

We laughed. "Dear Lord," I said. "People really are that stupid sometimes."

"Which is why you and I have jobs. Okay, I'm sending you some links. His Facebook, Twitter, and Instagram are all public."

I fired up my laptop and started looking over more of Jackson's life. Going to the beach, complaining about a hangover, joking with his friends. A photo he'd posted of Karl with devil horns added on and the caption, "Happy sucky father's day."

Terri said, "We might want to listen to this." I clicked on the link she'd sent and found myself on the Twitter page of some podcast called "4/20 Confessions." The logo was some sort of collage of pot leaves and kids' faces. One of the faces was Jackson's.

I groaned. "Not great, but his pot use isn't relevant to the crime. I should be able to keep any evidence of it out."

"I'm listening to the May 5 podcast. Check out the title."

I scrolled down. It said, "The Per420ct Murder." Not even witty. I clicked and was treated to the sound of Jackson himself opining on the awesomeness of marijuana, then flicking a lighter to start smoking.

I said, "He clearly had his college applications in mind when he recorded this."

She laughed. Then she said, "Oh, uh-uh. No. Leland, go to about the four-minute, twelve-second mark."

I scooted ahead. We listened in silent horror as Jackson described a dream he'd had after smoking a blunt. He'd dreamed of committing a brutal murder, he said, beating a guy half to death and then finishing him off with a baseball bat. The phrase "I turned his face into fuckin' hamburger" stuck in my head. All the kids were laughing.

I stopped it and asked her, "Was that hard to find?"

"No. It's one of his friends' pinned tweet, and it mentions Jackson's Twitter handle."

I looked at the clock. We hadn't even been on the phone twenty minutes. Ruiz was going to find this for sure. Even though it was most likely inadmissible as evidence, I knew from my own experience that things like that could make a prosecutor truly believe the defendant was guilty. It could put Ruiz on a crusade, making him less likely to go along with my bail request or offer a good plea deal.

But the real problem wasn't Ruiz. Hearing Jackson laughing like a hyena while he described beating a man to death made me have my own doubts.

10

THURSDAY, JULY 11, MORNING

On the morning of Jackson's bond hearing, Noah and I met Mazie outside the courthouse. It was a pompous-looking building, two stories, plain brick with some Greek columns thrown on the front to let you know it was important. We passed under oak trees hung with Spanish moss, then came back into the blazing sun beside the tattered-looking palm trees out front. I was telling them both what to expect, but Mazie hadn't said a word besides hello. She was terrified.

Once I'd deposited them in a pew in the oak-paneled courtroom, I went to the pen, where prisoners were held until their hearings were called. Through the plate glass I saw Jackson in an orange jumpsuit and cuffs. In a tote bag I'd brought an old suit from law school, when I was nearly as skinny as him. I was hoping they'd let me lend it to him so he could appear in court looking like a decent man instead of a prisoner.

I chatted with the guard. When I asked, he shrugged. "Put it through," he said, indicating the X-ray machine's conveyor belt. He sounded like it had been a long while since he cared about anything.

Jackson changed in full view of the guard and half a dozen other prisoners. When he was in his skivvies, I discreetly looked him over for bruises. I was glad not to see any.

In the courtroom, I was dismayed to see a couple of local reporters and some rubberneckers. Ruiz was shuffling papers at the prosecutor's table and whispering to his sidekick. When I got to the defense table, the bailiff deposited Jackson beside me. He wasn't wearing the necktie I'd brought. I wanted to kick myself for not showing him how to tie it. Karl probably never wore a tie in his life, and even if he had, he wasn't the kind of man to take the time to teach his son.

Jackson leaned over to me and said, "This is freaking me out."

"It always does, the first time," I said. "Try not to let it get to you." Courtrooms were designed to look intimidating. They put you in your place.

Judge Chambliss was still in chambers. In front of his empty bench, set lower than it but higher than us mere mortals, his clerk was at her desk. She looked young and a little nervous. With our small-town crime rate, I wondered if this might be her first hearing in a murder case.

It was my first time before Judge Chambliss. I was at a disadvantage. Back in Charleston I knew which judges wanted incisive legal argument and which ones would let off any defendant who said he'd found Jesus while in jail. But since coming home, I hadn't set foot in criminal court. I didn't know which clerks and bailiffs liked a friendly chat and which didn't. I wondered if this bailiff, who was standing at attention with his back to the chamber's door, had been assigned to General Sessions—that is, criminal court—on account of his size. He was a Black man with a face as impassive as an Easter Island statue,

76

and he looked like he could lift the front end of a Buick off the ground with one hand.

I turned to give Mazie and Noah a reassuring smile. He gave me a nod, but she didn't see me. She was glaring at Ruiz like her greatest wish was for him to drop dead on the spot.

She was going to need some coaching. I did not want the jury to see that expression on her face.

The bailiff called out, "All rise." The judge, an energetic little white-haired guy, scooted up the steps and took his seat between two flags: the Stars and Stripes and South Carolina's indigo with its white palm tree and crescent moon. I couldn't tell if his pink face was from sunburn or exertion.

The clerk announced the case. The judge leaned back like he was sitting in a recliner and said, "Morning, Mr. Ruiz. What you got for us today?"

"Morning, Your Honor. Well, as you know, our peaceful little seaside community had a murder last month." He paused to let the gravity of his words sink in.

Judge Chambliss shook his head like it was a damn shame. "I'm familiar, counsel. And may God rest his soul."

Ruiz said, "Amen, Your Honor."

I didn't normally send good wishes on high when child-abusing drunks died, but perhaps His Honor wasn't aware yet of what kind of man Karl was. I would need to make that clear.

"We're here to talk about bail," Judge Chambliss said. "Anything you want to say on that, counsel?"

"Yes, Your Honor," Ruiz said. "Mr. Warton here is a repeat offender with convictions for drugs and vandalism, two of them from just last year, right before he turned eighteen. And now he's charged with murder, and the victim is his own father."

Judge Chambliss was shaking his head with his lips pursed. I half expected him to say something about the folly of mankind.

"Not only that," Ruiz continued, "but when the police came to inform him and his mother that his father was dead, this young man"—he was pointing at Jackson—"fled out a back window and remained in hiding for more than a week. So even if the general rule was to grant bail in murder cases, which of course it isn't, the facts here weigh powerfully against granting it."

"Okay, thank you." Judge Chambliss looked at me and said, "And good morning, uh..." He glanced at something on his desk. "Mr. Munroe. I don't believe I've seen you in my courtroom before."

"No, Your Honor. I was with the solicitor's office in Charleston until recently, so today's the first time I've had the privilege."

"Well, welcome. Okay, you got anything you want to make of record?"

"Yes, Your Honor. I appreciate that. While it's not relevant here, I do want to make sure it's clear that when Mr. Ruiz suggested my client had some sort of drug record, he must've meant the $200 fine my client paid for possessing a single marijuana cigarette shortly after his seventeenth birthday. And the vandalism was a moment of teenage foolishness with some spray paint. He worked hard and paid for that small amount of damage."

Judge Chambliss asked, "That true, Mr. Ruiz?"

"We'll stipulate to the marijuana fine, Your Honor. And while I'm dismayed that Mr. Munroe is making excuses for vandalism, it's my understanding it was spray paint on the wall of a local bar."

"Thank you," I said. "Now, Your Honor, as Mr. Ruiz is aware, my client has no history whatsoever of violence. This is the first time he's ever been accused of laying a hand on anybody. And I know this isn't the time to enter a plea, but he denies any involvement—"

Ruiz stood up. "Your Honor—"

I said, "Mr. Ruiz, that's just for context. The point I was getting to is that as far as I understand the solicitor's theory, what he's going to allege here is that a boy with no history of violence was provoked until he lashed out at the father who'd abused him badly enough to break his arm."

"Your Honor, I—"

"Mr. Munroe," said the judge, "this is a bail hearing. You'll get your chance to argue for lesser charges later on. At this stage, I'm not going to second-guess Mr. Ruiz on charging this as murder rather than some degree of manslaughter."

I said, "Of course, Your Honor. My point was just that there's nothing here suggesting my client poses any danger to the community. And he's a local boy, just nineteen, with deep ties to the area. His entire family lives within an hour of this courthouse, and he's never set foot outside of South Carolina. He's a hardworking kid, and far from wealthy. Up until his arrest he was working nearly full-time at Barrett's Hardware here in town, earning just $7.95 an hour. In short, Your Honor, he's about as low a flight risk as he could be."

Judge Chambliss said, "But the first thing he did was flee. He went out the back window and went into hiding—am I wrong?"

"Your Honor, he slept in a friend's shed for a few days. He does have, I'm sorry to say, some fear of the police due to some perceived mistreatment that he feels he experienced during those previous incidents Mr. Ruiz stipulated to. But I've explained to him that there's nothing to fear."

"Okay," the judge said. "You finished?"

We both said we were.

He said, "All right, given this is a murder case, and particularly since the defendant already fled once, I'm denying bail." He banged his gavel and stood up.

"All rise," the bailiff called out.

As soon as the judge was gone, Mazie made a beeline for Jackson. They hugged; she cried. Noah came up too, and this time he smiled at me.

"You told us not to get our hopes up," he said. "You said there was no way he'd get bail. But you fought for him anyway." He stopped abruptly, gave me a nod of approval, and turned to say hi to Jackson.

I was fighting for both of them, I realized. And if I could give Jackson a shot at getting his life back, I had a shot at being redeemed.

"Excuse me, Mr. Munroe." Ruiz knocked my train of thought right off its tracks. He held out his hand. As we shook, I saw Mazie glaring at both of us. I'd warned her about this, told her me being polite to the prosecutor was in Jackson's best interest, but I was pretty sure she still saw normal attorney collegiality as some kind of betrayal.

Ruiz said, "I assume you'll be wanting a preliminary hearing?"

He meant the probable cause hearing. "Yep."

"We'll be sending over some more discovery as it comes in," he said.

"Thanks." I saw the bailiff coming over to get Jackson and excused myself.

We all went down to the pen with him. When Mazie saw him starting to undress in front of everyone, I could tell it was taking everything she had not to bust out crying. He traded my suit for his prison garb, gave her a hug, and let himself be led back out to the van.

She cried all the way back to her car, and then she started shouting in anger.

"Aw, man," Noah said. I followed his gaze and saw what he was reacting to: Mazie's car had been booted. She was parked just fine, but I remembered what she'd said about all the unpaid tickets Jackson had stuck her with.

"Dang," I said. "Listen, Mazie, you want a ride home?"

"I ain't going home," she said. "I finally got a new job, and I got to be there in fifteen minutes. Leland, I am never going to get out of this hole!"

"You will. My car's right here. You just tell me where to drop you."

She gave me directions to a roadside restaurant where, she said, everyone was passing through. There were no regulars to whisper about her son's murder charges and stiff her on tips.

As we drove, she said, "Leland, was that normal, how the judge treated him?"

"How do you mean?"

"He never even looked at him. When you said Jackson didn't do it, it was like he didn't want to know."

"Oh, that's because you don't enter a plea until the preliminary hearing. We weren't supposed to talk about that yet. I just wanted to plant a seed of doubt in the judge's mind, on account of that bit of character assassination we heard from the solicitor."

From the back seat, Noah said an enthusiastic, "Yeah!"

Mazie said, sniffling, "It's like he's not a person no more. When I call the jail, they ask for his inmate number, not his name. It's like nobody cares if his life gets wrecked."

"Well," I said, "we care. And the preliminary hearing will be different. The judge will hear us out. It won't be for a little while—I want to wait until the last day to request it, which would give us nearly three weeks to dig up more info and find the holes in the prosecution's case."

She nodded, looking numb. We'd arrived at her highway restaurant. She glanced in the wing mirror, wiped off her smeared mascara, said thanks, and got out.

Noah took her place in the front and said, "I was hoping for lunch, but I guess now I need to get to my PT appointment."

I turned around and headed north. "I'll bring you a sandwich when I pick you up. How's PT going?"

He sighed and looked at his lap. "Well," he said, "last week the therapist was talking about this case, actually. Everyone's talking about it. He said trials these days are done before they start. People see your Instagram and it's like, case-closed."

I thought of Jackson's podcast and winced. "Most of that stuff doesn't come in as evidence," I said. "And we question the jurors to get rid of the, you know, the tainted ones."

He didn't seem too convinced. We drove in silence for a bit. Then he said, "Does he have an alibi?"

"You know I can't discuss the details of a case."

He exhaled irritably. "Okay. I just meant, has he told you where he was that night?"

Something in his tone made me think he had something in mind and was checking to see if I had it too. When we stopped at a light, I turned to him. He kept looking straight ahead.

"Noah," I said, "do you know something?"

He didn't answer.

"Okay," I said. "But if you do, if you know anything, the best thing you can do is tell me." The car behind honked at me, and I accelerated a little too fast, throwing both of us back in our seats.

"Smooth move," he said.

"Well, nobody hired me for my driving," I said. "I get hired for my legal skills, but I can't do my best unless I know the truth. If you know anything, you got to tell me. Even if you think it's bad for Jackson's case, you telling me means I can be prepared to deal with it, instead of getting ambushed."

"Look, I'm not your goddamned spy," he said. "I'm not going to narc on my friends for the rest of my life just because you caught me doing stupid shit in high school."

He sat with his arms crossed, not talking, until I pulled up in front of the physical therapy place. My alarm bells were ringing. I knew there was something he wasn't telling me. I also knew I couldn't keep pushing, or he'd leave.

As he got out of the car, I said, "Have a good session. I hope you know I'm just trying to help Jackson."

"Yeah. Whatever." He slammed the door, then said through the window, "I thought the prosecution had to prove its case. Why do you want me to tell you all his private business like it's on us to prove he's innocent?"

I had no answer. He knew it. He walked away.

11

FRIDAY, JULY 19, MORNING

S itting in my office at Benton & Hearst, watching the raggedy palm fronds outside my window sway in the breeze, I listened to three or four rings of Aaron Ruiz's phone. I'd made an appointment to meet him that morning to, as I put it, "see what we can work out here." Jackson was still dead set against any kind of plea, but Aaron didn't need to know that.

"Solicitor's office," he answered. "Ruiz here."

"Hey there. I'm about to swing by, if it's still a good time, and wanted to check if I could bring you a coffee. I always hated the coffee we had at the office back in Charleston."

He laughed. "Yeah, nobody up here appears to have any idea how to make a good cup, either."

"We got other priorities, I suppose. What do you want?"

"A latte, I guess, if you don't mind."

After we got off the phone, I took another look at the notes I'd made for the meeting. My goal was to find out what I could about the evidence Ruiz had and what he thought about the strength of his case. The probable cause hearing was coming up, so it was a logical time to start feeling each other out for maybe reducing the charges or doing a plea deal. If he offered one, I would tell him I'd run it past my client.

As I was getting up to leave, Roy popped his head in the door. "Morning, Leland. You got a second?"

"Just barely," I said. "I have an appointment, but a couple minutes won't kill me."

He held out a big manila envelope. "I hate to ask," he said, "but is there any way you could run this up toward Charleston for me today? Not into the city, just one of the gated communities on the islands. I have so much going on, and then I thought, this might be a nice opportunity for you to connect with this client."

"Who's the client?" I had no desire to drive anywhere, but apart from meeting with Ruiz, my schedule was clear. Ample free time was a side effect of my lack of business development skills.

"Collin Porter. The major investor in Blue Seas. Henry's buying two more yachts, and we got some papers for Porter to look over and sign."

"Okay, will do." I took the envelope.

"Great. Uh, try and be a little more enthusiastic, maybe?" He was smiling, like he was teasing me, but I could tell he was bothered. "I'm trying to help you build your future here. Mr. Porter's an important man, and I want him to like you."

"Oh, thanks much," I said. "I'm sorry. I'm just distracted. Lot going on."

"That murder case?"

I nodded. I wished I hadn't opened the door to talking about that.

He sighed like he was about to lecture someone young and foolish. "Leland, I'm sorry to tell you, but that case is a dog. You'll never hear me say that outside this office, of course. I been telling people you're trying to make a name for yourself. Take on something big to show you can do a lot more than get somebody out of a DUI."

"Well, thank you," I said. "I appreciate that. Uh, who's been asking?"

"Just about everybody. On top of it being murder, the Wartons are notorious. You know how it is."

"I do," I said, in my poker voice. I had my views on what it said about a man's intelligence to mindlessly go along with small-town prejudice, but he didn't need to know them.

"Okay then," he said. "Anyway, I'll have Laura text you Porter's address and the times he's available today. Just try not to be too distracted when you're there."

Ruiz's office was on the second floor of the courthouse. He was the same rank I'd been, assistant solicitor, so it was nothing fancy, just the usual hand-me-down cherry-veneer desk and wall of legal books that nobody ever read. He'd tossed his necktie on the windowsill and undone the first button of his shirt. I took that as a good sign. It was the opposite of aggressive.

When we'd got through the niceties and about half of our coffees, I leaned back, crossed my left ankle on my right knee and said, in an apologetic tone, "So, I hope you'll forgive me on this, but I'm still not getting why the office charged this as murder." I was careful not to say *you* charged it. Blame made folks defensive, and I knew it was his boss's decision anyway. "I mean, we got a teenage boy with no history of anything like this, and no evidence placing him on the boat, so..."

He was shaking his head a little, side to side, like he could see my point but there was more to it. I sensed from his reaction that I was probably right about the boat: they didn't have any evidence Jackson had been on it that night.

"Well," he said, "we do have a police detective who placed him at the marina. *And* said he was carrying something that could be used as a weapon."

"Oh, I hear you," I said. "I mean, that isn't good for a defendant. But can you really look at it in a vacuum? I mean, without considering the defendant's record or the fact that folks can make an honest mistake about what they've seen? Or who?"

"Well, no," he said. "But when you got someone who had a fight with the victim earlier that evening, and he's walking down to where the victim is with some kind of blunt-force instrument in his hands, I have no basis to call that manslaughter."

"Mm-hmm." I nodded, taking that in. I would've seen it the same way if I were sitting on his side of the desk. Going to find somebody at night, for no good reason, with a weapon in your hand, certainly looked like malice aforethought. Unless the coroner's report clearly pointed one way or the other, it was all going to come down to Detective Blount's testimony.

"I mean," he said, "you've been in my shoes before. What would you do on these facts?"

"I'd do the same thing you are," I said. I had a good enough sense of who Ruiz was to know that if I wanted him to believe a word I said, I had to answer that one frankly. "On just those facts, if I was looking at it in a vacuum, I'd do the same thing. And maybe your Mr. Ludlow," I said, meaning his boss, "is looking at it in a vacuum. But back at the bond hearing, you know, I was speaking the God's honest truth. We got hospital records. That kid was beaten, had his bones broken, the works. Karl was… I mean, would you want any sister of yours to marry a man like that?"

"Oh, hell no. Look, I prosecuted Karl myself, nine or ten years ago, for breaking and entering and illegal possession of a firearm. That's public record, and I know a lot more things that aren't."

"I'm sure you do," I said. "That man was a blight on God's green earth."

"Sure, but murder charges don't depend on whether the victim was a good guy."

"Not whether he was a good guy exactly, no," I said. "But would I be lying if I said the difference between the thirty-year minimum sentence for murder and the two-year minimum for manslaughter does sometimes come down to whether the sumbitch was asking for it?"

He chuckled despite himself and said, "Nope, you wouldn't." Prosecutors tended toward brutal humor. When you spent every working day dealing with atrocities, it was a necessity.

He finished his coffee and asked, "So is that what you're saying? That what we got here is an abused boy who finally snapped?"

"*If* he did it at all," I said, "then yeah, that's how I see it. And I can tell you we're looking at a not-guilty plea. I plan to put Jackson on the stand." He would know that meant Jackson had not confessed murder to me. I wasn't allowed to put a man on the stand who I knew intended to perjure himself.

He took that in, nodding like he could see a jury buying that story. If we did end up getting offered a plea on manslaughter, Jackson would hate me for it, and his mother might too. But two years was a hell of a lot better than thirty.

"Well," said Ruiz, "I can't reduce the charges just on your say-so. We got some steps ahead of us, and we got to go through them, and I have to run it past Ludlow."

"You getting pressure from above?" It was odd that he hadn't come into this meeting with permission to at least sketch out some options.

"Oh, you know," he said. I didn't know, and he seemed a touch uncomfortable, like he wanted to get off the subject. "But I do hear what you're saying. And I like the way you work. I had some guy in here last week shouting Bible verses at me. You should tell your friends on the defense bar they'd help their clients a lot more by taking a cue from you."

"Oh Lord," I said. "I don't have friends on the defense bar, and I don't intend to. Soon as this case is over, I'm going back to trying to launch myself in business law and civil litigation."

"This isn't where you want to be?" he asked. "I figured that's why you took the case. I mean, I know you know the family, but a murder case that's all anyone's talking about is a quick way to make a name for yourself."

"Aw, hell no," I said. "If I'm going to be in criminal law at all, I want to be putting bad guys away."

"Yep, yep, yep," he said, nodding. "I hear you on that." Ruiz was a straight arrow. Even back in high school, I remembered, he kept his hair cut like a forty-year-old businessman, and he declined all invitations to get drunk or high. He tossed his coffee cup in the trash and asked, "So why you doing it? Just loyalty?"

"Partly that, yeah," I said. "And partly, I do not think the kid did it. At all."

"I mean, the abuse thing, though," Ruiz said. "There's motive right there."

"He had that motive all his life," I said. "And never did anything."

"People can snap, though," he said.

"Lots of people," I agreed. "Karl was a nasty drunk, and his own brothers don't care that he's gone. I'm not saying that to cast aspersions on a dead man. I just mean there's any number of people who might've had a grievance against him."

"Only one who was seen by a police detective down by the marina, though."

I nodded. Blount really was the linchpin. If Jackson wanted to be a free man, instead of going down at least a couple years on manslaughter, I was going to have to find some way to make Blount look like a liar.

But I also wanted to figure out why Ludlow was getting in the way of a plea. What did he stand to gain from seeing a teenage boy imprisoned for thirty years?

12

FRIDAY, JULY 19, AFTERNOON

Heading up toward the highway to Charleston, I decided to swing past the Broke Spoke. I'd never been inside. When I was young enough to be interested in strip clubs—young enough to overlook how desperate most of the girls looked—the Broke Spoke was still just a twinkle in the eye of Dunk McDonough, one of our sleazier local entrepreneurs. He owned the highway truck stop, and at some point he'd had a storage shed behind it expanded and converted into a strip club. With all the passing truckers, I had to admit it was probably a good business move.

In broad daylight the club was plain ugly: a box with tiny windows and shabby siding the color of pea soup. I figured Dunk must've gotten a hell of a deal on that siding. It didn't take much expertise in erotica to know that pea green was not widely considered a sexy color.

There were only a few cars in the lot—at four p.m., I wasn't expecting many—but one of them was a red Mustang convertible. It had South Carolina plates. Perhaps Karl's brothers had accurately intuited that his missing sports car was with his waitress girlfriend.

I didn't think it'd be a good investigative move to show up at a club I'd never set foot in and ask her questions about her dead boyfriend. That kind of thing made witnesses bolt, especially a witness who had inexplicably retained the dead man's thirty-thousand-dollar car. I scribbled the plate number in my notebook and got back on the road.

Going to Charleston wasn't easy. They say people who've lost a limb can still feel it. They can tell you what position their phantom limb is in, and feel pain in it. My life up there was like that: a phantom family living in the house we'd lost. At this hour on a Friday, phantom Elise was on her way home from work, listening to classical music on WSCI, 89.3 FM.

Thoughts like this were why I didn't like long drives.

I scrounged for a CD in the console and popped Tom Petty & the Heartbreakers' greatest hits into the player. Elise had never shared my enthusiasm for that band, so it worked pretty well to numb the phantom pain.

The address Roy had given me was in one of the gated communities on the islands. Golfer paradise. It was exactly where I'd expect someone to live if the word "investor" was part of their job title. I was glad to get off the highway before I got too close to my old exit.

The road wound through a thick growth of palmettos, oaks, and hick-ories. At a couple of bends, the dense woods opened onto pools of water dotted with cypress trees draped in Spanish moss. I rounded another bend and saw the gatehouse. It looked like a Swiss chalet and was tastefully accented with summer flowers. When I pulled up at the window, the slow blink of the uniformed man inside reminded me what a piece of crap I was driving. I also got self-conscious about

Tom Petty belting out "Refugee." I turned it down to a more civilized volume.

The guard disappeared with my license for a second. When he came back to return it, he said, "Mr. Porter will see you." He sounded surprised as he pressed the button to open the gate.

I emerged beside a rolling green golf course with a clubhouse that could've passed for one of Queen Elizabeth's country getaways. Beyond it, the ocean glittered. As I followed my GPS, the houses got larger and the yards got deeper. All of it was lush and beautiful in the way a place can only be if you hire a team of landscapers to curate every blade of grass.

Mr. Porter's home was one of the biggest yet, set on a low hill, its rising half-circle drive lined with palmettos. I didn't see a single dead frond on any of them. I pictured his squad of gardeners sending guys scooting up the trunks like ninjas to remove anything unsightly. I parked my piece of junk at the bottom of the drive, where I hoped no one in the house would see it, and started the hike to his massive front door.

As I got closer, I heard shouting coming from inside. It sounded bad. I couldn't see anyone through the sparkling glass on either side of the door, but somewhere in there, two men were snarling at each other. I touched the doorbell, figuring they'd stop when I rang. Then I would pretend not to have heard.

They didn't stop. The door swung open, revealing a smiling fortysomething man in a tux. "Ah," he said. "Leland? Collin Porter. Pleasure to meet you." He reached out and gave me a firm alpha-dog handshake. He was a sturdy guy with a weathered face. As we crossed the marble entryway, I saw what the shouting had been. In a room off to the side, *Scarface* was playing on a TV screen the size of my car. I didn't see anyone watching it.

I followed him into a kitchen. The ceiling looked about fourteen feet high. On the other side of the kitchen island and its vast expanse of some fancy stone, a plate glass window showcased the ocean view. French doors led to a deck big enough to host a wedding on.

Something moved at the corner of my eye.

"Oh, Anthony," Porter said. "Get Leland a drink."

The other guy, walking toward a built-in bar, was also wearing a tux.

I said, "Thanks for making the time, Mr. Porter. I can see you folks have plans this evening."

"Oh, it's no trouble. Thanks for driving up. I'm always glad to get a deal closed." He reached for the envelope, and I handed it over. "What do you take? Something light, since you're driving? Gin and tonic?"

"Thank you much. Yes." Roy had schooled me on the rule that barring medical orders, drinks offered by clients couldn't be refused. I figured I could get away with just a couple of sips.

Anthony had turned his head to make sure he got the order right. My gut sank at the sight of his face. We'd worked together in Charleston. He had to know the circumstances of my departure. Everyone there did. I hoped he wouldn't mention it to Porter.

I said, "Hey, Tony! How you been? Still with the solicitor's office?"

"Oh, yeah. Same old, same old." He looked at me for about half a second too long. Then he crossed the room with my drink, almost tripping on a rug that appeared to be the hide of an animal about the size of an elk.

I would not have pegged Tony as a pink-cummerbund man, but that's what he had on. The color reminded me that his last name was Rosa. I asked, "You two gentlemen going to a wedding or something this evening?"

Porter looked up from the papers he was initialing and cocked his head. "Oh, no," he said. He seemed surprised at my ignorance. "Tonight's the joint fundraiser for Henry Carrell and Sheriff Gaillard's campaigns. Don't tell me you're not attending?"

"Well, unfortunately," I said, "I won't be back to Basking Rock in time tonight." Of the various lies and truths at my disposal, I thought that one would make the best impression. Being too broke for a ticket was pathetic, and he'd think I was a fool if I said I'd calendared it wrong.

"Too bad," Porter said. "Well, it's a foregone conclusion they'll both get reelected, but it's a nice event. Much too nice to be dealing with legal papers while I'm there, and I've only got a narrow window to get down there and back tonight, so thanks for helping me get this off my desk." He pulled the last sticky arrow off the last of many pages and signed with a flourish. Gold light flashed off the nib of his fountain pen. I wondered if there was a place all wealthy professional men went to get their accessories: fountain pen, chunky gold watch, understated $200 haircut.

I asked my former colleague, "What's your interest in the election, Tony?"

"My sister lives in Basking Rock."

"Oh?" I started flipping through the documents, checking that Porter had signed and dated everywhere he should. "Anyone I know?"

"Her husband's the mayor."

"Huh," I said. The mayor was old enough to be Tony's dad. "Well, that must be nice."

Porter chuckled. "And this must be nice for *you*," he said. "More pleasant than investigating that sad little murder case I heard you're on."

I gave him the required smile. Apparently every damn fool was a rubbernecker now. "Well," I said, picking up my glass for a sip, "I tell you what, the liquor on your case is definitely better."

They laughed and clinked their tumblers together. I tucked the papers back into their envelope and raised my glass to theirs. When we'd taken our sips, I said, "Well, Mr. Porter, it all looks good. I'll get this to Roy tomorrow morning."

"Thanks much. Now, just so I have a scoop for everyone at the fundraiser, tell me, will you?" He threw a glance over his shoulder, a theatrical gesture to show he was making fun of all those *other* rubberneckers, then asked in a stage whisper, "Did Jackson murder his father?"

I chuckled politely. Tony laughed so hard I could see his molars. I wondered why a local prosecutor would be sucking up to some yacht investor. How'd they even know each other?

As the laughter subsided, Porter suggested we head for the door. We hadn't gone two steps when his phone rang.

"I've got to take this," he said, turning to shake my hand goodbye. "Thanks again. Anthony, would you see Leland out?"

Porter stepped through the French doors and closed them. Tony and I headed the other way. As his dress shoes clacked across the stone tiles of the entryway, he asked, "So, how's life after the solicitor's office?"

"Oh, different," I said. "But good."

"Putting everything else aside," he said, "I do want you to know we were all sorry to hear about your wife."

"Thank you."

"Glad to hear your boy's doing better," he added.

I wondered by what route that information had reached him. "Well, thank you again," I said. "It's a relief, that's for sure."

He came out the front door with me, to my chagrin. I glanced down the driveway and was relieved to see that a row of yucca plants blocked the view of my Chevy.

He stopped on the porch, reached into his chest pocket, and said, "Porter doesn't like me to smoke indoors."

"Huh," I said. "Well, I guess that's understandable." I was getting very curious about why these two were friends. "Anyway, got a lot on my plate this evening, so I'll be seeing you. Let's stay in touch."

He nodded, lit his cigarette, and raised one hand to say goodbye.

As I drove past the Swiss chalet and through the overgrown woods, I realized I was stuck. I'd said I wouldn't be back in time to attend the fundraiser, so I couldn't very well risk being spotted in town. Just before the forest road crossed the highway, I pulled over to check my email for the invitation. I needed to see what time it started.

Turned out I'd have to wait about an hour.

As I sat there wondering where the hell to go in the meantime, something light blue caught my eye out the passenger window. It was a clump of Stokes' aster, Elise's favorite flower. Each one looked like a three-or-four-inch firework the color of the flame on a stove.

Elise was never big on bouquets, or boxes of chocolates or other traditional things. She'd made our front yard and part of the back look like a meadow, with these asters and a hundred other wildflowers whose names I'd never know.

I remembered a night in our living room. No lights on, just the street-lamp casting shadows inside. Noah was upstairs. Elise was wearing a dress in some dark color and holding a wine bottle, which I was trying gently to get away from her. I'd come home to find her drinking. To cajole her, I'd put on Sinatra, something slow from the Capitol years. There was hardly any music written in the last hundred years that she liked, but his was an exception.

I'd gotten her up off the couch. I was tugging on the bottle, making some kind of joke, trying to surprise her or relax her so she'd let go easily. Through the front window I could see a clump of these blue flowers in the yard. When I heard Noah's feet on the stairs, I pulled Elise close and started swaying with the music. I didn't want Noah to see that his mother was drunk.

He was staring at his phone. When he looked up and saw us, the look on his face, lit up by whatever web page he'd been on, was a flash of surprise and then pure contempt. Of course he knew what was happening. He was sixteen years old; he'd gotten home long before I did. He'd seen her drunk a hundred times.

13

FRIDAY, JULY 26, AFTERNOON

I met Terri at the dog park for an update. It was a good place to talk, with just a few benches eight or ten yards apart, overlooking a green slope down to the lawn where folks tossed balls or Frisbees for their pets. She was standing by a bench holding a ball for her new puppy to jump at. When we got close enough, Squatter got excited at the sight of his friend, so I stooped to set him down. Her puppy ran over and did happy circles around him.

I asked, "He's not going to get to the size of a purebred rottweiler, is he? What's he mixed with?"

"No, that would definitely be too big for me to control. His mom was a black Lab."

"Still a full-sized dog, though."

"Well, no offense," she said, looking at Squatter, "but I wanted a dog that could scare people."

"That's understandable, in your line of work."

"Mm-hmm." She sounded like it wasn't just work she was thinking about.

She didn't continue. I didn't want to intrude, but I said, "Some folks think lawyers are scary too, so if you need more help than that puppy can provide, you let me know."

She laughed it off. "I'm good," she said. "But, speaking of work, I have some information."

"Oh, yeah?" We sat on the bench.

"So, first off, Jackson's alibi. There's about zero chance he spent the night on the beach."

I sighed. "Yeah, I had my doubts."

"Remember the ice cream stand that burned? Same night? The beach was crawling with cops and firefighters and all the tourists, plus the local gawkers. The cops swept the beach for witnesses, because it looked like arson right off the bat."

"I take it nobody saw Jackson sleeping rough. Or otherwise."

"Not a soul. I also checked with the shops near the marina, to see if anybody'd spotted him after Blount did. Or before, for that matter. No luck, although one cashier said Karl had bought a case of beer around 7:45."

"What time did the ice cream stand burn?"

"The 9-1-1 call came in at 10:09 p.m."

"Huh," I said. "Mazie said she drove down to the marina looking for Jackson, but she didn't mention seeing the fire."

"Hmm." She tossed the ball, and her puppy flung itself downhill. Then she pulled some papers out of her tote bag. "I also got some intel on that Mustang. It's in Karl's name, but there's no car loan on his credit report. I checked all three bureaus."

"You did?" I looked at the papers. "How? Is that legal now because he's dead?"

She hesitated. Then she gave me a look and said, "Let me rephrase. Some intern of mine went crazy and pulled his credit reports."

"Oh." I smiled. "Yeah, interns. Sometimes they just go rogue." I added her credit-report maneuver to the list of secrets I planned to take to the grave. Then I realized what she meant about the lack of a car loan. "Wait," I said. "You saying he paid cash for it?"

"Or someone just *gave* him a Mustang convertible." We both laughed. She said, "Maybe if Karl was a cute young woman, but…"

"Yeah," I said. "Karl definitely had a more limited appeal. What's this address here?" The car was registered someplace a few towns down the coast.

"That's his girlfriend, Kitty Ives, the Broke Spoke waitress. He registered it at her place."

"Huh. I want to talk to her, but I thought barging into the strip club wasn't the best approach."

She laughed. "Yeah, you'd better be discreet. I've had run-ins with the guy who owns that place, Dunk McDonough. He's a control freak, doesn't like anybody messing with his business. If he knows you're asking questions, he'll make trouble for her. He tried to get the Jump-start halfway house shut down. It's a block from the Broke Spoke, and he said it made the neighborhood look bad."

"Worse than a strip club?"

"I know! It's just women trying to get their lives together. But he was always calling the cops on fake noise complaints. I've got a feeling he's why one of my ladies there got arrested the other week."

"So Kitty'd probably be scared of him," I said. "Okay. I'll reach out to her someplace else." Squatter, tired of playing, limped over and curled up in the sunlight. I scratched his ears and said, "I need to talk to Jackson too. Whatever he was doing that night, I need to know."

"Yeah. It's too bad he doesn't understand that." Her pup brought her the slobbery ball, and she hurled it back downhill. "Or does he? I know you can't answer that. I'm just thinking out loud. Is he scared of something? What's he trying to hide? Anyway. That's what I'd be wondering."

I was shaking my head, but not because I disagreed. "I don't know," I said. "I can't even remember how long ago it was that I lost my faith in… in *reason*, basically."

"How do you mean?"

"Folks don't decide anything based on reason. They decide what they want to, or jurors believe what they want to, and then they come up with an excuse for it after the fact."

She sighed. Even the wriggling puppy dropping his ball at her feet didn't get a smile.

"Not to be depressing," I said, leaning over to get the ball. "Although if you want inspiration and uplift," I said, tossing it downhill, "you probably need friends who've never been prosecutors. Or criminal defense lawyers."

That made her laugh. "Or cops," she added. "I don't think we realized, when we were in high school, that the careers we wanted came with a side of losing faith in humanity."

"They never tell you that, do they. Speaking of cops, you find anything on Blount?"

"Not much. Nobody I talked to saw him at the marina that night. For background, I already knew he's married, three sons in their teens, been a cop for twenty years. He started around the same time I did. And I don't know if this matters, but some of us called him the Enforcer. In a good way. Sometimes, in child abuse cases, he'd take it on himself to warn the perps that whether the law got them or not, he would, if they didn't knock it off."

"Damn," I said. "I hope the jury doesn't get wind of that. They'd come to whatever verdict he wanted them to."

"Yeah," she said with a smile. "Most folks love that kind of thing. I mean, somebody's got to stand up for those kids."

"Wonder why he didn't stand up for Jackson."

She shook her head like she wondered that too. "He didn't do it in every case. And he could've scared off just about anybody, you know? He's like six foot four. I don't know how he picked which perps to go after."

"Great. So the main witness against us is a superhero. That helps."

She laughed. Her dog was back again, and she got a treat out, holding it just out of reach: "Sit! Sit!"

The puppy sat.

"Good boy!" He licked the treat until it fell off her hand. "Oh," she said. "I don't know if you remember this—you'd been gone for years when it happened—but his sister-in-law was murdered fifteen or twenty years ago."

"Oh, yeah. God, that was an awful case. They ever catch the guy?"

"Nope. So there's your uplifting story of the day."

I said, "I imagine he's not a fan of folks getting away with murder. Little ax to grind, maybe." I wanted to ask what she thought of Jackson's theory that Blount had it in for him ever since his high-school marijuana arrest, but I never wanted to put attorney-client privilege at risk. Instead, I said, "I checked Jackson's arrest reports to see if he'd had any run-ins with Blount before, but he wasn't the arresting officer on any of them."

"Well, it could've been his partner. Or if Jackson was brought to the station, they could've had some interaction there." She put a dog bowl on the ground and poured water into it. "I didn't work that closely with him when I was on the force, but he seemed like the angry type. Joins the police for the power, you know? Even when he used it for good, I could see what a charge he got out of it."

"Huh," I said. "Doesn't sound promising for getting him to agree to an interview." As Jackson's lawyer, I had the right to ask prosecution witnesses for an interview, but they didn't have to agree.

"Yeah," she said. "I do remember that he hated defense lawyers. Thought they got in his way."

Before I could answer, my phone rang. I showed her Aaron Ruiz's name on my screen.

I said, "Hello, Aaron. How you been?"

"Afternoon, Leland. Glad I caught you before close of business. I thought you'd want to know, I just got the coroner's report on Karl Warton. Got a copy here waiting for you."

I parked down the street from the courthouse and ran. It was about two minutes before five, and if the solicitor's office here was anything like in Charleston, by this time on a Friday there'd be tumbleweeds blowing through it. Ruiz had done more than he had to by phoning me and waiting, and I didn't want to make him regret his courtesy.

I all but skidded into his office. He was leaning against his desk, ready to go, with a fat manila envelope in his hand. We nodded hello.

"Thanks much," I said, taking it. "I appreciate it."

He patted his pockets, checking he had everything. "Sorry I have to run," he said. "My boy's got a baseball game."

"Well, best of luck to him."

We were parked on opposite sides of the building, so we didn't go out together. I was walking down the courthouse steps when I ran into Henry Carrell.

"Oh, hey," I said, wishing I weren't sweating like a pig from my mad dash to Ruiz.

"Leland! Good to see you! I was hoping you'd be at the fundraiser last week."

"Wish I could've made it," I said. "I'm parked up this way, so—"

"Oh, me too." He was so tall I had to work to keep pace with him. "So, I have a pancake breakfast on Sunday, if you want to put in an appearance. Not a fundraiser, just a little social thing. There's some people I think it'd be good for you to know."

"Well, thank you." He sounded like he genuinely wanted to help me, though I wasn't sure why. "Where's it going to be?"

"At church, of course. Victory Baptist." We stopped at the corner, waiting on traffic.

"Oh," I said. "Sunday morning. Of course." I couldn't remember the last time I'd set foot in a church. "Thanks much. I'll come by."

He clapped me on the shoulder, smiling, and said, "It'll be good to see you getting involved around here." The light changed. As we headed across, he looked around like he was about to say something confidential, then added, more quietly, "You don't need to keep such a low profile, Leland. Feeling ashamed is only natural, but you just don't need to. Not many of us here know what went down in Charleston, and those of us that do aren't judging you for it. That's not Christian. We're all sinners."

I stepped up the next curb and kept going. "Thanks, Henry," I said, wondering what the hell he knew and how he knew it. "That means a lot to me."

"Well, I'm glad," he said. "This is my car." He bleeped his keys at the Mercedes. "See you Sunday morning. Nine a.m."

I gave him a nod and walked back to my car. This wasn't the time to worry about what he'd said. The envelope with the coroner's report was heavy in my hand. I needed to find out how Karl Warton had died.

14

FRIDAY, JULY 26, EVENING

At home, I waited until Noah went to play video games in his room before taking a look at the coroner's report.

I winced at the photos, but that wasn't the worst part.

I had to call Terri.

"It's not good," I told her. I was in the kitchen, looking for chips or chocolate or something to distract me. "Let's put it this way: I knew we were going to lose at the preliminary hearing. They have probable cause. But I didn't know we were going to lose this bad."

"What's it say?"

I cracked open a Coke and went to the table. "Well, if I were prosecuting this, here's what I'd say: 'Shortly after the night Karl died, a police detective gave a statement about what he'd seen on the night of the murder. He said he saw Jackson walking toward the marina with a crowbar in his hand.' And I'd let that sink in." I looked out the window at the twilight sky, at nothing.

"Okay…"

"And then I'd say, 'Ladies and gentlemen of the jury, when that officer spoke, he hadn't seen the coroner's report. It wasn't completed yet. But fully six weeks later, when it finally was, it said the victim's injuries were consistent with being beaten with a crowbar.'"

"Oh, shit."

"Yeah. And that's not all of it. It was pretty violent. The coroner said there were so many blows he couldn't count them."

"Oh," she said. "Oh no. There goes manslaughter."

"Most likely, yeah. Hang on." I went through the basement door and pulled it shut behind me to make sure Noah wouldn't hear even if he stopped blowing away cartoon soldiers on his screen. "It's hard to tell a jury my poor abused child of a client didn't mean to kill his dad when he whacked him in the head three dozen times with a crowbar. Or however many."

"Mm-hmm."

"And for another complication," I said, "they couldn't narrow down a time of death."

"Had he eaten?"

"Yeah, but they don't know when, so knowing that the food in his stomach had been digesting for however many hours didn't help pin down what time he died."

She sighed. "Any drugs? Alcohol?"

"Just alcohol. But that can keep fermenting after death, and the samples weren't great because of the decomposition, so they can't say for sure how drunk he was."

I heard her moving around. I could tell she was thinking something through.

On a hunch, I asked, "You find out anything on Blount?"

"Not yet." She paused. "But, okay. I'm wondering about this crowbar sighting. I mean, I spent eight years out on patrol. I've seen about every damn thing a person can have in their pocket or their hand. I've thought cell phones were guns. I once thought a bulge in some guy's pocket might be drugs and it turned out to be, I swear as the Lord is my witness, a chipmunk."

I almost spat out my Coke. "A what? Was it *alive*?"

"No!" She was laughing. So was I. "What kind of fool d'you think I am? Those critters never stop moving. If it'd been moving, I wouldn't have thought it was drugs, would I."

"It's good working with you, Terri," I said. I was leaning against the stairway wall with my eyes closed. When a case was doomed, or when the facts were more horrifying than usual, a colleague who could crack a joke made it easier.

"So keep working," she said. "You see where I'm going with this? I want to know how Blount was so sure he saw a crowbar. I mean, that's real specific." I heard her clicking away at her keyboard.

"Oh," I said, getting it. "It's nighttime, he's driving, presumably at a normal speed. He passes some kid…"

"And what's a crowbar look like? I mean, from that distance, it could be a stick, a shadow..." The keyboard clicking stopped. "Okay, Leland, I just looked at the sunset times and weather that day. Depending exactly what time Blount says he saw him, it was either nautical twilight or astronomical twilight. Which is basically straight-up nighttime. Can you get away right now?"

"Uh, sure."

"It's nautical twilight for another half hour," she said. "Then astro-nomical. And there's no moon, same as on that night."

"I've got a crowbar in the basement," I said. "I'll see you there."

The last bit of road down to the marina still looked rural. When I'd left for college it was barely even paved, but when Henry Carrell's charter company took off, they'd spiffed it up and added palmettos down either side. When I turned onto it and spotted Terri's Jeep parked a hundred yards down, I saw it still didn't have sidewalks. Part of it was lined with oaks that cast dark shadows from the few streetlights nearby. I'd have to ask Blount where exactly he'd seen whoever he saw.

I parked, and we got out. While Terri's dog trotted off to do his business, she leaned over her hood and messed with something. When she stood up, I saw she'd attached a little camera to her windshield wiper. "Well," she said, looking down toward the marina with her hands on her hips, "we got about a quarter mile to cover. This could take a while."

It took almost an hour. I walked, holding the crowbar, while she drove past, filming. Sometimes I turned my head to see her Jeep pass; sometimes I didn't. I walked out in the open and under oaks. After every shot, we'd confer through the passenger window about what she'd seen and what to try next.

Afterward we swung by the McDonald's drive-through off the highway before heading back to my house to look at her footage on my laptop. Her camera's three-inch screen was too small to get a sense of what Blount could've seen.

We sat at my kitchen table, divided a burger between our two dogs, and ate dinner while watching my shadowy figure walk past some palmettos. Terri had a pocket notebook in front of her, and she checked it after we watched each clip.

"That camera's good in low light," she explained, "but I took notes in case my eyes were better."

We were deep at it, hashing our theories out while the dogs napped at our feet, when I heard Noah limping across the living room. When he saw us he looked surprised—and a little embarrassed, probably because he was dressed for bed in boxer shorts and an Anthrax T-shirt.

I hit pause on the video and said, "Oh, Noah, this is Terri Washington. She's the private investigator I hired for Jackson's case."

"Evening, ma'am. I'm sorry; I should've got dressed. I heard voices but figured it was Jackson's mom."

"Evening," she said. "Don't worry about it."

"For the record," I told Terri, "Mazie doesn't hang out here at midnight."

Noah said, "No, I just meant, who else do you ever see?" He went to the cabinet, steadying himself on the counter, and pulled out a box of cereal.

I could tell Terri was trying hard not to laugh. She looked at me and whispered, "Harsh!"

Noah dumped some cereal in a bowl and said, "What's that you're watching?"

I said, "Oh, we went and reenacted something from the night Karl was killed. Just wanted to check what a witness could've seen at that time of night."

He looked—there wasn't another word for it—scared. "There's a witness?"

"I'll know more on Monday," I said. "At the preliminary hearing I get to cross whoever they put on, so I'll know a whole lot more about their evidence after that. But yeah, there is."

In disbelief, he said, "Someone who says he *did* it?"

"No, as best I know they've got nobody saying they saw the actual crime."

He was looking past me, at the laptop screen. "Somebody saw him on the road there?" he asked.

"I'll see what exactly the witness says tomorrow."

He looked at the counter, shaking his head. It hadn't really hit him before, I guessed, that his friend might not get out of this.

When he'd taken his cereal back to his room, Terri said, "He's taking it pretty hard, isn't he."

I nodded. "All his friends back in Charleston left for college. Now they're back after freshman year, but he hasn't seen them because he feels like they don't have much in common anymore. Jackson's pretty much all he has."

"That's rough."

We went back to work. After watching it all, it seemed pretty clear that with so few streetlights and so many trees, there were only two spots on the road where Blount could've gotten a good enough look to identify both the crowbar and Jackson. Both of them would've required Jackson to look toward the car as it passed, but that seemed like a natural enough thing for a person walking down a road at night to do. Even so, Blount still wouldn't have seen much unless he was going under twenty-five miles an hour.

Terri said, "I guess you know what to ask Blount on Monday."

"Yeah. Thank you."

Her dog, asleep under the table, gave a muffled bark. She reached down to scratch him and said, "I'll see if I can get Kitty's cell number for you tomorrow. Meanwhile, it's past time for me and Buster to get on home. He's going to wake me up at six for a walk."

"Oh, man," I said. "I'm glad my dog's too old for that."

"I thought a puppy would make me feel young again," she said. "Lesson learned."

I walked them to the door and stood on the porch until they were safely in her Jeep.

15

SUNDAY, JULY 28, MORNING

In the basement of Victory Baptist Church, I found myself standing in a prayer circle holding hands with true-believing local business leaders. The pancake breakfast had come with a side of ministry. Henry Carrell was opposite me, his eyes closed, listening closely to the preacher's words. Two men down from him, with his eyes shut tight too, was Pat Ludlow. He ran the local solicitor's office. As Ruiz's boss, he had the last word on what crimes to charge Jackson with. I was starting to see the point of getting out in the community.

"Oh Lord," the preacher said, "we know that we are sinners. We turn from our sins again today."

"Yes, Jesus," Henry said.

My spirit did not move. I was distracted by Ludlow's hair. It had a fluffy, blow-dried look that I associated less with prosecutors than with high-end car salesmen.

"Take control, Lord," said the preacher. "Take control of the throne of my life. Make me the kind of person you want me to be."

"Please, Lord!" Henry looked up, his eyes still closed, his face contorted. He looked sincerely in pain. I knew you never could tell what was in a person's heart, but it still surprised me. He had more money than any man needed, a marriage that by all accounts was solid, and three kids who all seemed to be doing well.

Afterward, as I was walking to my car, I wondered if he'd invited me to Victory Baptist so I'd see him in that state. Was he just showing me he'd gotten right with the Lord? Or trying to tell me something else?

It was a little strange to go from there to a meeting with a strip club waitress. Terri had come through with a cell number for Kitty, who'd agreed to talk to me as long as it happened somewhere else. Not Basking Rock, because Dunk—or anyone else who knew her from the Broke Spoke—might see her. Not where she lived, a few miles down the coast, because that town was even smaller and more gossipy than Basking Rock. We settled on a Starbucks in downtown Charleston. On a summer Sunday, I thought, only tourists would be around.

I arrived early so I could find a good corner seat. The place was half-full and loud with chatter, the hiss of milk steamers, and coffee being ground. I spotted Kitty as soon as she walked in: a big-haired brunette, skinny legs, stonewashed jeans.

The first thing she said after hello was, "I want you to know right up-front that I was working at the Broke Spoke the night Karl died. There must've been sixty people there, and they got security cameras. So if there's—I mean, I know you're trying to keep that kid out of jail—but if this starts getting weird, I'll just leave. Okay?"

"Oh, absolutely. Ma'am, I am not looking at you that way at all. And you are free to go at any time. Matter of fact, that's why I suggested we both drive, so you could do that."

Her hackles went down a bit.

"Now, what can I get you?" I asked.

When I came back with my coffee and her diet Frappuccino, her jittery nerves had a new outlet: she was folding a napkin into tiny pleats.

"So, what I wanted to talk with you about," I said, "was just some background on Karl. How well you knew him, if you knew of anybody he might've been in conflict with. That kind of thing."

She stopped folding and thought for a second. "I don't know when exactly we got talking. Last summer? It was at the Broke Spoke. He used to drink with this trucker, Pete something. He was a good tipper. I just talked to him every time he came in. He figured out what section was mine and always sat there." From her smile, it was a bittersweet memory.

"And how'd you two end up getting together?"

"I don't normally date customers," she said. "I just—in a place like that, you see how men are." She shook her head, looking at nothing in the middle distance, like she'd seen about all she ever wanted to. Then she tossed her hair and continued, "But he was always talking about his kid. Like, he was proud when he graduated from high school, because Karl hadn't. So I thought he was a good guy."

Something in her tone made me ask, "Thought? Do you still think so?"

She glanced at me with a flash of anger. "Doesn't matter," she said. "Nobody deserves to die like that. You wouldn't do that to a rabid dog."

"No, you wouldn't," I said. I took a sip of my coffee to give her anger time to pass. When it had, I tried a different subject. "That other guy you mentioned, Pete? You know much about him? Any idea how well he knew Karl?"

She shrugged. "They were drinking buddies. They shot the shit, you know. 'Scuse me."

I nodded to let her know that language was fine with me. "He from Basking Rock?"

"No. I don't know where, but he was a trucker. You know how it's set up: families stopping at the truck stop to eat would never see the strip club, but if you go back by the truckers' showers, there's a door. It takes you across this little alley and you're at the back door of the Broke Spoke."

I nodded like I knew. I didn't. I'd never set foot in either place.

"If you remember his name," I said, "I'd like to look him up. Just, you know, cover all the bases."

She looked at me like she was trying to figure me out, and said, "Did that boy really not do it?"

"Uh, ma'am, no, I don't think he did."

"Wow," she said. "I mean, everybody's saying he did."

"I've heard the gossip," I said.

"Wow."

"Oh," I said, "speaking of gossip, I'm sorry to bother you about this, but is it true you've still got Karl's Mustang?"

She looked at the door. I thought she might bolt.

"You're not in trouble," I said. "I'm just trying to figure things out."

She stirred her Frappuccino and look a long sip through the straw. I thought if she had wings, she would've hopped up like a sparrow to perch on the crown molding and dart out the door as soon as it opened.

"If I tell you," she said, "do I get immunity? Or something?"

"Ma'am, I'm not trying to get you in trouble at all. Quite honestly, you could tell me you sold it for scrap, and I wouldn't call the cops. I'd even put a good word in for you if anybody did get upset. I just want to understand what's what."

"He registered it at my house," she said, defensively. "That's where it, like, lives."

I nodded. "Uh-huh. Now, do you know why he did that?"

"To keep it away from his bitch ex. He owed a lot of back child support, and even though his boy was a legal adult by then, he thought she still might come after him for it. She's not going to get it now, is she? He wouldn't have wanted that."

"Well, they were never married, so it certainly wouldn't go to her automatically."

"He would've wanted me to have it. He told me." She looked like she might cry. "He wanted a lot of things for him and me."

"Miss Ives," I said, "I'm sure he did. But he was brought down before his time. Is there anyone you can think of that might've wanted to do that?"

"Yes. His ex. She called when he was at the Broke Spoke, two days before he died, and threatened him. She was screaming so loud I could hear it."

"My goodness," I said. "And do you recall what she was saying?"

"Just insults," she said. "I heard a few when he held the phone away from his ear. The rest just all ran together."

.   .   .

118

Driving home from Charleston, I wondered if what Kitty had said was true. By her own account she hadn't heard any threats herself, so I figured Karl had told her that. It was hard to imagine Mazie having the energy or the time to harass Karl. She was already working two exhausting jobs at that point, but then again, exhaustion sometimes made people do crazy things. I made a mental note to check Karl's cell phone records, once I got them from Ruiz, to see if Mazie had called him then.

At home, Noah was immersed in his video games. I took Squatter for a walk and then got down to prepping for Monday's preliminary hearing. I knew we weren't going to get the charges knocked down to manslaughter. This hearing was about nothing other than the evidence Ruiz had, and what he had pointed to murder: a violent beating, a kid with a grudge, a cop who said he'd seen him heading toward the scene with a weapon in his hand.

I was so absorbed in planning out my questions for Blount, and for everyone else I could think of who might be there, that I forgot to eat. Noah came out of his bedroom around nine o'clock, made his way to the kitchen, and put some water on to boil. He took a box of mac and cheese out of the cabinet and asked, "Want some?"

"Oh, sure. Thanks."

He limped over, sat on the couch, and asked, "You gonna get him out tomorrow?"

I looked at him. He was only half joking.

"No," I said. "They've got what they need to keep him in."

"So what's the point?" He sounded angry.

"Well, what I'm there for," I said, "is to find out everything I can about the evidence they've got. I get to cross their witnesses. I get to lock down their testimony, so they can't change it later to fit any new facts we might dig up."

He thought about that for a second. "Like what?"

"I don't know," I said. "Whatever comes up that says Jackson didn't do it or points to someone else."

He closed his eyes and took a breath. "Dad," he said, "I need to tell you something. But you got to promise not to get mad."

"What is it?"

"I said you got to promise. If you flip out about this, I'll just, I don't know. I'll leave. I'm not putting up with that."

"I won't get mad."

He looked at me. Deciding whether he believed me, I thought. Then he pulled out his phone. "I'd bring this over," he said, "but it'd be easier—"

I went to the couch and sat beside him. On his screen was a clumsy selfie—I could see part of his thumb over the lens—of him and Jackson laughing. Noah was holding a bong.

I took a deep breath. I was determined not to break the promise I'd just made. The sight of my kid doing drugs again, even pot, was straight-up terrifying given his history. And his mother's.

I asked, "What's the time stamp on that? And where was it?"

"Beachside Park," he said, touching the photo to bring up the date. It said June 6, 10:48 p.m.

"What's that on his shirt?" I asked. Jackson had on a white T-shirt with what looked like soot marks, as if he'd wiped his dirty hands off on it.

Noah sighed and looked down. "It's from the, you know, the fire."

"The ice cream stand?"

"Yeah. He smelled like smoke when he got to the park. You can't see the beach from where we were, but I'd heard the sirens. He said he might've done something stupid, but he was smiling, like he was bragging."

"You ask him what he meant?"

"Yeah, but he just shrugged it off. He did say something about practicing for Karl. He talked about those Viking funerals, you know, where they set a boat on fire and let it float away."

"Funeral?" I asked. "He was talking about Karl and a funeral? Goddammit."

"No, not like that. He's into all this Viking metal—"

Something in my expression must've told him he was going to have to explain that. "It's, like, heavy metal from Scandinavia. They sing about that kind of stuff, and he's got a T-shirt with this flaming boat on it. That's where he got the idea. He said he'd like to do that to Karl's boat and then be there to see the look on Karl's face when he found out."

"Okay," I said. "So just destroying Karl's boat?" That would still be a crime, if he'd actually done it. But it wasn't murder. "And the ice cream stand was practice?"

"I guess."

I heard the water boiling in the kitchen. "You sit here," I said. "I'll get it." I went to dump the macaroni in. I didn't have high hopes for what a jury would think of testimony that the defendant was talking about using the victim's boat for a Viking funeral on the very night when, at some point in time that the coroner had not been able to narrow down, the victim died. Especially a jury around here, where one look at those T-shirts decorated with fire and skulls might make them worry about

Satan. I could see it now: *Jury concludes local man killed in Satanic death ritual.*

When I came back, Noah asked, "So, does that get him off?"

"I don't know," I said. I didn't feel like sharing my view that such evidence might do more harm than good. "It doesn't get him off tomorrow, anyway. The hearing's all about their evidence, not Jackson's defenses."

"But, I mean, at some point," he said, "they got to admit if he was setting a fire and smoking a bong, he wasn't killing Karl."

"Yeah, they might."

"They *might*?"

I shrugged. "I'd have to present that evidence at trial. And that time stamp might be helpful, but we don't know exactly when Karl was killed."

"I have some texts too," he said. "It's not just that photo, for the time stamps. And his cell phone must know where he was when he texted me. But, Jesus, does he really have to rot in jail for—how far away is a trial?"

"Could be six-plus months, easily."

"Oh, goddammit. I can't believe an innocent person could be stuck in jail so long." He let his head fall back against the couch. His eyes were closed.

I didn't want to depress him by telling him how many innocent people ended up convicted. Or, for that matter, how much jail time Jackson might be looking at just for the arson.

I stirred the macaroni with a tablespoon, trying not to burn my fingers. Organizing the kitchen had not been my job when Elise was alive, and it was low on my list of priorities now.

From wherever she was, on some other plane or just inside my head, she nudged me. She wanted me to make sure he was okay.

I said, still stirring, "Now, I promised I wouldn't get mad, and I'm keeping that promise. But I just want to know, how often are you using?"

He sat back up and glared at me. "I'm not *using*. That wasn't even mine. Jackson brought it."

He'd always been quick with an excuse. It was always someone else's pills or some outside circumstance.

I rooted around the cabinets looking for a strainer. "Unless you want to end up like that boat," I said, "drifting around St. Helena Island— or floating out to sea on fire, if Jackson had his way—there has to come a time when you take responsibility. No matter who brings stuff. Or what your friends want you to do."

"I don't just do what they want. You think he wanted me to tell you that?"

"I know he didn't," I said. "So, thank you. The more I know, the more I can do to help him."

He let his head fall back on the couch again and said, "Whatever."

16

MONDAY, JULY 29, MORNING

Terri and I headed up the courthouse steps with Mazie between us, doing what we could to shield her from the local reporters and busybodies. Aaron Ruiz trotted past without so much as a hello. We caught up with him when he got stuck at the X-ray machine, unpacking his pockets and discussing the contents of his briefcase, but he only gave me a curt nod as he picked up his bag. I couldn't think why he'd be out of sorts. Any prosecutor knew cases hardly ever got thrown out at this stage.

As I put my bag on the conveyor belt, Mazie gave a weak smile and attempted a joke. "Should I be worried about my parking tickets? I don't want to walk out of here in handcuffs."

I reassured her, and we went through. She'd insisted on coming, and I thought sitting through it would be good practice for her, for whenever the trial rolled around. I had warned her, though, that Jackson wasn't going to be there; defendants didn't normally come to these hearings, especially not when they were in jail and their transportation cost the state money.

Terri went into the courtroom to get situated at the defense table. Court reporters weren't present at preliminary hearings, so she was going to be taking notes. The judge's clerk was too—that was standard procedure—but I wanted a second set of ears, and one that knew what I was looking for.

In the hallway outside the courtroom, I took Mazie aside for a quick reminder. "You're going to hear a lot of bad things about Jackson," I said. "More than you'd ever hear at trial, since hearsay and whatnot are allowed at this type of hearing. So this is going to sound a lot worse than the real thing."

She nodded, but it didn't look like she was really listening.

"Leland," she asked, so quietly I could barely hear, "are they going to make this a death penalty case? Do they want to kill my boy?"

"Oh, Mazie, no. Mazie, put that right out of your head. That's for kidnappers and, you know, pedophiles and whatnot. For that, it's got to be more than just a, uh, a regular murder."

"Really?" She looked up at me, her pale eyes wide. "Even though Karl was his father? The Bible says it's a sin not to honor your father and mother."

"Well, that's not the law," I said. "You don't have to worry about that."

She took a deep breath and relaxed, but she still looked haunted. The dark circles under her eyes made me wonder how long it'd been since she'd gotten a good night's sleep.

Ruiz made his case the way I expected him to, except for one thing: he had trial-worthy exhibits already prepared. Photos of Mazie's shabby little house with clouds of bugs darkening the air behind it. Blown-up quotes from neighbors describing the worst things they saw or heard during the fight. A bird's-eye view of the neighborhood, with blood-red arrows to show which way Karl must've gone back to the marina afterward. A map of the town to show that if Jackson was spotted on the street leading to the marina, there wasn't any place else along that route for him to go.

Exhibits like that cost money and time. In Charleston, none of us ever prepared them this early. You didn't need them to convince a judge you had probable cause, and it'd usually be wasted effort, since most cases got resolved with a plea before trial. I thought about Ruiz's boss, who hadn't authorized him to make a plea offer, and wondered what had that man so interested in this case.

Ruiz kicked off with a map on which Jackson's mug shot was shown in various places around town, based on cell phone location data.

I stood up and objected. "Your Honor, we've had no showing on how reliable that data is or what it's based on. If it's just pinging one tower, for instance, instead of triangulating, it could be off by twenty miles."

Judge Chambliss looked at me like I must be confused. "I'm not sure what you're saying there, counsel. Just by way of example, I use my phone's GPS to get directions when I'm driving, and it knows right where I am."

Of course, I thought. He's a small-town judge. He's probably never tried a murder case, and in a lot of his cases, technology probably doesn't even come up at all. I was going to need to explain more to him than I would to a judge in Charleston.

"Yes, Your Honor," I said. "I know just what you mean. I use that myself. But that's a different technology than what Mr. Ruiz is relying on here. GPS data comes from satellites, not cell phone towers. It's a whole different thing."

The judge looked at Ruiz. "Counsel, I know things are a little relaxed here, compared to at trial. But we got to have some standards. What type of data is this?"

"It's cell-tower data, Your Honor. Triangulated, I believe, as Mr. Munroe indicated it ought to be. And it tracks just how you'd expect if Jackson went from his home down to the marina."

"Your Honor," I said, "even in Charleston, that kind of data was at best only accurate to within a few blocks, and there's a lot more cell towers there than there are down here in Basking Rock. A few blocks here is the difference between the marina and the beach."

"Okay," he said. "Mr. Ruiz, unless you can trot an expert in here to show us why that's reliable, I'm just going to consider that data neutral. So it doesn't point one way or the other as far as telling us if he was or wasn't there. What else you got for us, Mr. Ruiz?"

I said, "Thank you, Your Honor." While Ruiz conferred with his second chair, I scribbled a note to myself to move to exclude that data at trial.

Ruiz then told the court he had some witnesses to present. The first was Karl's brother Tim. Ruiz had apparently spruced him up; a suit would've been too much, but he was wearing a collared shirt that looked brand-new. He testified about the supposed Christmas dinner death threat. It looked like Ruiz was going to paint Jackson as a kid with a grudge and then use Detective Blount's testimony to show Jackson had finally carried it out. Ruiz needed the grudge to help show it wasn't manslaughter. A murder charge required malice afore-thought.

When my turn came, I said, "Morning, Tim. You mind if I call you by your first name?"

He stared at me like he was noticing me for the first time and said, "I talked to you before!"

"Yessir. Uh, Your Honor, for the record, I spoke to the victim's brothers as part of my investigation."

Judge Chambliss said, "Uh-huh. Noted."

Tim said, "I asked you about the insurance, and you never did get back to me."

"I'm happy to address your concerns at a different time," I said, "but for now, we got this whole courtroom full of people waiting to look into your brother's death."

"Jackson did it," he said.

I heard Ruiz sigh.

Judge Chambliss said, "Mr. Warton, we're not asking for your opinion on the ultimate issue here. I'm going to ask you to answer the questions put to you."

If this was the Warton brother Ruiz chose to put on the stand, I thought, the other one must've been even harder to control.

"Okay," I said, "so back to your name. There's a number of Mr. Wartons in this case, so to keep things clear, could I just call you by your first name?"

"Everybody else does."

"Thank you. Now, Tim, at this point I'm not questioning your recollection of what was said, but I do want to ask, was that the only time in your life you ever heard anybody say they wished somebody was dead?"

He laughed. "Oh, hell no." He glanced at the judge's young clerk. "Sorry, ma'am. Heck no."

I felt the mood in the courtroom lighten. I smiled as I said, "People say that a lot, isn't that true?"

"Well, yeah. But—"

"And you've probably said it yourself, right?"

"Sure, but—"

"And did you then go out and murder anybody?"

"No, of course not."

"Of course not," I said. "Thank you, Tim. Now, getting back to that Christmas dinner, isn't it true that Karl nearly died that night? From choking?"

"Yes, it is," he said. "He turned blue and everything. I thought he was done for."

"And isn't it true that Jackson did the Heimlich maneuver on him?"

"The what?"

"The, uh, where you come up behind someone who's choking and kind of punch them in the gut—"

"Oh, yeah. Yeah, he did that."

"So Jackson did the Heimlich maneuver to save his father. And did it work?"

"Yes, it did."

"So isn't it true, then, that—regardless of what he or anyone else may have said—Jackson, watching Karl about to die, chose to save his life?"

"Well, that one time, yes."

"Thank you," I said. "I have no further questions."

As I walked back to my table, Ruiz would not meet my eye. In the front row, Mazie was smiling at me. I gave her a nod.

I sat down, wondering why Ruiz had put Tim on the stand. If he'd done any witness prep at all, I didn't see how he could've not known the Heimlich maneuver story. Why would he put a witness up whose own testimony could blow a hole the size of a 747 in the prosecution's allegation that Jackson wanted his father dead? I scribbled on my notes to call Tim to the stand myself if Ruiz didn't put him on his trial witness list.

Next up was the police detective who'd found Jackson's pothead podcast. At trial, I was going to object the hell out of that, and I expected the judge would exclude it. Ruiz had to know that. I didn't appreciate his taking advantage of a preliminary hearing, where the rules of evidence didn't strictly apply, to parade this junk before the assembled crowd.

Next, Ruiz tried to call Mazie. I objected.

"Your Honor," Ruiz said, "the defendant and the victim were involved in a physical fight on the night of the murder. She was a witness to that."

"She was inside," I said. "The fight was mainly outside, on the porch. We'll stipulate that a fight occurred." I doubted it would help Jackson's case to let Ruiz grill his weeping mother. Testimony from emotionally distraught witnesses could go haywire fast.

Judge Chambliss said, "I think that's sufficient. Or do we need specifics, Mr. Ruiz? A time of day?"

Ruiz said, "About six in the evening, Your Honor. And afterward, the victim left."

"We'll stip to that," I said.

The last witness was Detective Blount. As he took the stand, in uniform, I wished their witness could've been almost any other cop. Blount was square-jawed, with ramrod posture and blond hair in a crew cut. He could've played an experienced cop who took his job seriously on any TV crime show.

On direct, he told his story well, with the right amount of detail and zero fluff. Ruiz didn't ask what time he'd seen Jackson, which to me meant that must be a weak point for them, but he did have Blount point out on the map where on the marina road he'd been. Beside me, on her laptop, Terri was clicking through her photos to find the spot. Ruiz's map didn't show any trees, but from the bend in the road, it looked like the spot was either right before the clump of oaks or under them.

Then Ruiz asked him about the day Jackson was arrested. I stood up and said, "Objection, Your Honor. What's the relevance of this to a probable cause hearing?"

"I'll allow it," the judge said, "but make it brief, Mr. Ruiz. And Mr. Blount."

Blount said, "We located the defendant in a shed on Dexter Street."

"And what did you do then?"

"We proceeded to arrest him."

"And what did the defendant do?"

"He used foul language and didn't cooperate. In other words, he resisted arrest. At one point, as we were attempting to place him in the police cruiser, he attempted to run, but he was in handcuffs at that point and didn't get far."

That wasn't in the arrest report. I made a note to think about either moving to exclude any testimony on that at trial or letting Blount say it and then using the arrest report to make the jury wonder if he was lying.

My turn came to cross him.

"Morning, Detective Blount."

"Morning, Leland. I mean, Mr. Munroe."

Judge Chambliss laughed and said, "It's a small town."

Jurors would probably react the same way. Stumbling over my name made Blount more personable. I was glad trial was several months away, because I was going to need time to think through all the ways I could handle him as a witness and how each might play to the jury.

There were no holes to poke in his work experience, so I didn't try. I kicked off with, "Detective Blount, could you tell the court about any encounters you've had with Jackson Warton in the past?"

He looked at Ruiz, who shrugged.

"I'm not sure what you mean by encounters," Blount said.

"Meetings. Interactions of any kind. Let's start with encounters in your professional capacity." I was leaving it open-ended so they wouldn't get a sense of what we knew and what we didn't.

"Uh, well, I've been present on, I believe, three occasions when Jackson was arrested."

"So, all the occasions? All of his arrests?"

"Yes."

That was a point in Jackson's favor, to me at least. He'd told me Blount was there, but I hadn't been able to check his memory or his honesty because the arrest reports only named the arresting officer.

"And isn't it true, Detective Blount, that until this last time, when you arrested Jackson in connection with this case, none of his arrests were for any type of violence or assault?"

"Yes."

"Yes, what?"

"Yes, it's true."

"They were for possession of a single marijuana cigarette, and for spray-painting a local bar? That's Jackson's entire criminal history?"

"That's correct."

"Your Honor," said Ruiz, "we've stipulated to this."

"I'll move on," I said. "Now, in your position as a police detective, did you ever have occasion to learn that Karl Warton had a criminal history?"

"I'm not sure what you mean," he said. I leveled an *Oh, come on* look at him, and he shifted in his seat. If he was going to waffle on something as basic as this, I could use that. Juries didn't like witnesses who tried to weasel out of questions.

"Your Honor," said Ruiz, "we'll stipulate to Karl Warton's record, although I don't see how it's relevant at this stage."

"Thank you," I said. "Some parts of his record are certainly relevant, but right now I'm not trying to establish that Karl had a record. I'm just trying to get a sense of what Detective Blount knew."

To Blount, Judge Chambliss said, "You can go ahead and answer."

"Uh, I was not the arresting officer on anything involving him, but yes, I was aware he'd been arrested."

"Multiple times?"

"Yes."

"For violent crimes?" I said. "Child abuse, for instance?"

"That's correct."

"Beating the mother of his child?"

"Yes."

"Bar fights? Plural?"

"I was aware of that, yes."

"Were you aware he'd broken his son's arm?"

"He was arrested for that, yes. And there was a plea."

"Okay. And you knew that at the time?"

"I think we all did," he said. "It's a small town."

"I'll stipulate to that," I said. Ruiz and the judge chuckled. "So, knowing as you did that Karl was abusing his son and beating the boy's mother, did you at any point intervene to protect them?"

"I'm not sure what you mean."

I gave him another look and let the silence sink in. In my experience, most people didn't like silence. They rushed to fill it. He was no exception.

"I was never called to the scene of any of that," he said. "If I had been, I would've followed procedures."

I cocked my head like I had my doubts. "Detective Blount, you knew Karl from high school, right?"

"I did."

"And you dock your own boat at the same marina he did, right?"

"That's correct."

"So you had occasion to see him around? Not just in your professional capacity?"

"At times, yes."

He was getting nervous. I didn't know why, and I wasn't about to derail my cross by asking questions whose answers I didn't know, but I made a mental note to look harder at whatever relationship he and Karl may have had.

"Okay. And isn't it true that you have intervened personally in domestic violence cases before? By which I mean, you've warned perpetrators to cut it out?"

He glanced at Terri. He knew where I'd gotten that information. I enjoyed the thought that to him, that little Oprah at her laptop might look like a ticking time bomb. They'd worked on the same police force for years, and if he had secrets, he had no way of knowing whether she'd uncovered them.

"I have done that, yes."

"You've warned violent men to stop beating their kids more than once, am I right?"

"Yes."

"And why'd you do that?"

He hesitated. It seemed he wanted to choose his words carefully. Finally he said, "The law is the law. On or off duty, I'm sworn to it."

"Okay. But not when it comes to Jackson Warton?"

"That's not what I said." He was getting irritated. I'd found one of his triggers.

"My apologies," I said. "Why don't you explain in your own words, then, why you left this particular abused child at the mercy of his violent daddy?"

"I did *not*—"

"Objection," Ruiz said. "Badgering the witness."

"Sustained."

"I'll rephrase. You knew Karl. You saw him around, in town and at the marina. You knew what he was doing. Why didn't you ever tell him not to beat his son?"

He paused, like he needed a second to calm down, and then said, "I can't answer that." He glanced at Ruiz and amended it to, "I just don't know."

"Okay." I looked at my notes and scribbled "*Annoyed, says doesn't know*" in the margin next to the questions on this topic. "Uh, moving on, Detective Blount, you've said on the night Karl disappeared, you were driving down the marina road?"

"I was, yes."

"Were you on duty?"

"No."

"What type of vehicle were you driving?"

"My personal vehicle. A 2011 Ford F-150."

"Okay. Were you heading to the marina yourself?"

He knew there was nowhere else to go on that road, and he was ready. "That was my intent, but I ended up turning around."

"Why was that?"

We were looking each other in the eye. I got the sense he was trying to intimidate me.

"I realized I forgot my cell phone," he said. "I'm supposed to have it at all times, even off duty. So I had to go back home."

That seemed awfully convenient. In about fifteen seconds of testimony, he'd explained why nobody had seen him at the marina. And he'd let me know that, even if I got my hands on accurate cell phone data for him, I couldn't use it to show he was lying, because at that critical moment in the case he just happened to leave his phone at home.

"Okay," I said. "About what time was that?"

He shifted and glanced sideways, at the judge perhaps. "I didn't look at my watch," he said. "At the time, I didn't know the importance of what I was seeing."

"About when did you get home?"

"Well, again," he said, "I didn't check. I didn't realize that night's timeline was going to be important."

"Was it dark?"

"Depends on what you mean by dark. To me, yes."

"Okay," I said. On my notes, I drew a star next to that line of questions. I'd typed up plenty more along those lines, but I didn't want to play those cards yet. I knew we weren't going to get the charges dismissed here. I just wanted to kick the tires to confirm their timeline was weak.

"So, Detective, you've said you were driving east on the marina road that night when you saw somebody walking?"

"I saw Jackson Warton."

"Okay. And about how far away was he?"

"Off to the side, where you'd walk. Maybe thirty feet when I first saw him, ten feet when I passed him."

I wrote those distances on my notes. "And at what point did you actually recognize him?"

"Well, he turned his head when I passed, so I saw his face. But I already thought it might be him from behind, when my headlights hit him. Tall, skinny kid, dark hair, always wearing those band T-shirts with the flames or skulls and whatnot."

"Uh-huh," I said. In my poker voice, I asked, "And how close were you when you noticed that?"

"Oh, maybe twenty feet."

I wrote that on my notes. I didn't really care about the distance. The detail that mattered, which I didn't want him to know mattered, was in the other note I made: "*Wrong shirt?*"

In the photo Noah had shown me, Jackson wasn't wearing any of the heavy metal band T-shirts he always wore. I didn't know why—maybe to make himself harder to identify when he burned the ice cream stand, or to avoid getting a shirt he liked dirty—but he'd been wearing a plain white one with nothing on it but soot marks. Nothing on the front, anyway.

I was going to need to get my hands on that T-shirt. Maybe Jackson was right to call Blount a liar. What I needed to figure out was how to prove it.

17

MONDAY, JULY 29, AFTERNOON

Mazie, Terri, and I all met up at my house after the hearing. I'd texted Noah we were coming, and as I opened the door, I saw him on the couch.

"Can you grab hold of Squatter?" I said. "Don't want any of us to step on him."

He scooped him off the floor and asked, "How'd it go? Can he get bail?"

I tossed my keys on a table and my briefcase on the floor, took the pizza and drinks Mazie'd been holding while I unlocked, and waved the two of them in.

"We brought a late lunch," I said. "Or an early dinner. But no, we didn't get him bail. That was not in the cards."

I was pretty sure I'd been clear with Noah that we weren't going to get the charges reduced, but he still had the ultra-resilient hope that kids his age usually did. It didn't feel great to shove that hope back down in the mud.

The light went out of his face for a second, but then he seemed to realize who else was here.

"Oh, Ms. Grant," he said to Mazie. "I'm so sorry we couldn't get him out for you." His hangdog look of self-pity had vanished; he was focused on her. My kid was acting, for the first time I'd ever seen, like a grown man.

"Oh, thank you," Mazie said. "Well, it's just going to take a while."

When I turned to bring our paper cups of Coke into the kitchen, I saw Terri smiling. She raised her eyebrows and gave me a little nod that seemed to say, "Not bad!"

I felt proud but also a little unnerved. I kept getting whiplash from watching my kid grow up before my eyes.

While I got plates out and poured our Cokes into proper glasses, the women told Noah how it had gone.

"Your dad fought hard," Mazie said. "He got Tim Warton to admit right in front of everybody that Jackson couldn't have wanted Karl dead, because last Christmas he saved Karl's life."

"Oh, that's great," Noah said. "Yeah, I remember him telling me about that."

"And the judge said something—what was it, Leland? You'll explain it better."

I sat down and handed out plates. "Yeah, Judge Chambliss said he had to let the case go forward, because with evidence that's consistent with either manslaughter or murder, he couldn't just toss the murder charges. But he told the prosecution that if the evidence still looked like it could go either way at trial, then he'd instruct the jury on manslaughter if I asked him to."

Noah said, "What's that mean?"

"Just that he'd let the jury consider manslaughter too. Which only has a two-year minimum sentence, instead of thirty to life."

"Dang," said Noah. "I mean, that's a lot better, but I can't believe he really might not get out of this."

Mazie slumped back in the armchair, eyes closed. I gestured to Noah to fix her a plate and pass it over.

Terri said, "We got a lot of good information too."

"Well, Ruiz gave me an envelope of stuff," I said, "but I don't know how useful it's going to be." As we were leaving, he'd held it out with a perfunctory "Here you go." I hadn't had a chance to look at it.

"I didn't mean that," Terri said. "I mean on cross." To Noah, she said, "You ever seen your dad do a cross-examination?"

"No, ma'am. He said I was too young."

"Leland, no! If he's interested, you've got to take him."

"It's a deal," I said. "Long as you can survive without your phone. They won't let spectators bring them in."

He shrugged like I was an idiot for even thinking that might be a problem. Then he seemed to realize that, even as he was sliding a piece of pizza onto a plate for our guest, his phone was still in his hand. It had been in his hand ever since we got home. He put it down.

Terri told him, "You've got to watch sometime. It's like martial arts. Or, no, here's what it's like: Picture a couple ballroom dancing, you know? So smooth, so nice, and then suddenly the guy flips his partner over his shoulder and you realize he was doing judo the whole time."

I said, "I can't say I'd ever choose Detective Blount as my dance partner. Or Tim Warton."

"Blount?" said Noah. "Is that the tall one? That cop who looks like Thor, but with a crew cut?"

Terri laughed.

I said, "Yeah. You know him?"

"Yeah, he's always patrolling the beach. He's, uh…" He paused—I thought he was adjusting his language for our guests—and then said, "He's not a nice dude. Unless you're the right kind of person, which I guess I'm not."

"Yeah," said Terri, "he picks and chooses."

Noah said, "Jackson told me Blount hated Karl. And him. Both of them."

"Huh," I said. I was going to have to ask Jackson about that.

Mazie sat forward and picked up her plate of pizza. "Blount had a thing for me in high school," she said. "For a little while. But I was with you at the time, Leland, and one day he called me a whore, and that was that."

Terri said, "He sure knows how to sweet-talk the ladies."

We laughed.

She shook her head, thinking about it, and added, "Sometimes I think it'd take a whole filing cabinet to keep track of all Blount's griev-ances. He doesn't lose his temper all that often, but he is an *angry* man."

That night, I asked Noah to show me the photo of him and Jackson again. Just as I recalled, Jackson was wearing a blank white T-shirt, not a skull or flame in sight.

"Okay," I said, "can you make sure that's backed up? And in a way that's time-stamped?"

"Yeah," he said. "I texted it to Jackson that night, after making him swear on his mom's life that he wouldn't post it on Instagram."

I laughed. "Good call."

"Does that picture help? That's awesome."

"It just might. Is there a way you can email me the file with its original time stamp?"

"Sure." He made his way over to his laptop.

I put a note in my calendar to ask Mazie about the T-shirt. To Noah, I said, "There's no blood on that T-shirt either, is there."

He peered at his screen. "No. Even zoomed in, I don't see anything red at all."

"Do you remember how he was acting that night? Or what he was talking about?"

"'Course I remember," he said defensively. "We only smoked that one bowl."

"Look, that's not even what I meant. It was two months ago. Anybody could forget the details in that length of time."

He glanced over at me, then back at his laptop. His eyes flashed anger and apology all at once.

"Well, he talked about Karl," he said. "He was mad as hell, on account of the fight they'd had. And I'm not gonna lie, he said he wished Karl was dead. But he was talking like he was still alive. He said he wanted to do that Viking boat thing and see Karl's face when he realized that was his boat on fire. And wasn't Karl already dead by then?"

I hesitated, then shook my head. "I wish I could tell you what we know and what we don't, but I don't want to, you know, influence what you actually remember."

He looked startled. "You gonna put me on the stand?"

"Oh, hell no." I wasn't even sure I *could* put my own son on; that wasn't something I'd ever looked up the rules for. But the idea gave me nightmarish visions of Ruiz raking him over the coals to show he was an unreliable witness: *Isn't it true that you're a drug user? Isn't it true that you stole prescription opiates and then spent two months in rehab as part of a juvie-court plea deal?*

Not to mention the stress testifying would put on his sobriety. He might be Jackson's only alibi, but I was going to have to find another way.

After Noah went to bed, I hauled my briefcase over to the kitchen table and pulled out Ruiz's fat manila envelope. The only thing in it was a report on the forensic examination of Karl's boat. I flipped to the back page and saw the expert had signed it more than a week earlier. It was annoying that Ruiz had held off on giving it to me, but since today was exactly thirty days after I'd made my discovery request for all the forensic reports they had, it wasn't technically late. Nothing I could complain about.

I flipped back to the start. The summary said the boat appeared to have been hastily or carelessly scrubbed down. The fatal confrontation had apparently happened on deck. The report noted a damaged section of railing with blood and hair still stuck to it, and extensive bloodstains that had soaked into the deck. On the facing page were gruesome color photos of that evidence. Test results said that blood checked out as Karl's.

Belowdecks was an impressive range of local flora and fauna. I scanned through a bullet list more than half a page long that identified various seeds, leaves, scraps of tree bark, and scales from several different species of fish. The next page itemized types of dirt and sand. I truly had not realized how many different kinds of dirt there are.

Then my eye stopped on an unexpected word: heroin. A trace amount had been recovered from the crack between two bits of Formica in a countertop. I wasn't sure what to make of it. Karl was a drinker; nothing I or Terri had dug up had pointed to his dabbling in any other substances, apart from the occasional joint. And Jackson certainly didn't strike me as a user. The gangly arms that stuck out of his death metal T-shirts—and now his short-sleeved summer prison uniform— had no tracks on them. He'd also been stuck in jail for nearly two months, with no source of money I was aware of, and he didn't act like a junkie in withdrawal. I'd seen my share of those in Charleston. It wasn't pretty.

Terri and I were going to have to look a little harder at Karl's friends. I was making a note of that on my yellow pad when I heard, outside, the unmistakable sound of breaking glass. I turned the lights off and peeked out the curtain.

The street was empty. I could see the blue flicker of TVs in a couple of the neighbors' houses.

My car was parked in the driveway. Something glittered inside. I turned off the porch light and stepped out to get a better look.

The rear windshield was shattered. The streetlights were glinting off the pile of broken glass on the back dash.

18

TUESDAY, JULY 30, MORNING

At work the next day I backed into a parking spot, hoping the dwarf palm tree on the curb would keep Roy from noticing the plastic-sheeting rear windshield that Noah and I had duct-taped to my car. It didn't work. Roy headed out around eleven for a lunch date, but within three minutes, he was back inside and hanging off my doorframe.

"Leland," he said, "you can ask Laura for the number of my car place. I'm sure they could get that windshield fixed for you today."

"Thanks much," I said. "Although I don't know when I'm going to be able to get around to it. Lot going on with that murder case."

The case, of course, had nothing to do with my inability to repair the damage. I'd already gotten a quote for $350, and it was safe to assume that wherever Roy took his Beemer would charge more.

He squinted like he thought he might not have heard me right.

"Well, now," he said, "perhaps there's more complexities to that case than I'm aware of, or perhaps you didn't know that Judge Chambliss takes the whole month of August off?"

"His clerk did mention that," I said.

"Okay, then," he said. "Just so you know, all the judges who've been on the bench about as long as he has takes three or four weeks off before Labor Day." After another second of squinting at me, his face cleared. He stepped into my office, touched the door as if to close it, and asked, "Do you mind?"

"Not at all."

He sat down in my guest chair and said, "Leland, believe me, I do not mean to pry. But that windshield of yours can't be more than, what, a $500 repair? So I have to ask, are you having financial difficulties?"

My gut sank. My dignity sank lower, to somewhere about the vicinity of my shoes.

"Okay," he said, leaning back in the chair. My face had apparently answered his question. He thought for a moment and added, "Well, building a practice takes time. And some folks are just not as gifted at that side of things."

With that remark, my dignity was now in Roy's basement.

He leaned forward like an athletic coach about to announce the next play. "Leland," he said, "I still believe you're an asset to Benton & Hearst, but I cannot have that redneck piece of junk sitting in my lot. The plastic sheeting is just—" He shook his head; it was beyond the pale. "So, here's what we're going to do. I have a client who owns a few auto dealerships. I'm sure I can arrange a very favorable lease. Not for the kind of car an attorney with your experience ought to be driving, but even something along the lines of a Chevy Malibu would be light-years better than what you've got. And probably under two hundred a month."

"Roy," I said, "I so appreciate that, but candidly, I have no wiggle room in my budget at this point. Even a lease—"

"That's not what I mean," he said. "I can lease it on behalf of the firm, take the business deduction, and let you drive it. Some of that'll be taxable to you, since the IRS always wants its cut, but that won't amount to much. In the meantime, I'll pass along a little more work for you to do. If you lighten my load a bit, I can take a vacation this month. And then you can roll that abomination you're driving into the nearest swamp and pray folks in Basking Rock forget you ever owned it."

I was floored. "Roy—I don't know what to say. Thank you so much. That is unbelievably generous."

He grinned and winked at me. "It's not charity," he said. "It's PR. If we don't look successful, clients won't think we're any good."

He rapped on my desk with his knuckles, drawing things to a close, and stood up. "I'm having lunch with Collin Porter, and we'll be golfing the rest of the afternoon. I'll have Laura give you a Blue Seas file to get started on. I never much enjoyed the research and writing end of things. The more of that you do, the more I get to take clients golfing."

I said, "Sounds like a win-win right there."

"Exactly."

An hour later, that good news was tempered by a frantic call from Mazie. Jackson had been hurt in jail and taken to the hospital, she said, but the hospital wouldn't let her visit because he was under armed guard. Only his lawyer, they'd told her, was permitted.

As I pulled out of the lot, I smiled at the thought that Roy would be happy, on his return from the golf course, to see my piece of junk had vacated the premises. On the causeway, the combination of my speed and the wind from the ocean loosened a corner of the plastic sheeting.

It slapped against the frame so loudly it was like having a seagull trapped in the car with me. Apparently, even with the most versatile tape on the market, I was still not capable of carrying out solid repairs. The law was truly the only thing I was good at.

I hoped I'd be good enough for Jackson.

Our county detention center, where prisoners awaiting trial were held, was too small to have an infirmary. It had experienced medical staff, though, so Jackson must have been pretty seriously injured to be admitted to the local hospital.

When I got to his room, I showed my bar card to the cop at the door. He nodded. A nurse was in the room changing IV bags. Something was beeping. She was blocking my view of Jackson's face, but I could see his left hand was cuffed to the bed rail.

As I walked in, I got a better view. His face was bruised to hell, and his jaw was wired shut. He glanced over when I said hello, then winced and let his head fall back where it had been.

"Oh God," I said. I could only think of one reason a person's jaw would be wired shut. I asked the nurse, "Broken jaw?"

She nodded. "Sorry I can't say more," she said. "There's a form he'll need to sign if he wants you to be able to get his medical information. I'll leave the two of you to talk. You can use his communication board, if you want."

From the foot of his bed, she picked up a plastic board with the alphabet and the numbers from zero to ten printed on it, plus a few words: Water. Hungry. Hot. Cold. Pain.

"He doesn't like using this," she said. "But maybe with you he'll feel more like talking. I did just give him his morphine, but he should still be lucid for at least another twenty minutes or so."

"Okay, well, thank you."

When she left, I followed her to the door and told the cop, "I'm just going to shut this while I'm here, to consult with my client."

He shrugged. I shut it.

I went back to Jackson and asked, "How you feeling?"

He gave me a look.

I picked up the communication board, scrutinized it, and said, "I'm not sure why, but 'I feel like shit' isn't one of the options. Just hot, cold, and whatnot."

I heard a little snort and saw a smile flicker, then turn into a wince. He'd laughed, but it hurt. I had a gut-wrenching flash of déjà vu from when Noah was hospitalized in Charleston.

"Goddamn," I said. "I'm sorry. Okay, listen, I'm not going to hang out here too long. That morphine's going to put you to sleep, and I'm sure that's what you need. But if somebody at the jail did this to you, you tell me. I can get you moved, or I might even get them to revisit bail."

His eyes stayed closed. He knitted his brows together, but I couldn't tell if it was from pain or, possibly, anger.

"How about this," I said. "Just tap the sheet with your right hand. Once for yes, two for no. Did a prisoner do this to you?"

His eyebrows were still drawn together. I wasn't sure he'd heard me, but then his hand moved. Two taps.

"Goddamn it!" I said. "It was a guard?"

A tap. Then another.

"No?"

He didn't move.

"Not a prisoner or a guard? Are you sure?"

He clenched his fist and pounded it on the bed. Three times, four times; it had no apparent meaning other than anger.

I tried another angle. "Listen, Jackson. I'm your lawyer. Anything you tell me is confidential. If you don't want me telling your mother what's happened, I won't. It's just between us."

He seemed to be pointing at something. The communication board, I realized, where I'd set it halfway down the bed. I held it up.

He opened his eyes a slit and jabbed his index finger at four letters: F-E-L-L.

"You *fell*?"

One tap on the mattress. Yes.

I stared at him. He had at least half a dozen bruises on both sides of his face. I didn't see how a person could hit his face in that many different places in a single accidental fall.

"Okay," I said, giving up for now. "I'm sorry if somebody back there's got you too scared to even tell me, but you're safe here, so I'll let you get some rest. In the meantime, I'm doing everything I can to tear apart this town and figure out how to make you a free man again."

He didn't say anything or even open his eyes.

"I'll check-in again tomorrow," I said. "And I'll get the nurse to put my cell number in your file. Actually, I'll put it right here too." On the wall facing his bed was a small whiteboard with the nurse's name written on it and a red marker attached to it with a string. I uncapped the marker and wrote across the bottom "Mr. Munroe (lawyer)" and my number.

"Okay," I said. "If you want me, just tell them to call me. Anytime, day or night."

. . .

That night, I took Squatter for a drive. He snoozed peacefully in his dog purse, which had a seat belt loop to keep him safely on the passenger seat. I sped down the causeway with the windows open, enjoying the racket and the salty air. I didn't know what to make of Jackson's unwillingness to confide in me, and I was hoping a drive might clear the cobwebs from my brain.

Since the marina wasn't too far off, I turned toward it. As I rounded the last corner and headed down the marina road, Squatter barked in his sleep. There was nobody on the road. My headlights skimmed bushes and the trunks of trees. If they hit a white T-shirt, I thought, I'd know it was white. All those death metal shirts Jackson wore were black.

Down toward the end, the road forked: right to the old marina, and left to the new dock and clubhouse where the yacht charters moored. One of Blue Seas' vessels was anchored there, a sleek white yacht with "Lady Jane" written on the side. I parked at the side of the road, eighty or a hundred yards short of the yacht, and got Squatter out to do his business. As he sniffed the bases of various palm trees, I watched a few uniformed men unloading barrels from some sort of opening in the side of the yacht. Waste barrels, maybe; they had biohazard symbols on the sides.

I realized I didn't know how to describe what I was seeing. The correct nautical terms were not in my vocabulary. When I was growing up, any boat with room for more than two or three passengers was for rich people, as far as I was concerned. As a result, I had a mental block when it came to port and starboard and whatever else rich sailing men talked about. I figured I should learn about boats now, since Roy was having me do more work for Blue Seas. Heck, I should've started learning as soon as I found out that the murder scene in Jackson's case was a speedboat.

There was an unpleasant, oily smell in the air. It had never smelled like this down here when I was a kid; all you could smell then was the water and, if you were close enough, the little bait hut that used to stand here, before the road was widened. Where the large dock and clubhouse now stood, there'd been tall rocks that we all liked to jump from. Henry's company had brought more prosperity to Basking Rock, and I myself was starting to benefit from that. But I still wondered at what cost it had come.

Squatter finished his business and curled up on the asphalt. I figured it must still be warm from the long, scorching day. I scooped him up, turned back to my car, and was startled half to death to see a man looking at me from the grass a few yards past the passenger side. He had on what looked like the same uniform as the crew members unloading the barrels down by the dock.

"Evening," I said. "Sorry if I startled you."

He scowled at me and took off walking toward the water.

I got in, locked the doors, and took a moment to get Squatter situated before turning the ignition and hightailing it out of there. I didn't know if that man had meant to scare me or if the scowl was because he hadn't wanted to be seen. Whatever it was, it left a bad taste in my mouth.

19

THURSDAY, AUGUST 1, EVENING

R oy told me the Malibu he'd leased for me would be ready to pick up on Friday at the dealership two towns over. That made me decide to visit the Broke Spoke again while I was still driving my beater. Somehow it felt wrong to take my brand-new company car to a strip club.

When I pulled up, around six-thirty, I didn't see the red Mustang. I parked anyway. Even if Kitty wasn't around, she couldn't be the only person there who'd known Karl.

Inside, the place was dimly lit and, at most, half-full. At the back, on stage in purple light, a girl was dancing to some pulsing electronic beat. It wasn't my kind of music. Then again, exotic dancing was probably not a great fit with the music of Tom Petty & the Heart-breakers.

I headed to the bar. Behind it, polishing a glass and occasionally glancing at the dancer, was Terri's nemesis, Dunk. Like anyone from Basking Rock, I knew his name and face even if I'd never talked to him. He was built like a pro wrestler, about six four, with shoulders that looked like they might actually be three feet wide. As befitted an entrepreneur in the truck stop/strip club industry, his blond hair was cut in a mullet: business in front; long, shaggy party in back.

As I took a seat down the bar from him, a red-haired waitress came up from behind me and yelled an order back to the kitchen, which was visible through a wall of stainless steel shelves.

She shouted, "Two wings, extra large, extra hot! And don't wimp out this time—I mean really fucking hot!"

As I shook my head, trying to get my hearing back after her drive-by shouting, she gave me a big smile and said, "Hey, babe. I'm Cheryl. Want something to eat?"

"Thank you kindly," I said. "You folks have onion rings?"

"Yeah. They're real good."

"Okay, then—"

She leaned across the bar and screamed, "Onion rings!"

Between the stainless shelves, I thought I saw a fry cook flip her the bird.

She smiled at me again and said, "You want ketchup, honey? Anything you want, you just let me know."

"You know what," I said, raising my voice because the exotic dance music was reaching its crescendo, "I'd actually like to know, by any chance is Kitty Ives working tonight?"

She pouted like a child, jutting out her lipstick-bright lower lip. "Aw, honey," she said. "Don't you like me no more?"

I laughed. She was fishing hard for tips, and I couldn't blame her. "Aw, Cheryl," I said, "course I do! I just wanted to say hi if Kitty was here."

"Well, she ain't. You'll just have to settle for me."

"Now, that isn't settling," I said.

"Aw, thank you."

I saw movement out of the corner of my eye. Dunk had come down to our end of the bar to hand her the platters of wings the fry cook had just flung onto the shelves. She took them, said, "Back soon, babe," and winked at me as she left.

Dunk growled, in a voice several octaves lower than Cheryl's, "Evening, Leland. Something to drink?"

"Yeah, thanks, Dunk." It hadn't occurred to me that our town's foremost businessman, or second foremost since Blue Seas Yacht Charter had come in and classed the place up, would know my name. "Wish I could order something good, but I'm driving, so it's got to be tonic water."

Without his blank expression changing one iota, he said, "You want a maraschino cherry in that? Or maybe a little umbrella?"

I wasn't sure if he was straight-up insulting my manhood or if I was supposed to be in on the joke. It seemed wise not to take offense at anything said by a man his size, so I laughed and said, "Sure. Make it a pink umbrella and a diet maraschino cherry, if you got some."

I heard a faint noise, like a car engine backfiring a couple blocks away, and then realized he was chuckling. "Diet maraschino cherry," he said, enjoying the line, and then he headed back up the bar to get my tonic water.

As he was coming back with a bottle of Schweppes and a glass of ice, the fry cook slung my plate of onion rings onto the shelf. Cheryl materialized out of nowhere with a bottle of ketchup, tossed her long hair, and started shaking the bottle up and down in about as transparent an imitation of a hand job as I'd ever seen. "It's hard to get the ketchup to come out," she explained, with a suggestive smile. "I just thought I'd help you get it going."

I resolved to leave her more of a tip than I could afford, partly out of pity for any woman so desperate for cash, but mainly because she seemed like the talkative type. I had long since realized that waitresses knew everything about their regulars, and for an investigator, a talkative waitress who liked you was pure gold.

Dunk set my rings and drink down. "Table six," he told her, pointing off behind me.

She looked. "Oh, shit," she said. She set my ketchup on the bar, smiled at me, and said, "Honey, I got some impatient folks over there. But you need anything, you just let me know."

To Dunk, I said, "Nice girl. Kitty's nice too. You hire good waitresses."

He shrugged and said, "I have standards. For them and the dancers."

"I guess you do." I took a drink of the Schweppes. "Say, when's Kitty on shift next? I was hoping to say hi."

He was wiping the bar with a rag but looking me straight in the eye. "I guess she didn't tell you," he said. "She gave her notice a few weeks back. She done hightailed it."

"Oh, yeah? Huh." I took another drink.

"For a guy that's been sniffing around," he said, passing someone's meal over the bar to Cheryl, "you don't know much."

"I guess not." I started in on the onion rings. "Cheryl was right," I said. "These are damn good."

"My grandma's recipe," he said. "And I will take it to my grave."

I nodded like that was the right thing to do. Then I said, "Karl Warton took a lot to his grave too. Lot of things I wish I knew."

"Hell of a thing," Dunk said, "getting offed by your own kid."

I chuckled. "Well, you're excused from jury duty, I can tell you that right now."

"I've never done jury duty." He sounded proud. He was rubbing the bar down almost gleefully. "Been called a couple times, but I always get out of it."

"Well, you got businesses to run. You're a busy man."

He stopped washing the bar and looked at me. I was chewing an onion ring and felt suddenly self-conscious.

"Munroe," he said, "I don't butter up easy." His voice was cold. "And I don't trust folks who try. What exactly is it you want from me?"

I washed the food down with a sip of my Schweppes. If he was suspicious of flattery, a straightforward approach was the only way. I asked, "You know Karl well?"

"Beers till five, then Jack straight up."

"You ever know him to indulge in anything else? Illegal stuff? I'm not talking about here," I said, waving an onion ring to take in the whole place. "Just anywhere."

I did not like the look he was giving me.

After a second, he said, "What folks do on their own time is not my business." Then, perhaps thinking a chess move or two ahead, he added, "But no, that's not something I ever recall seeing Karl do. Why, would that get his kid out of jail?"

"It's not that simple."

"Sure it is. Life is simple. If there's smoke, there's a fire. If it quacks, it's a duck." He turned to the array of bottles behind him, poured himself a finger of Johnnie Walker Blue, and turned back to face me. "And if I'm thirsty," he said, "I drink." He swallowed half the whisky and sighed with satisfaction. "Life ain't some TV show with plot twists and all that shit. It is what it is."

"That why you think Jackson killed Karl? Because it's simple?"

"Sure!" He shrugged and shook his head like asking that question didn't make sense. "I mean, who the hell else even cared enough about Karl to bother?"

I wasn't about to say I agreed with him, but he had a point. I went for the hint of a joke: "Doesn't seem like he inspired much in the way of passion."

He snorted with laughter. "What do you expect? He drank. He fished. He fucked. It ain't much of an obituary."

"No, it isn't." I finished my Schweppes. The music got louder; another dancer must have gone on stage. I half yelled, "Speaking of drinking, you ever see him hanging out with a guy named Pete? A trucker?"

"Hard to say," he yelled back. He finished his whisky. "We're right on the highway. No way I can remember everyone who passes through here."

He was looking at me like he dared me to prove otherwise. I wondered how much experience he had, if any, on the wrong side of the law. He sure seemed well versed in the fact that if you don't want to get caught in a lie, saying you couldn't remember was your best bet.

"Well," I said, swirling my last onion ring in the ketchup, "my compliments to your grandma. I've never had better rings."

Out of the corner of my eye, I saw him jut his chin to signal someone. Seconds later, Cheryl appeared and set the bill down on the bar. It was a ten-dollar tab. I handed her a five-dollar tip.

"Oh my goodness," she gushed. "Honey, thank you! I want to see you back here, okay?"

Dunk snorted and walked back up the bar, shaking his head.

Watching him go, she leaned close to my ear to ask, "Darlin', did you make him mad?"

"I might have." I stood up and stuck my wallet back in my pocket. "Didn't mean to."

"Oh, honey," she said. "Don't do that. You just do whatever you got to do to get along with him."

"What, does he hold grudges?"

She hesitated. Her eyes flicked to the side, making sure he was far enough away. Then she said, "He does a lot of things."

I nodded, thinking on that. "Thank you," I said. "Now, you take care of yourself, okay?"

"I will."

The parking lot outside was deserted, and it was dark. I got in my beater, slammed the door, and dialed Kitty Ives's number. Then I thought better of calling her from here, where Dunk might come out the door at any moment. I headed toward Roy's office for the Blue Seas file he needed me to work on and called Kitty on the way.

I got an automated message: her number was not in service.

Dunk wasn't kidding. She'd really gone to ground.

20

WEDNESDAY, AUGUST 7, AFTERNOON

I took a break from researching maritime law for Blue Seas and drove down to the beach to meet Terri, swinging by my house on the way to get Squatter. For all the digging I'd done on Jackson's case, my shovel kept coming up empty. He was reasonably safe—when the hospital sent him back to jail, I had him placed in solitary instead of in the general population—but my investigation was stalled. I thought if Terri and I sat on a bench eating lunch, watching the dogs play and talking about things, maybe the sun and the sea breeze would clear the fog out of my brain.

In the parking lot, Terri checked out my new silver Malibu and said, "Nice car. You can tell it's new by that big old towel on the seat."

I laughed. The fear of damaging Roy's car had made me put a folded-up towel on the passenger seat to prevent Squatter and his dog purse from ever touching the upholstery.

We got lunch at the hot dog stand, which was about ten yards from the ice cream stand that, I remained convinced, Jackson had set on fire. It was already almost completely repaired. A sign announced a grand reopening next week. I pointed it out as Terri loaded up her first hot dog with onions, relish, banana peppers, and every other topping available.

"Good for them," she said. "At least they'll catch the last part of summer. It's family-run. They'd probably go under if they missed the whole season."

"Seems like you know everything about this town," I said. "I couldn't have said who ran that place."

"Even though it's part of your case?"

"Yeah, I should know." I shook my head, wondering what else I'd missed.

Her pup, smelling the food, stood on his hind legs and pawed at her hips. He knocked her off balance; he had to weigh at least forty pounds. "Buster!" she said. "Down!" He sat right back down in the sand, perfectly behaved. I would have too, if she'd aimed that voice at me.

I was impressed. "You training him yourself?"

She gave me a look. I laughed. She didn't need to put words to it, but she did anyway: "No, Leland, I got Buster his own private tutor. And I take him for a hot-stone massage and doggy acupuncture every week. Because that's just the kind of person I am."

I was still laughing as I ordered my food. Pocketing my change, I told her, "I'm working on my obliviousness. But it could take a while."

She smiled. "We all got our crosses to bear." She took her second hot dog, which was topping-free, out of its wrapper and held it down to Buster. "Wait," she said, and he did. When he'd waited long enough, which was a while, she said, "Okay," and in a flash of black fur the snack disappeared.

Squatter's ears wilted. As he searched the sand for crumbs that might have fallen from Buster's mouth, I broke off one end of my hot dog and bun for him. The sight of it made his day, if not his week.

As we headed over to a bench on the side of the beach where dogs could be off leash, I asked, "Any luck tracking down Kitty Ives? Or that trucker she and Karl knew, Pete?"

"Not yet," she said. "You'd think a bright red Mustang would be easier to find."

"You sure she took it, then?"

"I think so, since she tried to sell it and couldn't. I traced it back to where Karl bought it, off a pretty nice used car lot over in Bluffton."

"Huh," I said. "Thought he bought it new."

"Just about. It's a 2019, but somebody else bought it new, then changed his mind and traded it back in. I went and talked to the owner of the lot, and he remembered Karl because he paid in cash. He remembered Kitty too, since she came with him. He told me she swung by ten or twelve days ago driving it, looking real pretty, asking if he could help her and what she might be able to get for it."

"Even though it isn't hers?"

"That's what he explained to her. From how he told me, he was real apologetic, and she was practically crying."

"The old damsel in distress thing?"

"Or she really could be scared of something. I mean, she's lived here going on ten years. It takes a lot to make a settled person skip town."

I looked around, making sure the few other beachgoers present on a weekday afternoon were far enough off, before asking, "You think the heroin was her?"

"It could be. But there's a lot of people it could be."

We sat down and unleashed our pups. As Squatter watched, Buster barreled back and forth between the stretch of sand we were on and some nearby rocks.

I said, "Maybe I'm out of touch, but heroin just seems weird. I mean, on some middle-aged yahoo's motorboat? When I think about the opiate crisis here, or anywhere in small-town America, I think OxyContin, fentanyl, that kind of thing."

"Yeah," she said. "Not some resin from a flower in Afghanistan."

I thought about that a second. "Did Karl know any veterans?"

"Of Afghanistan, you mean? Hmm. I'll look into that."

"I imagine there's a few on the police force."

She nodded. "Yeah, several I can think of off the bat. Not Blount, but some folks he works with. Or used to, at least."

"Or it could just be some junkie friend of Karl's. He came over, they got high. Maybe Dunk is right, and things are mostly pretty simple." I'd told her about my encounter with him at the Broke Spoke.

Squatter curled up against my foot to sleep. He'd used up his daily quota of energy.

She flicked a chunk of onion off her finger into the sand and said, "I wouldn't go looking to Dunk McDonough for crime-solving tips. Or life advice, or whatever that was supposed to be."

I said, "I don't love the guy, to say the least. But I am curious what you got against him."

She looked out at the breaking waves, thinking. I had the sense she was doing what I sometimes did: parsing through an answer to remove sensitive content before she spoke.

Finally she said, "Would you agree if I said you get the measure of someone's character when you see how they treat folks who aren't any use to them? And how they treat someone that they could get away with hurting?"

"Yeah, I think that's a damn-good barometer."

She nodded. "So, the problem is, Dunk fails on both counts."

I could tell from her voice that that was all I was going to get. The details were confidential.

I said, "You think we should be looking at him? About Karl, I mean?"

She shrugged. "I think we need to be looking for somebody like that," she said. "But unfortunately, there's a lot of people like that around here."

"Damn. It must be hard knowing what you know." With her eight years on the force, plus a decade as a private eye and however long volunteering in social work, I thought she probably knew the underbelly of this town better than most anybody else.

"It can be," she said. "Hard, I mean."

I looked out at the water with her. A couple of families with kids were playing in the surf. I figured if they were locals, she could see right through them: she probably knew if the kids were safe and if anybody was a wife beater, a druggie, or a drunk.

She looked up toward the rocks and said, with a smile in her voice, "That's why I got myself a big old cheerful puppy."

I followed her gaze. Buster was jumping around, trying to grab seagulls out of the air. The effort was futile, but he looked happy as hell.

. . .

I drove back to Roy's office, trying to figure out where Karl had gotten the money to buy a $30,000 car in cash. The simple answer, the Dunk answer, would probably be that he was dealing drugs—or running them in his boat. But Karl had no history of any type of drug arrest, and in all our digging, nothing had come up about his ever being involved in drugs or having friends who were. The Mustang was his only luxury, the only sign of money. And, given how thoroughly the forensic report had analyzed every last fish scale found on his motorboat, I at least knew the boat couldn't have been command central for any type of drug operation. That would've left far more than one solitary trace amount of heroin.

After work, I thought, I might swing by the fishing supply store where Karl's brother Tim worked part-time, to see if he was there. He had his own preoccupations with the Mustang and with money, as I recalled. And he was the kind who seemed to say whatever the heck was on his mind, without thinking first. People like that were like peach trees you could just shake to make fruit fall. Of course, a lot of what fell was pure BS, but if I could get one peach out of the deal, the shower of manure would be worth it.

The Rusty Hook Bait & Tackle Shop wasn't far from the causeway. It was an oversize hut with an old, cracked oar hung over the doorway. Inside, antique corks and bobbers hung from blue-painted rafters. Tim was at the register bagging up someone's purchase, so I went down one of the two aisles, pretending to browse. I knew a lot more about fishing than I did about boats—I had to; as a kid, it kept us fed—but I didn't want to spend more than necessary to get Tim talking. The extra work Roy had set me up with was a big help, but not that big.

When the customer left, I grabbed a Super Sally lure and headed up to the register.

Tim looked up as I approached. I said, "Oh, hey."

"Hey there, Mr. Lawyer."

"Oh, I'm just Leland when I'm not wearing a tie."

"Didn't know you was a fishing man."

"Thought I'd take my son out, see what we can get. I'm hoping for some largemouth bass." I tossed the lure on the counter.

"Uh-huh," he said, ringing it up. "These Super Sallies, them bass, just jump right on 'em. But you know," he said, tapping the blue-and-black skirt of my lure with his fingertip, "I've had better luck with the chartreuse than with this color."

"That so?"

"Mm-hmm. Much better. Round here, it's just what they seem to like."

"Well, thank you. I'll be right back."

I took the lure to the shelf where I'd found it and swapped it for a chartreuse one. Handing it to Tim along with a ten-dollar bill, I said, "I could've used one of these when I was a kid. We would've eaten a damn sight better, I'm sure."

He nodded. "We were the same way," he said. "Three of us used to fish together—me, Pat, and Karl—and when our uncle took us out with the, you know, the original one of these, the smaller one, I swear, we thought it was magic."

He sighed at the memory.

I said, "I sure am sorry about your brother."

"Yeah, well." He shrugged and handed me my change. After a second's pause, staring at the counter or maybe the floor beyond, he said, "You know, that did make sense, what you said back in court.

About Jackson saving his daddy's life. He could've just let him choke."

"Yeah, he could've."

He looked me in the eye and said, "So, I just don't know."

I nodded to say I understood.

"Thing is, though," he said, "who else could it be? And why?"

"Well, that's what I'm trying to figure out."

He put my lure in a plastic bag, shaking his head at the puzzle. "It's just, I ain't never seen nobody but Jackson get that mad at him. Apart from Mazie, and I mean, she's so little she couldn't kill a dang cat, much less Karl."

"Yep," I said. "You know, one thing I'm trying to find out, which might help figure all of this out, is where he came up with the money for that Mustang."

He chuckled and shook his head. "Naw, he didn't need none. He straight-up won that car in a card game."

"Did he?" I figured Karl had told his brothers that story so they wouldn't know about the money he had. "Dang, what kind of high rollers was he playing cards with?"

"Don't rightly know," he said. "I never went myself. He went most every month, up in Charleston, and most always came back flush. He was a hell of a poker player. I don't think I ever beat him once in my life."

"Well, isn't that interesting. You know, anything else you might happen to remember about those card games, if you could let me know, it'd be much appreciated."

"You could ask Pat," he said. "He went with him at least once that I recall."

"Well, thank you much," I said, picking up the bag with the lure. "I'll do that."

"Go down the Broke Spoke," he said. "He's there three, four nights a week, I'd say."

21

THURSDAY, AUGUST 15, AFTERNOON

It was yet another glorious, sunny day. I'd driven down to the beach to get a paper cone of fried shrimp for lunch. I wondered sometimes if living in this perfection of ocean breezes, seafood, and endless summer days made people a little crazy. We were living in Eden, but instead of enjoying it, some folks were running around whacking people in the head with crowbars, abusing their own families, and, according to Jackson, trying to frame teenage boys for vicious murders. And on top of that, as I'd learned from the Blue Seas work I was doing for Roy, our eminent councilman Henry Carrell was playing some kind of barely legal shell game with offshore subsidiaries, all in the name of squeezing a few more dollars out of his already-lucrative company. It seemed like most every trouble that existed in the world was right here too, quietly poisoning our idyllic-looking seaside town.

What I hadn't learned yet was any more about Karl's monthly poker games in Charleston. I'd cruised past the Broke Spoke a few times, looking for Pat's battered pickup in the parking lot, but hadn't seen it. I could've gone back to the trailer park and looked for him there, but I thought I'd get more out of him if I could catch him half drunk at the strip club.

Here on the beach, the ice cream stand was doing great business. Even though it was a weekday afternoon, the line was almost twenty people long. Once Jackson's jaw was healed enough for him to talk again, I was going to need to badger him a little more about the arson. If he'd cop to it, I could narrow that night's timeline and maybe create reasonable doubt about whether he'd even had time to commit the murder.

My phone beeped with a text: Mazie letting me know she got off at five. I texted back that I'd swing by her house. Before talking to Jackson, I wanted to find out what I could about the white T-shirt he'd been wearing in the photo and see if she had any idea whether the ice cream stand had some sort of meaning for him. I was just trying to understand the kid. If I could do that, maybe I could get around whatever it was that had him too scared to talk to me about the arson. Not to mention too scared to tell me which prisoner or guard had been involved in the so-called fall that broke his jaw.

I knew Mazie always showered and changed after work—she didn't want to smell like a greasy spoon all night long—so I didn't show up at her place until close to six. She hollered to me to let myself in. When I got into the kitchen, she was pulling a cup of coffee out of the microwave. Two plastic-wrapped slices of pie sat on the counter. "The diner was just going to throw them out," she said, "because they're from yesterday. You want cherry? Or key lime?"

"Oh, whichever one you're not having."

We got situated and started eating. I said, "This is good, but I doubt it holds a candle to what you make yourself. Karl's brothers had high praise for your pie."

She laughed. "Yeah, tastes great, and it almost killed Karl. That definitely wasn't part of the recipe."

"Well, there's things drunk people just shouldn't do. Wolfing down pecan pie is one of them, I guess."

"And going sailing at night," she said. "Are they really sure he didn't fall and hit his head?"

I winced at the memory of the photos in the coroner's report. "Yeah, they're sure."

She sighed.

"It's all down to Blount, then," she said. "Ain't it."

"As far as evidence against Jackson, yeah. Speaking of which, I know he's always wearing those death metal T-shirts, but does he have any white ones?"

"Oh, yeah," she said, taking a bite of her key lime pie. "I tried to get him out of all that fireball-and-death stuff. At least for work, because I mean, skulls with worms crawling out of the eyeholes and whatnot, that just ain't professional. He won't go anywhere in life looking like that. So I bought him a pack of plain white shirts, three of them. And he did wear them sometimes."

"Any idea where those shirts are now?"

She screwed her eyebrows up like she'd just remembered something. "Oh," she said, and looked at me. "He came home in one of those the next morning. Or, you know, right before dawn, right after Karl died. Oh my God. Not one of them black shirts like Blount was talking about."

I nodded. "Tell me more."

"Well," she said, "I remember because it was such a mess. I had to put detergent on the stains and soak it a while before I could wash it. And it still didn't come out right."

"What kind of stains?"

"Just—" She caught herself and stopped. As she took a sip of coffee, she looked at me warily over the rim of the cup. Then she set it down and said, "I mean, it could've been from a campfire."

"Mazie—"

"Look, my son is in enough trouble already. I don't see how it helps to add arson to the neck-high pile of crap he's already standing in."

"It could change the timeline," I said. "It could make it less likely that he would've had time to kill Karl."

She nodded slowly, seeing my point. Then she covered her eyes with one hand and said, "Oh, Lord. Lord, I don't even dare hope, but thank you for this. Thank you for helping me remember this."

When she finished her little prayer and took another sip of coffee, she said, "He was wearing one of them skull T-shirts before, that same night, but it got messed up in the fight with Karl. Blood, dirt, and I think it even got tore up a little bit. That's why he changed."

"Was there anything else on the white T-shirt when he came home? Any blood?"

"Not one drop. All the stains were black or, like, dark gray."

"You still have it? And the one he had on during the fight?"

"Yeah. I washed them both, but yeah, they're in his drawer."

"Okay, hang on to them."

I made a mental note to formally ask Ruiz to hand over any footage from the day of the murder that the prosecution might have. Most of the shops along the beach had security cameras, and the ones trained on the entrances would also pick up people walking past outside. If I could get a glimpse of Jackson wearing a white T-shirt that night, before the murder, then the selfie Noah had shown me from hours later would be even more powerful evidence. Ruiz was legally obligated to turn over any evidence that might exonerate Jackson—I didn't even have to ask him for that—but I could see why, from his perspective, security-cam footage from hours before the murder wouldn't seem to be in that category.

I drained my coffee, set it down, and asked, "About that ice cream stand. It's been there since I was a kid. Do you remember anything that might have happened to him there? Or anything about the folks who own it? I'm trying to get a sense of why he might've targeted it."

She sat back and crossed her arms. She was mad. "If we got the T-shirt," she said, "if Blount was lying about what he was wearing that night, then what do we need the fire for? I didn't ask you to help put my boy in jail on some other charge."

"A first-time arson with no victims—and not even any possible victims, since the place was closed when it burned—is nothing like murder in terms of the sentence he could get. If he pleads to it and keeps up the good behavior, I mean, they probably wouldn't let him out on time served, but I doubt it'd be that much longer."

She looked at the ceiling like the answer to all her troubles just might be there. Then she sighed: it didn't seem to be. She looked back at me and said, "If he burned that thing down, would that mean for sure they couldn't get him on the murder?"

I sighed. "I wish it was that simple. As of now, no, it's not definitive, because we're not exactly sure when Karl died. But it's an important piece of the puzzle, because it makes it a whole lot less likely."

"I tell you what," she said. Her arms were still crossed, and she'd tilted her head, cocking her jaw at me defiantly. "If you find some other piece of your puzzle, so I know this'll help him instead of

174

hurting him, then you come back and let me know. Then I might just remember something else about that night."

I looked her in the eye. I could tell she wasn't going to say one more word right now.

"Okay, then," I said. "I'll keep digging."

That evening, when I did my nightly swing past the Broke Spoke, Pat's beat-up gray pickup was out front. I toured the lot for a minute, trying to find a parking spot that made me feel confident nobody was going to bang into Roy's Malibu when they came out drunk and yanked open their door. The lot was crowded, and there was no such confidence to be had. I pulled back out and parked on the side street.

Inside, there had to be twice as many people as the last time I'd been there. A dozen or more guys were crushed up against the stage, stuffing some woman's thong with bills. It seemed darker, somehow. As my eyes adjusted to the dimness, I looked around for Pat. I didn't see him, and the colored lights didn't help; they were flicking back and forth across the crowd, making the place feel like some shabby little knockoff of a rock concert.

Dunk wasn't at the bar, and I didn't recognize the angry little man who was. He glared at me when I ordered my Schweppes.

After a minute, my talkative waitress came and found me. Over the music, she yelled, "Hi, honey!"

"Hey, Cheryl! How you doing?"

"Better now you're here!"

The bartender slammed my tonic water down—just the bottle, no glass—and went away. Cheryl threw her head back and laughed. "Oh my goodness," she said. "Don't pay him no mind."

I smiled and said, "He doesn't seem to like me much."

"Oh, he doesn't like nobody."

I laughed. "Hey," I said, "tell me—have you seen Pat Warton tonight?"

"Why you always looking for somebody other than me?"

"Somebody in addition to you," I said. "And there's no competition."

She laughed and pointed him out at a table by the wall.

"Thank you." I pulled out my wallet and handed her a ten-dollar bill. "This here's all I'm ordering tonight," I said, holding up the tonic water, "so please keep the change."

"Aw, thank you!"

I gave her a nod and headed over to Pat.

"Hey there," I half yelled. The music was louder here.

I could tell he didn't recognize me for a second. When he did, he wasn't friendly.

"I was talking to your brother the other day," I said. "He said I should come over here some night and talk with you."

"What about?"

"Mind if I sit down?"

He hesitated, then shrugged. When I set my Schweppes down, he smiled at it like I was an idiot and asked, "What the hell is that?"

"Got a medical condition," I said. "It's a damn shame, but it is what it is." Lately I'd decided that was going to be my excuse. If I told a man who was drinking that I didn't want to drink and drive, he might take it as an insult to his own choices. And if I told him I could not bear to drink after what had happened to my wife… well, at that point I might as well go straight to an Al-Anon meeting and give up on any kind of normal conversation.

He was watching the stage show without much interest. If he was really here that often, maybe it was all too familiar by now but he was still trying to avoid interacting with me.

"So, your brother told me something interesting," I said. "About that Mustang Karl had."

Without looking away from the stripper, he said, "Why the hell you still so interested in that?"

"I was just wondering," I said, "were you at the card game where he won it?"

He turned his head so fast I thought he might get whiplash. It was too dark to be sure, but I could've sworn I saw a flash of fear in his eyes.

"Okay, I don't know what you're up to," he said, pulling out his wallet. "But I got nothing to say to you." He peeled off a twenty, slid it under his half-empty beer glass, and stood up.

I was glad I'd already paid Cheryl. Pat wasn't three steps away when I stood up myself and followed him.

Out in the parking lot, the door slammed behind us and he turned on me. He looked around like he was making sure nobody else was in the lot, and then he hissed, "I don't know what the hell you're playing at, but I got nothing to say to you. The card games, that was Karl and Pete's thing. I never had nothing to do with that."

I deployed my poker voice. I didn't want him sensing that all my attention had zeroed in on that name, the trucker Kitty had mentioned. Terri was still trying to track Pete down.

"Look," I said, holding my hands palms-out to say I was no threat, "I have nothing against you at all. If I saw you doing lines off a stripper's ass, I'd look the other way. I do not care. All I'm interested in is how your brother got killed."

"He beat his kid, goddammit, and then his kid got big enough to whup him for it." He looked like he truly believed that: indignant, and frustrated as all hell that I somehow couldn't see that simple truth.

"Well, I just don't think so," I said. "And I don't think Karl would want to see his son jailed for life for something he didn't do. You already lost a brother. You want to lose your nephew too?"

He shook his head. I could see it kind of tore him up.

"They told me," he said, "I mean them detectives, he probably wouldn't go down for too long. Because it's probably just manslaughter, right? With all that Karl done to him, that ain't really murder."

"Well, it depends," I said, deploying the poker voice again. "Was this Detective Blount? He try to get you to testify to something?"

"Yeah, that crew-cut guy," he said. "The tall one. The resident asshole. But, I mean, he's just trying to do his job."

It sounded like someone in the strip club was approaching the door, about to join us in the parking lot, so I cut to the chase. "If you'd tell me a little more about that, or about Karl's friend Pete, it'd be much appreciated."

"Look, why you got to root around in all this shit? Best thing for anyone to do is forget it and move on."

The door pushed open, pouring electronic music into the parking lot. A few men stumbled out as Pat stalked off to his truck.

22

TUESDAY, AUGUST 27, AFTERNOON

After Jackson got the wires removed from his jaw and let me know on the jail phone that he could talk again, I went over to visit. The sun was streaming through the high windows of the visiting room, highlighting how pale he was. The lower half of his face was still a little swollen, but apart from that, he was even skinnier than he'd always been. I realized why when he complained about eating nothing but smoothies and vegetable puree all month. His old bravado was gone; he slumped in his chair, discouraged.

I knew from all my mistakes with him and with Noah that I was not exactly a master in the art of relating to teenage boys, so I tried to take off both my lawyer hat and my dad hat and just listen. It wasn't easy. Dispensing advice seemed second only to breathing in terms of things I did automatically. I kept my hands under the table so I could gouge my palm with a fingernail whenever I felt that urge coming on. It didn't work perfectly, but it helped.

When he fell into a quiet funk, I told him, "I talked to your uncle Tim at work. He's having second thoughts. I mean, since testifying at your probable cause hearing."

"Huh." He gave a shrug and said, with maybe one-tenth of his usual feistiness, "Well, that's big of him."

"He's been thinking about how you saved Karl from choking. And thinking, you know, a killer wouldn't have done that."

He sighed and shook his head. "You know what, though? I shouldn't have. 'Cause then none of this would've happened, and I'd be out living my life."

"Yeah. It didn't turn out right, did it. But it says something about you that you'd save a human life, even if you didn't like the guy."

"Don't know where I learned that from. Not him, for sure."

"Your mom, maybe. Or maybe it just comes natural to you."

He looked at me. His hazel eyes were so shiny I thought he might be holding back tears. "How's my mom? I mean, she comes here, she acts strong, but…"

"She is strong," I said. "She loves you more than anything in the world, and she won't rest until you're home."

He nodded. He was looking me in the eye, and I had the sense that his fiery defiance was just about extinguished. Then he said, real quiet, "If there was something I could plead to, if they'd give me just a couple of years, maybe I ought to. That way she'll know I won't be gone too long, and she can—I don't know—have some hope."

"Well, I can talk to Ruiz," I said. "That's always something they could put on the table, and they normally do." I jammed my fingernail into my palm about a second too late; by the time I felt the pain, I was already saying, "But you don't have to make that decision now. We'll cross that bridge when we come to it."

"I'm tired of waiting, though," he said. "I'm tired of not knowing."

The look on his face reminded me that for a young man, sometimes "tired of" was code for "scared of."

"Yeah," I said. "It's hard."

He sighed and picked at the hem of his orange prison shirt. Shaking his head, not looking at me, he mumbled, "I looked up the arson stuff. There's a computer in the little library they got here."

I waited. He didn't say anything.

Finally I said, as casually as I could, "Oh, yeah?"

"I mean, you can go away for a long time for that. Like, longer than I've been alive."

I waited. He looked up at me but didn't say anything. The look on his face, the *how-does-this-law-make-sense* expression, made me think that despite being a teenage boy, he actually might want a little advice from a grown man for once.

"Okay," I said. "So, for an arson that damages a building but doesn't cause any injuries, that's second degree, and it gets between three and twenty-five years in jail."

"Yeah, that's what I saw. I don't understand that. I mean, if you're going away for twenty-five years, you might as well be convicted of murder."

"Oh, you're not looking at twenty-five years. If you set fire to, like, a historic mansion or a museum or something, if you caused $10 million in damage, that's what the high end of that sentencing range is for. But, my God, a little ice cream shack on the beach? A place they built back twice as nice in six weeks? That's literally what the low end of the range is *for*."

"But three years is still a long time."

I nodded. This was one of the situations that came up sometimes and made me question the priorities of the criminal justice system. I'd seen rapists get shorter sentences than that.

"And what if I got sentenced for both? What if they say, okay, you burned that place down, and then you went over to the marina and fought with your dad and—you know?"

I nodded. I had to acknowledge that was a risk. The autopsy hadn't been able to pin down a time of death for Karl, partly because of decomposition and partly because, although he had food in his stomach at a certain stage of digestion, there was no evidence as to when he'd eaten it.

We sat in silence for a minute, long enough that I could've sworn I saw the sunbeam across our table slide over a little bit. Then, just to break the silence, I asked, "Did you know the family that runs that ice cream stand? Or did Karl?"

A shield went up in his eyes. He said nothing.

I shrugged and said, "I was just wondering."

"They ain't good people," he said. "Or the dad ain't."

I waited. After a second, I said, "How so?"

He winced and looked away.

"It doesn't matter," he said.

I left the jail later than I'd meant to, close to dinner time, and had to stop by Roy's office to get a Blue Seas accordion folder full of old contracts to review that night. When I got home, I saw Terri's car parked out front and remembered that I'd suggested she stop by for some pizza and a check-in about the case. When I walked in the front door, apologizing, she and Noah were sitting at the coffee table talking up a storm, with half a pizza left in the box between them.

"Dad," he said, "she's like a spy! She literally spies on people!"

"He was asking me about my job," she explained.

I couldn't remember the last time I'd seen Noah looking enthused about anything. He said, "It's like something out of a movie! How cool is that? I mean, if you ask any of my Charleston friends what they do, they'd all be, like, 'Oh, I'm majoring in business at Clemson' or something. Like, 'I'm a frat boy in cargo shorts majoring in business.' I mean, who cares? But anyone asks *you* that, you get to say, 'I'm a freaking *private eye*—'"

She laughed. "Yeah, that is the best word for it. It's more fun than saying detective or investigator."

Over his head, I smiled a silent thanks to Terri. For a couple of weeks, Noah had been moping about his old friends in Charleston, how they were about to head back to college for their sophomore year while he was still stuck here doing physical therapy and not much else. Their lives looked amazing on Instagram, and he felt like a loser. It was good to hear him poking fun at them. He'd finally realized they weren't actually all that cool.

He looked from Terri to me and sighed. "Well," he said, "I guess you guys got to talk about stuff I'm not allowed to hear."

"Yeah, sorry," I said.

Terri said, "That's where the 'private' in 'private eye' comes in."

"That's awesome," he said. "I'm going to go look some of that stuff up online." He put two more slices of pizza on his plate, got up, and made his way carefully down the hall to his room. It had been months since the last time he'd fallen, but he was still very careful how he moved.

I sat down across from Terri and got myself a slice of lukewarm pizza. I flipped the TV on to the news to make it harder to overhear our conversation.

"Thanks for that," I told her. "I can't remember the last time I saw him excited about... well, anything, really."

"Yeah, he seemed a little down when I got here." She slurped the last of her soda, looking thoughtful. "I think he must've been on social media or something, because he was talking about how all his friends he hadn't seen in a year were heading back to college again without him. I just said writing term papers wasn't nearly as interesting as investigating a murder, and it went from there."

"That's great," I said. "He always did love that Hardy Boys and Scooby Doo stuff when he was little. He used to sit in his window and watch the neighbors with binoculars."

She laughed. "So it's not my fault. If your kid skips college to become a private eye, don't blame me."

"I won't," I said. "I'll credit you. Any productive path that gets him out of his funk is fine by me."

For a second I felt Elise there, smiling with me. She'd given him the binoculars, for his seventh or eighth birthday as I recalled, and she would listen with exaggerated interest whenever he came to her and reported on what he'd seen the neighbors doing. I'd thought it was a little weird, but she was determined to support him in whoever he was becoming. It had taken me a while to get there, as a parent, but I was learning. It felt like she approved.

Terri was looking at the TV. She said, "Is that anyone you know?"

The newscaster was saying something about the Charleston solicitor's office. It took me half a second to recognize Tony Rosa, maybe because he wasn't wearing his pink cummerbund. He was standing at a podium, about to give a press conference in pinstripes and a blue tie.

"Oh, yeah," I said. "We weren't work friends or anything, but I knew him. I actually saw him recently, over at Collin Porter's place." She looked at me quizzically, and I realized she didn't know who that was. "Porter's some big investor in Blue Seas," I said. "Rich as all hell. Lives in a mansion in one of them gated communities on the islands."

"Huh," she said. On-screen, Tony announced a major heroin bust outside Charleston. As he spoke, she asked, "That guy's not, I don't know, the chief solicitor or anything, is he?"

"No, he's junior to me. Or was junior."

"His family rich?"

"I don't think so. His oldest is a couple years younger than Noah. They were at the same high school."

"It just seems weird that he'd be friends with somebody rich enough to back a yacht charter. If he was in private practice, I could see it, but a prosecutor? How'd they even meet?"

"I don't know. I wondered the same things myself."

Tony congratulated local DEA agents on their successful investigation. It made me wonder what an old friend of mine was up to, a law school buddy who'd become a federal prosecutor specializing in drug crimes. Most of what I knew about the DEA came from him. We'd hung out sometimes in Charleston, and I'd sent him an email with my new address when I moved back to Basking Rock. The thought of what he must know about the local drug scene made me wish I'd kept in touch.

I asked Terri, "Speaking of investigating, any luck on Kitty Ives?"

"Not much. I did trace her stuff to a storage unit north of Charleston, not too far from her mom's house. But no sign of her or the car, and she went dark on social media right around the time she disappeared."

I thought about that a second. "You think she's okay?"

"You mean alive?"

"Yeah."

She shrugged and said, "I have no reason to think otherwise. I mean, if she'd disappeared without moving her stuff into storage first, then I'd wonder."

"That makes sense."

"Yeah, and from what I can tell, she was real close to her mom—she posted tons of pictures of them together before she went dark. I think they must still be in touch. Her mom hasn't filed a missing person's report or even said anything on her own social media about Kitty being gone."

"Well, that's good." I thought for a second. "I guess us reaching out to her mom would just scare her off more."

"That's what I was thinking. Maybe give her time to relax instead. She'll get less cautious, and I'll have a better chance of finding her."

"I guess that's the one good thing," I said, "about the wheels of justice turning slowly. We got a little time."

She nodded. "In the meantime, I'd like to track down that trucker," she said. "Last year I heard from a few different women about a trucker who went by Pete, and a couple of times by other names. I wonder if it's your guy. He was some sleaze who came through town a few times and traded drugs for sex, mostly with married women. I know of at least two women who switched from oxy to heroin through him. Soccer-mom types who were so ashamed about it all that he must've known they wouldn't report him."

I said, "You ever feel like there's way too many bottom-feeders in this world?"

"All the time."

"I guess that's why we have jobs."

"I guess it is."

"Well," I said, "that particular bottom-feeder may or may not be my guy. Karl's brother Pat knows him—my guy, I mean—and he drinks, or at least used to drink, at the Broke Spoke when he was in town. So I think the Broke Spoke is where we got to look for him. But I'm wondering if maybe you could step in for me on that. Apart from this one friendly waitress who's desperate for tips, I get a real strong sense of not being welcome there. They're getting tired of me. Maybe it's time to change it up."

She gave me a look. I wasn't sure why.

I sensed from her voice that I was about to be schooled.

"Yes, ma'am?"

"How often do you think a woman walks into the Broke Spoke by herself to have a drink? And what sort of attention do you suppose she'd get if she did?"

"Oh, of course," I said. "Sorry, my brain must have left the room for a moment."

"Now, beyond that. Think back on whenever you've been there. Okay? You picturing it in your mind?"

"Yep."

"When you were there, did you see one Black face?"

"Oh," I said. "No. No, I didn't."

"Not even a dancer, right?"

"Uh, nope. I don't think so. Not that I recall."

She was nodding. "And just so you know," she said, "at least one of Dunk's bartenders is a Proud Boy. Swastika tattoos and everything. The little bald guy."

"Oh, shit," I said. "They're bad news. Five or six years ago I prosecuted a couple of them for a hate crime up in Charleston."

She gave one last nod. Her case was closed.

"So," she said, "there's things I can do that you can't. Places I can go, people I can talk to, just because of who I am. Okay? But then there's also places I can't go, and people I can't talk to."

"Understood," I said. "I'm sorry. And look, I appreciate the bluntness. If I do anything like that again—I mean, if I'm asking you to do something that don't make sense or makes you uncomfortable, please just smack me upside the head."

She said, like it was a promise, "Oh, I will."

I chuckled. Even back in high school, I'd always liked the sense she gave me that I knew exactly where I stood with her. She had some sort of force field around her that made lies and BS just wither and die.

Then I sighed and leaned back in my armchair, closing my eyes, resigning myself to my fate. "I guess I have to go see Dunk again," I said.

She didn't say anything. I sensed an undercurrent, something serious, in her silence. I looked at her.

After a second, she said, "Don't talk to him. I just—to say the least, I don't think it'd be helpful. I understand you've got to find this Pete guy. But stay away from Dunk, if you can."

23

MONDAY, SEPTEMBER 9, AFTERNOON

Sitting in my office at Benton & Hearst, I had the window open for a breeze. The sweltering summer's heat was fading a little; it was only seventy-nine degrees. Roy had returned from his vacation a few days earlier, after Labor Day, deeply tanned and so relaxed that for two days in a row he actually came to work without a necktie. He'd gone down the coast on one of Henry Carrell's yachts, ocean fishing the whole way.

He was back to ties now, and back from lunch, lounging sociably against the frame of my office door. "You have got to come sailing with us," he said. "I know you're not a sailing man, but you will be. Blue Seas will convert you."

"That'd be great," I said. "I have nothing against it, just never got into it."

"I'm thinking the shrimp festival," he said, referring to the town's annual week-long party in late September and early October. "He'll have some charters going then. A short pleasure cruise, dinner on the water, that kind of thing. He's been happy with your work these past few weeks, and it's time you got the social end of things going with him too. I mean, it's way past time, but you got to start somewhere."

"I really appreciate that, Roy. I mean, if I'm ever imposing, you let me know, but I really do appreciate all your help."

"Hell," he said, "I'm helping myself, here! I been sitting in this office for twenty-five years. I'd much rather be out sailing and golfing, but somebody's got to sit here writing and researching while I'm out doing that."

I said, "Happy to oblige."

"Well, then," he said, "we got us a win-win. But you got to get out in the community, let people know who you are. How are they going to trust you otherwise? And if they don't trust you, you can sit here all you want with your little computer fired up, but there won't be any work."

"Yup," I said. "Well, sign me up for the shrimp festival. Whatever Henry's got going for that, I'm in."

After Roy went off to do whatever he did in the office these days, I closed my door to concentrate and got back to work on Jackson's case. I had six Redweld files of discovery: the autopsy and the forensic report on the boat, a partly redacted but unremarkable personnel file for Detective Blount, arrest reports, piles of paper I'd read many times before. Ruiz had put a few surveillance-camera videos online in Dropbox for me, and I'd watched them a dozen times each, changing the brightness and contrast in case it helped, and concentrating on different parts of the frame. I hadn't spotted Jackson in any of them. No magic bullet had emerged. The mess remained a mess.

A knock came at the door—Roy was genteel enough to always knock —and I said, "Come in." When I looked up, it wasn't him; it was Mazie.

"My goodness," I said, unfolding myself from my habitual slouch and standing up to gesture her to a seat. "Hello. What can I get you? Water? Coffee?"

For once she wasn't wearing a waitress uniform or her other staple, sweatpants plus some decorative T-shirt featuring kittens, flowers, or both. She had on a skirt and blouse. It looked like she'd dressed up for this visit. I could see she was intimidated by the surroundings.

She wanted coffee, so I hit the button for Laura's phone to ask her to bring a cup.

"Oh, no," Mazie said, waving her hands like she was trying to erase what she'd just said. "I don't mean to be any trouble. Forget it. I had coffee already."

"It's no trouble," I said. "Besides, we have to finish the pot. The day's almost over."

"Well, if you're sure," she said. "If it's no trouble."

"Not at all."

When the drink was brought and Laura shut the door on her way out, I asked, "Everything okay? Is something going on?"

"Well, I just visited Jackson at lunchtime," she said. There was pain in her face. "Leland, what's happened to him? He's not himself. I thought he'd feel better when his jaw got healed up, but he's still so low. It's like the fight's gone out of him."

I nodded. "It's taking its toll."

"How long does he have to be in there?"

"Well, the solicitor's office is pushing to fast-track his case—"

"Oh, good," she said.

"So that means his trial could begin as early as December."

She stared at me. "That's fast?"

"For a murder trial, yes."

She shook her head and slumped in her chair, looking at her hands in her lap.

I reached back to my bookshelf to get the box of Kleenex I figured she was going to need and set it on my desk so she could reach it.

"Leland, he's so thin," she said. "He barely talks, and he's had bruises on his arms the last couple times I was there. Something's wrong in there. I have got to get him home."

I didn't know what to say. There was no way of getting him out of jail short of waiting for trial and then winning when it finally rolled around. And, based on the evidence we had today, I wasn't at all sure we would win. On top of that, Ruiz hadn't reached out with so much as a hint at any kind of plea deal. I didn't know what he was playing at.

While I was contemplating the whole sorry situation, she opened her purse, found a folded dollar bill, unfolded it, and pushed it across the desk to me.

"You're my lawyer now, right?" she said. "That makes you my lawyer, so everything's confidential?"

"Uh, well, it doesn't really work that way outside the movies. But what's going on? You need legal advice?"

"If it's just between us."

"Well, look," I said. "Your son's my client, so on the off chance you tell me something that goes against his interest, we got a problem. But otherwise, I guess, fire away."

She took a deep, shuddering breath, like she was preparing to get something bad off her chest.

"Okay. I don't know what it was," she said, "but Karl was doing something. I mean, something illegal."

"Uh-huh," I said. "Well, that don't surprise me. What all did you know?"

"Can this be used against me? Or my boy?"

"I'm not a cop," I said. "I'm not telling anyone unless it helps him."

She nodded nervously. "What I know," she said, "is that he had money all of a sudden. A lot of it. I don't know from where, if it was drugs, or stolen... whatever people steal and sell, I have no idea. But he was doing something, and he was real proud of it, almost. I mean, like he was getting away with something."

"He tell you he has money?" I asked. "Or show you? Or what?"

"My washer died," she said. "Back in the springtime. And he heard— from Jackson, I guess. He came around with a fistful of hundred-dollar bills for me to buy a new one. He was cocky about it, but I took it. I mean, I can't live without a washing machine."

"Of course not."

"And then he bought Jackson a new bed," she said. "Because he was still sleeping on the little, you know, the twin bed we got for him when he was maybe six years old."

"So Karl was stepping up? Trying to make up a little bit for what he hadn't done before?"

"That's how he saw it," she said. "And he thought, you know, since he was buying things we needed, I should—" She winced and looked away. "Like, he's stepping up as a father, for once, so I ought to be… you know… available."

I shook my head, angry at him and at the same time feeling like it was a waste of energy to be angry at a dead man. I wished to hell he could've just fallen off his boat and drowned, instead of causing his family even more problems in death than he had in life.

She said, "That's what the fight was about. I mean, the night he died. Or part of what it was about."

"Oh," I said, connecting the dots at last. "That's why he was there yelling that you owed him money?"

"Yeah. He figured if I wasn't going to… you know… then he wanted his money back."

"Goddamn him."

She took a Kleenex and blew her nose. I looked at my Redwelds of papers about Jackson's case. Everything she was saying made sense, but I wasn't sure it helped. If anything, it could make a jury think Jackson had all the more reason to go after his daddy that night.

When she'd dabbed her eyes and pulled herself together, I asked, "You were saying that's part of what the fight was about? Was there something else?"

She looked at me and said, "Leland, this cannot leave this room."

I nodded. "It won't."

"The reason I kept this to myself before is that I didn't know—I still don't know—if Jackson was involved at all. I mean, in whatever illegal things Karl was doing. When Karl came into money, he started coming around a lot, asking Jackson to hang out with him. They went places together. And it seemed like Jackson had a little more money too."

"Uh-huh," I said. "Any idea what they did together? Or where they went?"

"I heard," she said, "not from them, but from a lady I know, that they went to the Broke Spoke a couple times."

"Oh? Huh. You ever talk with Jackson about that?"

"No. I told Karl off. I mean, my son is—he was eighteen years old at that point, and that man was taking him to a strip club? That's how he steps up as a father? I told him to cut it out or stay the hell away from both of us. But, I mean, I couldn't control what Jackson did with his time."

"Nope," I said. "You can't, can you. I know exactly what you mean." I thought for a second and then added, "Jackson ever mention any card games or trips to Charleston with his dad?"

She shook her head.

"He ever say anything about Dunk McDonough? Or any of his bartenders, or anything?"

"No, I don't think so. I mean, you hear about Dunk, just around, but I don't think I heard anything from him. It's not like he was gonna tell his mama what he was up to down at the strip club."

"No, I suppose not."

She took a sip of her coffee and looked out the window. Some of the fronds on the palmetto were brushing against the glass.

"I did hear him arguing once, though," she said. "On the phone with Karl. He was in the backyard, and I don't know why he was so riled up, but he said something about somebody named Pete."

I froze. "Oh?"

"Yeah." She was shaking her head, with her eyebrows screwed up like she couldn't quite make sense of it. "He said, 'You keep Pete the hell away from her.' I don't know who he meant, though. I mean, I don't know who Pete or the woman were."

24

FRIDAY, SEPTEMBER 27, AFTERNOON

I was glad I'd decided to get lunch at the '50s-style diner downtown. Roy's advice to "get out there more" had led me to bring peanut butter sandwiches to work most days so that once a week I could afford to head over to the diner where judges and successful lawyers liked to eat. Apparently Ruiz was one of those lawyers. When I walked in I saw him a couple booths away, sitting by himself, and gave him a nod.

Jackson's second appearance, where he would enter a plea on the murder charges, was two and a half weeks away. I still hadn't heard word one from Ruiz about a possible plea deal, which was strange. It was a good time to run into him.

I gave him a, *Mind if I join you?* gesture, and he shrugged. Not a real welcoming shrug, but I wasn't going to be picky.

He had a cup of coffee but no plate yet. As I sat down, the waitress came over to top up his cup, pour me one, and hand me a menu.

Ruiz said, "You going to the shrimp fest tonight?"

"Absolutely," I said. "Shrimp is my weakness. I've yet to taste a way of making it that I don't like."

He smiled and stirred two packets of sugar into his coffee. "You are a local boy," he said, "through and through. And I hear you. Me too."

I looked at the menu. "I guess for once I won't have it for lunch," I said. "That'd be kind of overkill, with what's going to be on offer tonight."

He sighed. He had something on his mind. After a second, he said, "You know, Leland, it's not my business, but I can't help wondering. Did you want to come back home, or did you have to?"

"Uh, how do you mean?"

"Well, would you still be up at the solicitor's office if what happened there hadn't happened?"

I wasn't sure how much he knew, but I figured there was no point being cagey. We were part of a small legal community in a small town; privacy was hard to come by. And maybe being straightforward with him would encourage him to do the same.

I said, "You mean if I hadn't gone over to the wrong side of the law trying to protect my wife?"

He nodded. There was not a flicker of surprise. Evidently word had reached him, most likely from someone he knew up at the Charleston solicitor's office. I had misused the powers of my office to keep Elise from being charged with a DUI, more than once. I'd put lives at risk trying to protect her from consequences. I'd been lucky to be allowed to resign in lieu of facing an ethics complaint.

I thought back to his question. "Would I still be there? Yeah, I guess. It's almost addictive, isn't it. You know, the caseload, the fast pace, the sense of putting bad guys away. On good days it feels like you're saving the world."

He smiled and shook his head. I got the impression it had been a long time since he'd felt that way.

I said, "Why do you ask? You thinking of moving on yourself?"

The waitress came back to set down his burger and fries and take my order. I didn't want him to feel obligated to sit there waiting for me, so I asked for a ham sandwich, hoping it'd be out quick.

He poured himself a mound of ketchup, started in on his fries, and said, "Maybe it's a small-town thing, but it isn't often that I get the sense of fighting the good fight. You know, I put some domestic abuser away, and a year later he's back out doing it again. To the same woman or a new one, it doesn't seem to matter to those jackasses."

"Yeah," I said. "Although I guess you still spare somebody a year's worth of pain."

He shrugged. "I might as well smack one mosquito down at the swamp, for all the difference it makes."

I nodded and took a sip of coffee. Then I asked, "You still on board for Jackson's trial, though? Hope you aren't going to leave me in the lurch."

"Oh, yeah," he said. He sounded tired of Jackson's case, tired of pretty much everything. "I have nothing lined up. I haven't even started looking yet. It's just, you know, something I'm thinking about."

On a hunch, I said, "I don't blame you. I haven't heard good things about your boss."

He laughed. "There isn't much in the way of good things to hear. Let's see, uh… he drives a nice car? He still has all his own hair, I think, although he might just have a really good hair-plug surgeon. After that, I kind of run out of compliments."

I laughed and thanked the waitress, who'd come by to set down my sandwich.

"I was wondering," I said, "if your Mr. Hair Plugs is the reason you haven't run a plea offer past us yet."

He dragged a fry around in his ketchup like he was painting a picture. "Uh, he's the reason for a lot of things. What, that totally innocent client of yours might take a plea?"

I didn't appreciate the sarcasm. "Oh, you know how it is. Given the possible sentence here, it's something I'm duty bound to consider and advise him on. And I know every solicitor's office runs a little different, so maybe it's nothing, but up in Charleston, that'd probably be on the table by this point."

He nodded slowly, still drawing with his fry.

"It's hard to know sometimes," he said, "why Mr. Hair Plugs picks one case to be a hard-ass on and not another. But that's his call, not mine."

"Him and Blount," I said, and he nodded. I could see he knew some of the pressure was coming from Blount, and maybe he even had some sense as to why, but he didn't say anything.

To fill the silence, I said, "It's like they think they got Osama bin Warton locked up in the county jail."

He laughed.

"By the way," I said, "that forensic report was interesting. What'd you make of the trace amount of heroin they found on the boat?"

He tossed his fry in his mouth and said, "Somebody went out for a sea cruise and got high. Party on the motorboat. You'd be surprised"—he looked at me with wide eyes, his voice dripping with sarcasm—"but people in Basking Rock get high all the damn time."

I laughed. "Up in Charleston, we used to joke that at some point they were going to have to declare that the winner of the war on drugs was drugs."

He picked up his burger, said, "You might as well declare war on the goddamn sun," and took a bite. After chewing for a second, he added, "No matter what you do, it's going to rise again tomorrow."

"It isn't rising by itself, though," I said. "I mean, oxy, meth, whatever —people make that or get it from a doctor. But who's bringing pure heroin into Basking Rock?"

He washed his burger down with a sip of coffee and said, "Where there's roads, there's smugglers. If there's a harbor, there's smugglers. People will do anything to make a buck."

He seemed so lost in his cynical mood that I felt I should join him there. I nodded and said, "Isn't that the truth." It seemed wise to get on his wavelength if I wanted him to keep talking frankly with me.

"It's just a game of whack-a-mole," he said. "You catch one guy bringing it in, a week later some other guy replaces him."

"Mm-hmm," I said. "I know the feeling. You guys catch anybody lately?"

"Oh, yeah," he said. His voice told me it didn't hardly matter to him at all. "You see that bust-up outside Charleston? Third-biggest in South Carolina history?"

"Yeah, I saw that on the news. I used to work with that guy."

"Oh yeah? Well, anyway, we helped with some intel on that." He shrugged. "So they whacked a mole, and now another one'll pop right back up."

It didn't sound like I was going to get any specifics from him. He knew where the lines were, in terms of what he could say to anyone outside the office, and he wasn't going to cross them. Ruiz had never been a line-crosser.

In his current mood, I thought, he might be receptive to my own suspicions. It couldn't hurt to drop some ideas on him and see where they landed.

"You ever think," I said, "that maybe Karl got caught up in any of that? And maybe that's what got him killed?"

From his frown and the tilt of his eyebrows, I could see he thought that was entirely possible.

"Of course, that isn't where the evidence is pointing." He looked me in the eye and said, "I can't try a case on evidence I don't have."

It might have been hope or desperation making me read more into it than he meant, but I had the impression that what he'd said was code. It seemed to mean that he wasn't going to dig into this, but if I did, if I could walk into his office and throw evidence on his desk that said the prosecution's theory was wrong, he would listen. He would do what he could.

He was an honest man, and a fair one. He always had been.

Which was probably why he didn't get along with his boss.

25

FRIDAY, SEPTEMBER 27, EVENING

I parked around a corner two blocks from the beach, trying to find a compromise between avoiding shrimp-fest traffic and walking farther than Noah could comfortably manage. He insisted a few blocks was fine, and while I wasn't sure I believed him, I knew telling him so would spoil the good mood that the prospect of the event had put us in. We'd driven there with our windows down, since it was still nearly seventy degrees, and before we could even see the beach—before we saw the crowd and the lights of a Ferris wheel twinkling against the dark sky—we could smell frying shrimp. His deep breath and relaxed smile reminded me that he had inherited my tastes in that regard: the aroma gave both of us an immediate sense of well-being.

As we headed down the sidewalk, I said, "I'm sure glad Basking Rock's got this tradition now."

"How d'you mean?"

"Oh, you weren't even in kindergarten yet, I don't think, when Henry Carrell came up with the idea. Everyone in town pretty much had their own family shrimp fest for white shrimp season, but he's the one who got the ear of someone at the county tourism office to get something bigger started. I'm sure he thought it'd be good for his boat business—and he was right. And, to be fair, also good for the local economy."

"That's so weird," he said. "I mean, this is a tradition, you know? It feels like we've been coming to this my whole life."

"Well, you pretty much have." We walked a few yards in silence before I added, "Even though your mom didn't like shrimp."

"What?" He laughed in disbelief. "How is that possible?"

"I know," I said. "But I married her anyway."

He laughed. "I guess you got to be open-minded," he said. "People can have other qualities even if their taste buds just don't work."

I chuckled and felt a flash of pride that my kid had a sense of humor.

"If I leave you nothing else," I said, "as my legacy, at least you love shrimp and you know how to crack a joke."

"It doesn't look like you're going to leave me much else," he said. "I mean, judging by that plastic-and-duct-tape window you put on the only car you actually own."

I laughed so hard I had to stop walking for a second. It wasn't just because my kid was damn funny. It was because joking around like this made me think that someday, when he was older, when we'd gotten through the fallout of Elise's death and his injury, we might be able to settle into something like friendship.

At the beach we stood in line, saying hi to familiar faces as they passed, and then walked around a while munching on mixed baskets of shrimp that had been fried in a half dozen different kinds of batter. The nightly breeze had started blowing toward the water, and in its coolness I could feel the first hint of fall. From the side of the beach where fairground rides and booths had been set up, kids screamed happily on a whirling teacup ride, and I saw Detective Blount trying to shoot rubber ducks to win a stuffed animal for his youngest boy.

He failed.

Instead of being a good sport, Blount rammed the butt of the toy rifle into the sand and taught his boy five or six swear words. I remembered what Terri had said about him being an angry person, or having anger problems, or however she'd put it.

I told Noah, "That's Detective Blount, there. Who we were talking about last week or whenever."

"Oh, yeah. He's… yeah, nobody likes him."

"Well, I share that sentiment. And by the way, anything you find out about him, or anything you remember, might possibly be helpful for Jackson's case. So let me know."

"Oh yeah?" It sounded like news to him that I wanted intel on Blount. "I'll do that," he said. "I'll think real hard."

Our father-son moment ended when he saw a gang of teenage boys standing around like they were too cool to actually enjoy the funnel cakes and fried ice cream that they were eating. He started talking with them, and I had the sense my continued presence would be embarrassing. I vaguely recognized one of the boys, though it took me a minute to realize from where: he was Jackson's friend who ran the idiotic podcast about the wonders of marijuana.

Not who I wanted hanging around with my son, but I knew saying so would put an end to any chance of a pleasant evening with Noah. And if I insisted on a house rule that he couldn't have any pot-smoking friends, that would eliminate most of the boys his age in town.

Noah asked for money—I slipped him my last twenty—and promised to keep an eye on his texts so if Roy came through on his suggestion of a yacht ride tonight, he could come with us. Yachts were apparently cooler than other teenagers, and he was looking forward to it.

I texted Roy, hoping to get that part of the evening to kick off ASAP. Then I pocketed my phone and strolled on down the beach. It seemed like half the town was there. It looked exactly like it had every other time I'd been to the shrimp fest, and the whole last decade and a half blurred together in my mind. I could hardly believe that Noah no longer only came up to my waist, or that Elise was gone.

A woman's voice called out, "Hey, doll!" It took her a couple tries before I saw her in the crowd and realized she was talking to me. Cheryl, my extremely friendly Broke Spoke waitress. She wasn't alone; apparently Dunk had an entourage, and she was part of it.

I said, "Oh, hey, Cheryl! And Dunk, and all y'all!"

Dunk grunted a grudging hello and said to one of his compadres, "Give him a shirt." The whole crew, all six or eight of them, were wearing Broke Spoke T-shirts. The compadre balled up a black one and tossed it to me. I opened it up and saw, under the club's name, a nude female silhouette bending over a motorcycle wheel. My life as I knew it did not contain any type of event at which I would wear such a shirt.

I said, "Thanks much!" When I looked up, I noticed the women's shirts were a little different: same illustration, but the club's name was written in sequins.

Cheryl said, with a big smile, "I hope you come on back soon, now!"

Before I could answer, Dunk told her, "You know he doesn't drink anything but water. With maraschino cherries sometimes."

The men he was with guffawed. One of them looked like a younger, less bulky Dunk. I'd heard he had a son.

Dunk told Cheryl, "Unless you're getting ten-dollar tips on two-cent cherries, you're barking up the wrong tree."

Her smile faltered. "But it's a medical condition," she said, looking to me for confirmation. "Ain't it? That's what Pat Warton told me."

I nodded, wondering how well she and Pat knew each other.

"Medical condition, my ass," Dunk said. His eyes narrowed.

"It is what it is," I said, with a shrug.

He looked friendly all of a sudden—not toward me, but toward whoever he'd spotted behind me. I turned and saw Henry Carrell staring clear over my head at him. Henry had a tight smile on his face, the kind of smile I associated with running into someone you owed money to. Or how I'd probably looked, I thought, when I'd run into Tony Rosa and worried he might tell folks I'd left our former workplace under a cloud of disgrace.

"Henry!" Dunk walked past me, holding out his meaty paw, and smacked a handshake on Henry that would've knocked some people over.

"Great to see you, Dunk." Henry's politician voice had kicked in, and he sounded sincere.

"Henry and I go way the hell back," Dunk told his entourage. "To when we were this high." He gestured. "Third grade, wasn't it?"

"Third grade," Henry confirmed.

"Nobody thought punk kids like us would be the economic future of this town. Or that you'd get so high and mighty. Look at him, a fisherman's son, on the beach in a goddamn suit!"

Dunk's buddies laughed.

Henry tried a little joke: "Well, we only have a week until the election, and I'm fishing for votes." I gave him a polite chuckle; nobody else did. He added, "Speaking of which, I should get going—"

I said, "Mind if I come with? You have my vote, and I have no problem telling other folks why."

"Well, that's mighty kind of you, Leland."

Over his shoulder, Dunk said, "Give me extra-large. Pink or pastel or some shit." His compadre tossed him a mint-green shirt, and he put it in Henry's hands.

Henry unfolded it and looked at the illustration. His eyebrows went up. "Dunk," he said, trying to hand it back, "you know I support local businesses. But advertising a strip club won't sit right with my wife, or my church."

Dunk crossed his arms on his chest. "Carrell," he said, "That is the *least* of your wife's worries. And I did not get my ass shot at in Iraq just to come home and get disrespected by some jumped-up fisherman's kid."

After a second, Henry said, "Course not." His arm dropped; he'd given up trying to get rid of the shirt. "And as I've said before, thank you for your service."

As we walked up the beach, Henry glad-handing every third or fourth person while I carried both T-shirts, I wondered but didn't ask why he'd let Dunk give him such a drubbing. I didn't remember them being friends, enemies, or anything else in high school. I hadn't realized how far back they went.

As we headed to the parking lot to meet up with Roy, I said, "I owe you for making my son think I might not be completely uncool. He's looking forward to this yacht trip so much, he's even willing to hang out with his dad."

He gave a sympathetic laugh. "How old is he, again?"

"Nineteen."

"Lord." He shook his head. "The teenage years are a special kind of hell, aren't they."

"How old is your daughter?"

"Eighteen next month. And she's a wonderful girl, doing great in school, but… Lord."

I laughed. "I hope for your sake she doesn't listen to Nordic death metal music."

He didn't know what that was, so I shared what little I knew.

In disbelief, he said, "Your boy listens to that?"

"Little bit. He picked it up from friends, unfortunately."

"Leland," he said, "if your boy comes near my daughter and she starts listening to that, I swear, I will rescind the invitation I was planning to extend for you to come to my Christmas party this year."

"On the yacht?"

He nodded.

"You have my word," I said.

Noah met us at the parking lot, and Roy drove us all down to the marina. The *Lady Jane* was at the dock, looking like a postcard, with graceful palm trees framing it as we approached. It was fifty or sixty feet long, and strips of lit-up windows showed it had two levels below the deck.

"Dang!" said Noah.

Roy pulled into a parking spot and asked, "This your first time?"

"I been on motorboats," he said. "And a sailboat once, and crawdad fishing. But nothing like this."

Henry, in the passenger seat, said, "Well, your dad made a strong case I should invite you."

"Awesome! Thanks, Dad."

As Noah got out, Henry looked back at me and winked.

We headed down the dock. It was as finely made and tastefully lit as any up in Charleston, with lamps casting golden pools on the wood and small spotlights in the sand illuminating the boat. Henry, or Blue Seas, had spared no expense. Down in the sand I saw a worker, judging by the blue shirt they all wore, talking with a man in a suit that I thought I recognized.

Henry was asking Noah what his college plans were, so I asked Roy, "Isn't that the investor you sent me to see? Collin Porter?"

Roy paused to peer down at them. "Yeah, that's him. I guess he'll be joining us tonight."

He didn't, though. Or, at any rate, he never joined us on deck.

26

SATURDAY, OCTOBER 5, AFTERNOON

I 'd finished drafting something Roy needed filed on Monday and was tapping a pen on the edge of my desk, thinking about Jackson's case. I'd left one stone unturned, and it was bothering me. Who was that trucker, Pete, who Karl had hung out with? If he was the same guy Terri had said was trading opiates for sex, was that my angle in, to show that Karl had been dealing and had made himself some enemies in the process?

That night back in August, when Pat Warton was heading to his truck in the parking lot of the Broke Spoke, he'd told me Pete was a poker buddy of Karl's. He'd also felt the need to add that he himself had "nothing to do with that," which was a strange thing to say about an innocent poker game. I wondered what all he knew.

The weekend seemed like a good time to find him at home, so I headed over to the trailer park.

When I turned up the dirt road to the Wartons' trailer, I saw Tim sitting in the mermaid chair with what I assumed was a bottle of malt liquor in hand. The only change since my visit in the summertime was that he had added a Hawaiian shirt to his shorts-and-tank-top ensemble, probably because temperatures had dropped to the low seventies. As I parked and stepped out, he gave a whistle of appreciation and yelled, "Check out the fancy new car, Mr. Lawyer!"

"Yep," I said. "Moving on up in the world, I guess." My silver Malibu had not sparked such enthusiasm in anyone else. I wondered if Tim was a little drunk already, even though it was only two in the afternoon.

We got to talking. I asked about the half-carved wooden sculpture behind him, which was nearly as tall as I was and portrayed a fish leaping out of waves. It was a striped bass, he explained, the official state fish of South Carolina, and the base of the sculpture, when he finished carving it, was going to look like our state flag. He had a lot to say about which woodworking tools he'd used and why.

Pat was nowhere to be seen, which I thought might be a blessing, since he had struck me as the more intelligent and paranoid of the two. Those weren't qualities I wanted to deal with just now. A man who was talkative even when he wasn't drinking, and who was most of the way through a forty-ounce bottle of what was indeed malt liquor, was much better.

"Hey, Tim," I said, as if the thought had just occurred to me, "you ever play poker with your brother? Karl, I mean?"

"Not in years," he said. "He wiped me out every time I ever did."

"Yeah, I heard he was good. Played with some folks up in Charleston, from what I understand."

"I guess. Oh, yeah, that's how he got the Mustang, I remember." He shook his head, smiling in admiration at Karl's luck.

"Did he win that off a guy named Pete? Or was it someone else?"

"Don't rightly know," he said, taking a swig from his bottle. "Wouldn't that be on the title? Who owned it before? I'd be interested to know where that car is, and who gets it now."

"Well, if I worked for the government," I said, "It'd be easy for me to look at the title. But I don't. So I just wondered if you'd heard anything about that."

He thought for a minute, tapping his foot like it might trigger a memory. He was wearing flip-flops, and his feet were spattered with what I figured must be wood stain.

Finally he said, "I don't think it was Dupree. All I ever heard about him was trucks and garbage. Not cars."

"Pete Dupree? The trucker?" I kept my voice calm, but my mind was in overdrive. I'd heard that name somewhere before.

"Uh-huh. Well, not a trucker like you're thinking of. He drove, but mainly he owned a little waste-hauling company, from what I recall. And I don't remember Karl ever mentioning him when he talked about that car."

"Okay," I said. "Well, I guess we can cross his name off."

After another ten minutes of chatting about Karl's poker buddies and how to find the car, I said I'd keep him posted if I found it and took my leave.

On my way out of the trailer park, I gave Terri a call. She wasn't familiar with the name Dupree but said she'd check with some of the women he'd victimized to see if it rang a bell with them.

If she didn't know the name, then clearly I hadn't heard it from her. But I'd heard it, and although I couldn't recall where, my brain had filed it under "work." It filed most things under work—one of the arguments Elise and I used to have was whether my being a workaholic was responsible for her drinking problem—but that still seemed like a good clue. I decided to head back to the office.

At my desk, I fired up my computer and then stopped. I leaned back in my chair, staring at the ceiling. If Pete Dupree was mentioned somewhere in Roy's client files, or if, God forbid, he or his waste-haulage company was a client, the state ethics board might have some thoughts about my actions right now. Those thoughts would not be positive.

Then again, I wouldn't know if there was a conflict until I figured out who Pete Dupree was. For all I knew, he'd been one of the protesters Roy had mentioned harassing Blue Seas a while back. That particular scenario seemed unlikely for a waste-haulage guy, but it was entirely possible his name had come up on the opposing side of some problem one of our clients had had. In that case, there wouldn't be any ethical issue at all.

I ran some searches. It didn't take long, because Roy, who preferred almost any leisure activity to actually working, had invested in some very solid practice management software. It warned us of all upcoming deadlines, kept everything organized, and applied various other bells and whistles with the end goal of leaving Roy free to golf.

And there, highlighted in blue on my screen, it showed me the name Pete Dupree.

He wasn't a client, thank God. He worked, or had worked—this file was from two years earlier—in waste haulage for Blue Seas.

I kept searching. A little over a year ago, I learned, Dupree, Karl, and a Blue Seas shipboard worker called Luis Garza had been arrested for trespassing at a salvage yard up in Charleston. Henry Carrell had vouched for them personally, and Roy helped get them off. The arrest report showed a Charleston address for Dupree, in a nicer neighborhood than my old one. I wondered if it was waste-haulage money or drug money that had allowed that.

I picked up the phone to call Terri, then put it back down to think. Blue Seas was Roy's client, which in terms of ethics rules meant mine too, since I worked for Roy. But employees or contractors of Blue Seas were not our clients. If their interests were in conflict with Blue Seas—and any drug dealing by Dupree would sure as hell fall in that category—then I had zero obligation to protect them.

I called Terri, got voicemail, and left her a message with the information I'd found. Within ten minutes, she texted back that Dupree had sold his Charleston house and moved on to parts unknown.

I sighed and shut my eyes. This case had been an obstacle course from the start, and it seemed like every new lead presented a new problem along with it. My brain just wanted to power down and forget it all. I stood up and took a little walk around the office. As I passed Laura's empty desk, I wished I'd thought to start up the coffee maker when I arrived.

It crossed my mind that if Pete did have some connection to Karl's murder, Henry Carrell would be pretty pissed off if cops showed up at his place of business without his lawyers warning him. And if I gave him a call, maybe he'd tell me more about Pete.

I headed back to my desk.

He picked right up. We shot the breeze, and then I got to the point: "I just wanted to give you a heads-up, an old contractor of yours might have some information about Karl's murder. I didn't want cops showing up at your door out of the blue—"

"Good Lord," he said. "Are you serious? Who?"

"Your waste-hauler guy. Name of Pete Dupree."

"Damn. He gave us enough trouble already. This past spring he flaked out on his contract, right before high season. You ever tried to get a reliable company to haul half a ton of waste per week, on three days' notice?"

I laughed. "That seems mighty ungrateful of him, after you and Roy helped get him out of those trespassing charges."

"The what, now?"

"Oh, that thing up in Charleston. He got himself arrested along with Karl and another Blue Seas guy by the name of Luis Garza, and Roy got the charges dropped after you vouched for them. Speaking of which, they might want to talk with Garza too. Any idea where to find either of them?"

He didn't say anything. I couldn't tell if he was thinking or had gotten distracted. Then he said, "Oh, yeah. I tell you what, so much shit hits the fan here sometimes, I have trouble recalling each specific turd. But that does ring a bell. Garza was one of my Dominicans, the D-visa crew. I let him go after the trespassing thing. Couldn't say where he is now. In theory, he should've gone back home."

He also had no idea where Pete might be. When we hung up, I yanked open my desk drawer for some Tylenol. Chasing leads that went nowhere was giving me a headache.

For dinner, I brought an extra-large pizza home. Noah ate half of it in about ten minutes and took another piece back to his room to power him through some online gaming. I looked out at the setting sun, thinking it might be time I went back to the Broke Spoke. I could swing past and check the lot for Dunk's obnoxious red Hummer and Cheryl's little light-blue Kia, or Hyundai, or whatever it was.

I checked my wallet. I had ten bucks left, enough for some sparkling water and a ridiculous tip. If Cheryl was there and Dunk wasn't, maybe I could find out a little more about Pete Dupree.

Saturday night, it turned out, was not a good time to go investigating at a strip club. The angry little White-supremacist bartender glared at me for occupying the last available barstool, and Cheryl was run off her feet. I nursed my expensive water, left her a tip that I hoped would buy a future conversation, and headed back to my car. I'd parked half a block down, across the street. I never wanted to have to tell Roy I'd damaged his car by leaving it in a strip club lot for some drunk idiot to dent.

The night air was pleasantly cool, and the streetlight by my car was shining through oak leaves and Spanish moss. I took a deep breath; even here, I could smell the salt tang of the ocean. For all the problems this place had, I thought, heading diagonally across the street, it truly was home.

A revving engine snapped me out of my reverie. I broke into a jog to get across the street, but a headlight beam lit my hands and then the asphalt in front of me. Some Saturday-night driver, probably drunk, was veering toward me. I burst into a sprint, praying he wouldn't swerve onto the sidewalk, and went airborne over the curb. As brakes squealed, I hit the ground hard. The engine revved again, and I looked back to see a black truck peeling away. It shot down the street, took the first corner, and disappeared.

As I scrambled to my feet, I saw blood on my hands and down the front of my suit. I had to get out of there—the hairs on the back of my neck told me that—so I ran to my car without even trying to clean up, turned the key, and took off.

At a stoplight six or eight blocks later, holding napkins to my bloody nose and feeling glad that the Malibu's upholstery was black, I realized what had me on edge. A drunk driver could easily veer toward a pedestrian; that happened all too often. But there'd been nothing erratic about that truck. A drunk driver wouldn't have shot down the rest of the block as straight as a bullet and taken the corner so tightly.

And if it wasn't some drunk, that meant he'd been aiming for me.

27

FRIDAY, OCTOBER 11, MORNING

I was back in Judge Chambliss's courtroom for the short proceeding known as a second appearance, when folks charged with crimes had their lawyers show up to let the judge know if they were pleading guilty or going to trial. Chambliss held these things every other Friday, so what looked like half the defense attorneys in the county were sitting in the courtroom's wooden pews waiting their turns. I joined them and spent an hour watching Ruiz do his thing at the prosecution table. I couldn't help but notice that of the five cases handled in that hour, four of them got plea bargains. That was normal. I still hadn't figured out why Jackson's case wasn't normal to Ruiz. Or, rather, to his boss.

When my case was called, I stepped over to the defense table, nodding to Ruiz as I passed. Judge Chambliss finished conferring with his clerk and said, "Well, counsel? You got this taken care of?"

Chambliss and I both looked at Ruiz. He moved some papers around on his desk, looking down at them like there might be an answer printed there, and said, "Your Honor, uh, it appears this case is going to trial. According to whatever schedule you impose, of course."

Judge Chambliss looked at me. I could tell he was puzzled.

I said, "Morning, Your Honor. Mr. Ruiz and I have conferred, but his office has not offered my client any type of plea. And my client maintains his innocence, so yes, we're proceeding to trial."

Chambliss turned to him. "Mr. Ruiz, I trust your office is aware of what I told you at the preliminary hearing? About, uh, the manslaughter jury instruction that I said, if the weight of the evidence still looked pretty much like it did then, I'd offer if asked?"

"Yes, Your Honor. Of course, Your Honor. I'm well aware, and I informed my superior."

"Okay. And, for the record, are you confirming you folks haven't offered a plea?"

"Yes, Your Honor. The solicitor general believes this case should go to trial."

"Well, okay then." He beckoned to his clerk, said something to her, and handed her a page from his desk. She sat back down and flipped a couple of pages over in her calendar.

"Mr. Munroe," Chambliss said, "as I recall, Mr. Ruiz had asked to fast-track this. And you were not opposed?"

"No, Your Honor. My client's been in jail since June, and he's eager to get this over with."

He nodded. "Okay, then." His clerk walked back to the bench and handed him the piece of paper. He looked at it and said, "Mr. Ruiz, you free in the last half of December?"

"Uh, let me… One moment, Your Honor." He fumbled for his phone and started scrolling. "Uh, you mean Christmas, Your Honor?"

"Courts are closed on Christmas Day, Mr. Ruiz."

"Yes, of course, Your Honor." I could see him deflate. He was a family man, and a trial was a twenty-four seven job. With four little kids, I knew, it would kill him to spend Christmas that way.

Chambliss said, "Monday, December 16 work for y'all?"

Ruiz nodded. "Uh, one week, Your Honor?"

"Let's make it two. If we don't need that much time, fine, but I'd rather schedule that so nobody ends up having to cancel holiday plans if we run long."

Ruiz deflated even more. When I picked my files up and headed out, he barely looked at me.

After work, I met up with Terri outside Mazie's house so we could retrace Jackson's steps on the night of the murder. Mazie was at work. Our plan was to see how long it took to walk to the marina, and to take some photos along the way that we might use in trial exhibits. Terri took a few shots from Mazie's porch and the sidewalk in front. The sun was starting to head down the sky and turn gold, making the neighborhood look prettier than it normally did. For trial exhibits, I liked that. Juries tended to make assumptions about people from bad-looking neighborhoods.

"You know," I said, "I've only ever driven through this part of town. It feels different walking."

"What I notice is how many windows there are. All these people, and they mostly would've been home at night. And the convenience store, the laundromat… The streetlights work, right?"

"We'll see when we get back. I never thought it was dark driving through here, though."

She paused on the sidewalk, hit the stopwatch she was using to get an accurate measure on the length of the walk, and took photos of the convenience store and a house whose front window faced the sun. You could see the whole living room through it, and several members of the family inside.

"We'll have to blur their faces," I said.

"Mm-hmm."

She started her stopwatch again, and we walked on. "So, all these people," she said, "and all the publicity about this case, but the prosecution doesn't have anybody other than Blount who saw Jackson walking with a crowbar?"

"That's a good point. And, I mean, it's quite the coincidence that the lead detective just happened to see the defendant acting suspicious that night."

She nodded. I could see her going over something in her mind. "I'm not going to get into specifics," she said, "but one of the reasons I left the force is that I saw a couple of fellow officers manufacture some real convenient coincidences. And they didn't get called out. The brass covered for them."

I shook my head. "I can see that driving out good cops. Sure, you nail the perp in the case right in front of you, but big picture, you end up corrupting the force and destroying public trust."

She laughed, a bit harshly, and hit her stopwatch again. As she snapped a photo of a crowded gas station, she said, "If you think there's much public trust left to destroy, your definition of the public must be different than mine."

"Oh," I said, realizing what she meant. "Oh, right." I had a mental image of the entire Black population of South Carolina standing on a corner several blocks ahead, looking at their watches and waiting for folks like me to catch up.

When we started walking again, I said, "Speaking of coincidences, it turns out Pete Dupree did some work for Blue Seas. Did you dig up anything on him?"

"Mm-hmm. Unless there are two truckers called Pete Dupree who spend time in Basking Rock, we're talking about the same guy. Or the same lowlife, I should say. What'd he do at Blue Seas?"

"Waste haulage. He's not just a trucker. He drove, but I guess the more lucrative end of his business was that his company got the contract for handling all the garbage from the yacht charters."

"I wonder how Henry found him. I mean, did he put it out for bids? Did he run a background check on Dupree? Because it wouldn't have come back clean."

"Huh. I don't know." I wrestled for a moment with myself, wondering if there was any way to rationalize pawing through the Blue Seas files again to see if I could find that out.

As she snapped a photo of a roadside restaurant and then zoomed in on the door to get a picture of the sign—the hours of operation showed it would've been open during Jackson's walk—a problem occurred to me. "Hey," I said. "I should've asked when we started out, but do you need me to be taking notes about exactly where we are at each photo? And how long it took to walk from point A to point B? I mean, so we can reconstruct that in the trial presentation."

"No. Every photo's geotagged and date-stamped. And I checked my camera settings this afternoon to make sure it was all up to date and accurate."

"I remember a guy I worked with up in Charleston talking about something like that." I tried to recall what he'd said. "I think he needed an expert witness to testify about the accuracy, but the basic gist was every digital photo had all that information hidden in it somewhere."

We turned onto the causeway. This part of the walk was going to be on the beach, because aside from one small parking area halfway along, the causeway was nothing but road.

"It's not exactly hidden," she said. "It's in what's called EXIF data. Which is, you know, searchable, viewable, depending on your software." We stepped into the sand, and she took a long shot of the causeway with the line of palm trees and the strip of beach leading to the other side of town, then put her camera back into its bag. "I don't want to get sand or spray in it," she explained. "And anyway, I don't think anyone driving down the causeway at night would've seen him walking on the beach."

I agreed. We walked without talking for a bit. The sound of the waves a few yards away was soothing. A couple of seagulls were wheeling in the sky. I looked out at the water, imagining Karl's boat adrift. It was white; it had been found pretty quickly, considering how remote the spot it ran aground was, because it was easy to spot against the wet sand.

I asked her, "That data you're talking about, can you search for it online? I mean, find photos that were taken at a certain place and time?"

"It depends where you look," she said. "Sites like Facebook strip that data out when you post photos, to protect privacy. But a lot of sites don't. Things on the cloud or those photo-storage sites could have it, if the user didn't tweak their privacy settings. Are you thinking we look for photos of Jackson that night?"

"Oh, that too," I said. Her idea was brilliant, but it hadn't crossed my mind. "I was just looking at the water and thinking about Karl's boat."

"Oh." She squinted out at the water. I could almost see the math she was doing in her head. "Well, the problem there is you're looking at a huge amount of possible coordinates. We don't know what path his boat followed, so we got a whole bay and part of the ocean to search."

I could tell by her expression that she wasn't giving up because of that. She was trying to figure out how to make it work.

"There's also accuracy issues," she said. "If people's phone settings are off, or their time zone didn't update or whatever, we'll get some results that aren't right and we'll miss some that are."

"I guess that's why my guy up in Charleston needed an expert witness."

"Mm-hmm. And if we did find anything useful, you'd need one too."

"I'm going to need a lottery win to get this case done right."

She laughed.

I sighed and shook my head. "I guess we cross that bridge when we come to it. If we come to it."

"You got me curious now, though. I want to figure out how to make this work."

"You like doing the impossible, don't you."

She smiled. "I already know I can do what's possible. What's the point in just doing more of that?"

"That seems like a good motto. If—" Before I could finish, I felt my phone vibrate. I pulled it out. Henry had texted me.

"Huh," I said. "Henry says he found a current address for Pete Dupree."

"Good," she said. "If your case doesn't give prosecutors what they need to put him behind bars, I am going to bring that man down myself. He's hurt too many women in this town."

"You got a hell of a to-do list."

She said, "I am not here on this earth to waste my time."

28

SUNDAY, OCTOBER 27, MORNING

Terri dropped by with Buster so we could walk the dogs at a little park near my house while discussing Jackson's case. I kept pace with Squatter, picking him up a few times to give him a rest, while her dog barreled off after thrown sticks and balls. It was a strangely wholesome thing to be doing while we discussed the sordid criminal record of Pete Dupree. Or "Lowlife," as she called him. We used nicknames when talking about the case in public, to keep from being understood by anyone who might overhear, but most of them were less colorful.

According to the mug shot she'd texted me, Lowlife Dupree was about six one and heavyset, with thinning hair gone mostly gray. He looked like I'd expect a guy who ran a waste-haulage business to look: nothing fancy, a regular guy. I wouldn't have looked at him twice if I saw him on the street. I certainly wouldn't have figured he had a rap sheet almost three pages long from states up and down the east coast. Various drug crimes, aiding and abetting prostitution, assault. There was even a human trafficking charge from last year, which got dismissed. Terri had forwarded me his record, along with a list of the original charges he'd faced each time, and I found myself wondering how his defense lawyer had worked the miracle of keeping this guy mostly outside of prison. Everything had been tossed out or pled down.

"Goddammit," I said. "To think Lowlife here is still walking around despite all this, but my guy's been in jail since June."

"Lowlife has money," she said, leaning down to give her dog a treat. He wolfed it and vibrated with joy. "Good boy," she said. "You're a good boy. If you and your dog friends ran this world, it'd be a much better place."

I laughed and agreed. Then, getting back to the task at hand, I said, "I guess there's not much point my warning Polly about this guy." We'd started referring to Henry as Polly, short for politician. "I mean, Lowlife doesn't work for him anymore, and he left on bad terms anyway."

She looked at me. "You don't think he already knows?"

I hadn't seen anything in the Blue Seas file about Dupree's record, but I didn't want to tell her I'd been looking there. "Well, you know," I said, with a shrug. "Folks sometimes don't do all the due diligence that they ought to. And I can't see an upstanding churchgoer like him doing business with somebody if he knew about that."

She nodded, but she looked doubtful. "Some of those churchgoer types, though," she said, "they go a little overboard on forgiveness. Some crook says he's found Jesus, they forget all about the people he hurt."

"Yeah, I've seen judges who do that. But I don't get the impression Polly works that way."

"Still," she said, "keep this between us. We don't want Lowlife hearing from anybody that you're looking into him."

Talking about Dupree's sleaze had put me back in my prosecutorial frame of mind, and my old habit of cracking jokes to relieve the bleakness was coming back. "What's he going to do if he does," I said. "Force me into prostitution?"

That got a laugh. As an ex-cop, she had the same habit and understood it coming from me. "I don't think you need to worry about that," she said. "Don't take this the wrong way, but I doubt he'd see you as a big income generator. At all."

"Did you really need to add the 'at all'?"

She laughed. "Sorry. But look, Leland, I am deadly serious. He's a career criminal with the resources to…" She stopped. I sensed she didn't want to say right out that he could pay someone to attack me. She'd been trying to track down the black pickup that tried to run me down, but I had almost no information for her to go on. I hadn't even noticed if it had South Carolina plates.

Finally she said, "Lowlife doesn't work alone. He can give orders, and his guys will listen." She glanced around like she was checking who was in earshot, then called her dog to make the glance look innocent. He came running, and she threw a tennis ball to send him off again.

No one was close by, but I kept my voice down when I said, "You got some intel on him you haven't shared?"

"Only because I haven't confirmed it yet. At least, not to my normal standard. But it's a little hard to confirm when someone's part of a major drug cartel."

"*That* yahoo? Damn. Really?"

She nodded and said, "It helps to look like a yahoo. People don't suspect."

"Yeah. So what the hell cartel is operating around here?"

"The same one your friend talked about on TV."

"Up in Charleston? Damn." I remembered Tony Rosa and his third-largest heroin bust in state history. "That's big."

"It's a lot bigger than a monthly poker game."

"Yeah. I doubt Karl knew what he was getting into."

"Well, maybe you can ask what he knew," she said. "Because I found Kitty."

"Are you kidding me?" She wasn't. "She resurfaced? What's she doing?"

"Going by Katie now, and dying her hair brown. She works at a restaurant up in Charleston, in the French Quarter. And if you got time to get there today, you might want to, because she usually works the Sunday brunch shift."

I whistled and said, "Damn, you're good."

She accepted the tribute with lowered eyelashes and a nod. I could see she was proud of herself, and rightly so.

I checked my watch. If brunch extended into the lunch hour, which I figured it did, it was doable.

On the drive up, I thought about how to approach a potential witness scared enough to skip town, dye her hair, and start going by a different name. The fact she'd done all that made me think she must have had at least some idea that Karl was neck-deep in shit. And the fact that, according to her, it was Dunk who'd told her to get out of town made it pretty clear to me that he probably knew that too, or else he knew how Karl died, and either way he didn't want the information to come out.

Or, of course, he knew both those things.

I parked on a side street near the French Quarter. It was a bright blue, sunny day, but down in the low sixties; there was no escaping fall. I was glad for the tweed jacket I'd grabbed on the way out.

The restaurant was in what had originally been a house, a pink Victorian with double-decker white porches. There was a short line out the door, and I took my spot. The street was lined with tall palm trees, and from the rose bushes and swirly cast-iron fence surrounding Chez Madame, I figured it was the kind of place that sold postcards of itself to out-of-town visitors. I found myself wondering how a strip club waitress like Kitty had managed to get through the job interview.

I didn't have to wonder long. I'd missed the brunch rush, and there were a few bar seats and a two-top to choose from. I asked the girl seating me, "Do you know which section Katie's working today? I always like having her."

She walked me over to the two-top and handed me a menu. I held it a little high so Kitty, or Katie, wouldn't recognize me from a distance. As I read it, I realized a year-plus of eating in Basking Rock had made me forget just how much an omelet could cost. To pay for this, I was going to be bringing peanut butter sandwiches to work for at least two weeks.

Kitty, when she showed up, played her part well. I saw her flinch when she recognized me, but just for an instant; the smile popped right back into place. She had transformed herself into a full-on southern belle: cute skirt, fluffy hair and all. She had classed up, and it suited her.

I said good morning, called her by her new name, and gave her what I hoped was a reassuring smile. She told me the specials and assured me the waffles were good. When she stumbled over a little speech about the crepes and apologized for it, I said, "Don't worry. Really, don't worry. I won't tell nobody." I looked her in the eye as I said it, hoping she'd understand I wasn't talking about the crepes.

I had decided to approach this gently. A person who skipped town once could do it again, and the surest way to make her do that would be to try to interrogate her while she was working. I ate my waffles with no coffee to accompany them, which felt like a sin against nature, but the greater sin would have been to spend six dollars for a single cup. If I was making that kind of investment, I figured, better to put it into a tip.

When Kitty came to refill my water, she went into some waitress chitchat about whether I was in town for business or pleasure.

"Oh, I do nothing but work," I said. "But, you know, I'm a lawyer. I'm just trying to keep an innocent kid from spending the rest of his life in jail."

Her smile flickered to a frown, then reappeared. She nodded. "Well, okay then. If you need anything else, you just let me know."

Apart from bringing the check, she didn't come back. I paid with my debit card so I'd have a reason to leave a piece of paper for her. I tucked both receipts into the little leatherette folder she'd brought: the signed copy for the restaurant and the copy I was supposed to keep. On that one, I wrote my cell number and the words, "Don't worry."

That night after dinner, Terri called, sounding more excited than I'd ever heard her. She was talking so fast I couldn't understand at first.

"Just a minute," she said, and I heard her take a couple of deep breaths. "Okay. Are you sitting down?"

"I am."

"Okay. Then let me—I'll just start from the start. I tried so many different things. All kinds of different searches. I was up almost all night. I swear, Buster was worried about me. I conked out in bed with my laptop and woke up with him sleeping next to me. He had his head right on the other pillow."

"What was going on? Did you track down that black truck?"

"Better than that. Or, I mean, not better—sorry, that came out wrong. I don't mean a threat on your life is less important."

I laughed and said, "I don't think I've ever heard you in such a tizzy. What's going on?"

Another deep breath. "I have photographic evidence of Karl's time of death."

"Oh my God. How—wait, when? What time?"

"He has to have died before 11:29 p.m."

I gave a low whistle of appreciation. If Jackson would admit to the arson, a time of death that early would mean it was almost impossible for him to have killed Karl. "I don't know how you did that," I said, "but it's a big help to the case."

"I know."

"But how'd you do it, though? What've you got?"

"I'll email the photo," she said, "so it's full-res." I heard her keyboard clicking as she explained what she'd done. She'd scoured every social media site for photos taken in Basking Rock and posted on the night of the murder or within two weeks after. Then she collected shots taken near the marina, and every photo where you could see even a bit of the bay or the nearby ocean. Tourists on boat rides or the beach, folks boarding yacht charters, everything.

I fired up my laptop. "Why'd you go on social media, though? I thought you said Facebook and those folks stripped out that data you need to see where and when it's from."

"Yeah," she said. "The EXIF data was step two. First I wanted to find people who'd posted photos they took from the beach or the marina or out on the water. Then I looked for their other shots from the same trip. The ones that didn't turn out good enough to post. People dump those on photo-hosting sites to free up space on their phones. That first one is from Instagram."

On my screen, two smiling fortysomething women were leaning against the railing of a boat, raising glasses of champagne.

"The second one—well, just look. That's from what she dumped on a hosting site, and it's still got the data. She took it out on the bay, at the right coordinates for what we're looking at. And the time stamp says June 6, 11:29 p.m."

It was one of those accidental shots, like it had been taken while one of the women in the first photo was putting her phone away. I could see part of the boat railing and someone's hand, both blurry. The background was in focus, though. And across the water, run aground on the sand, was Karl's empty boat.

29

TUESDAY, NOVEMBER 5, MORNING

Trial was starting in less than six weeks. En route to the jail for a talk with Jackson, I waited at a stoplight and fantasized about how many paralegals I would hire if I won the lottery. The houses, cars, and other purchases that most people daydreamed about seemed beside the point. All I wanted was someone other than myself to deal with the physical logistics of preparing for a trial. Someone else to make and print out lists of exhibits, put together binders with tabbed copies of all the exhibits in order, and organize all the photographs, the maps, the timelines and forensic reports. Binders with detailed tables of contents so I could find the police report, witness statement, expert bio, case law, or statute that I needed on the fly, in front of the jury, to catch a witness in a lie or dispute some legal point with Ruiz.

I was picturing where in Roy's office each paralegal could sit when the car behind me honked to let me know the light had changed.

In the jail, I asked for a private room and waited for Jackson. When he came in, he looked about one-third cocky teenage boy and two-thirds exhausted. For what was left of the teenage boy in him, I wanted to fight.

He slumped in his chair, looked through his bangs at me, and tried a wisecrack: "So, you proved me innocent yet?"

"Actually," I said, "Terri found something. It's not a home run, okay, but we really got something this time. And we tracked down the person we need. She's a wedding planner up in Charleston. She's a little reticent, so we might need to subpoena her, but at least we know who she is."

I told him about the photo this woman had taken, but since the jail-house guard had divested me of my cell phone, I couldn't show it to him. A good paralegal, of course, would've anticipated that and printed out a nice big color copy for me to bring.

He looked at me blankly. "I mean, cool," he said, "but so what?"

"Well, it comes down to the arson. And the selfie from when you were with Noah. The first 9-1-1 call about the arson came in at 10:09 p.m., and that selfie is time-stamped at 10:48 p.m."

"Oh," he said. His eyes brightened a touch. "Wait, so that's like forty minutes before that photo of the boat?"

"Uh-huh. And I don't know how fast you walk, but from where you two were on the beach, it's just under a mile to the marina. And that's to the entrance. From there, you still got to get to where he moored his boat, and then you got to unmoor it and ride out to halfway around St. Helena Island."

"Halfway—oh, that's almost impossible." He sat up straighter in his chair.

"You got it. That's the point."

"So wait. If you got the photo, why do we need this lady in Charleston?"

"To authenticate it. To get up on the stand and say, yeah, I took that photo on June 6 when I was out celebrating whatever she was celebrating on that yacht. And the prosecution is probably also going to want to take a look at her phone, which she's not happy about."

I could see he was thinking about something, but it wasn't what I expected. Instead of saying anything else about the wedding planner or the prosecution, he asked, "But doesn't it sound—I mean, who wouldn't confess to an arson if it 100 percent, for sure, got them out of murder charges? What if they think I'm just saying I did it to get out of thirty years in jail?"

"You know what," I said, "you got a good head on your shoulders."

He laughed. "I like how you sound surprised."

With a smile, I said, "You got me there. I'm sorry. We haven't talked about much other than what happened when, so I don't suppose I've had that much opportunity to see how you think."

He flicked his eyebrows up and down. I got the sense that my apology would do for now, but to him I was just one more old man who didn't respect him. I'd added to the chip on his shoulder, and I regretted it.

I said, "Tell me what you think might help. I mean, to get the jury past that problem."

He shrugged but said nothing. I waited. After a solid thirty or forty seconds, he leaned forward and put his elbows on the table, head down, like he had something to confess. "Okay," he said. "Well, I didn't sleep on the beach that night."

"Oh? Where'd you go?"

"You know down past Broad Street, that little block of boarded-up stores?"

"Oh, yeah." It was the derelict part of Basking Rock, about a mile inland from the beach.

"There's one where kids go a lot, to smoke. The one in the middle. It's boarded up, but one of the boards you can just slide right out. And then behind that, there's… I guess it used to be a bait shack?"

"Uh-huh." I nodded. "That's what it was when I was a kid. A shop, I mean, not a shack, but I guess it's falling down a little now."

"Yeah. So I slept in the store in front of it, and then before I went home, when the sun was coming up, I saw my jacket had burn marks on it. So I took it off and hid it under a pallet in the bait shack."

"Oh, so could that be evidence? The jacket? I see where you're going with that. Yeah, it could."

He sat back, crossed his arms over his chest, and gave me a look that said, *See? You can think I'm dumb all you want. That won't make it true.*

"Yeah," I said. "That's a good idea. I'll stop by there now and take a look."

"It's a little gross in there," he said. "Ain't been taken care of in I don't know how long."

"That won't bother me."

It seemed like about time to leave, but first I checked the pocket notebook I scribbled reminders in. "Oh," I said. "I did have a question about something."

He was peering across the table at my notebook, twisting his head to see it more right side up. "What *is* that? I mean, are those *words*?"

I smiled. I was proud of my chicken-scratch shorthand. "To me they are. I write this way to maintain confidentiality."

"Huh," he said. "I'd have flunked out of school for that." He thought for a second, then added, "You better take care of yourself, then. If some public defender or whatever had to replace you, your notes would be no help at all. They'd have to start from zero."

I looked at him. He didn't say anything more.

"Jackson, did someone in here say anything about my safety?"

"Not you, exactly." He was looking at the table, and in that moment I saw the little boy in him. He was scared.

"What'd they say?"

"Just… that there's people of mine on the outside who could get hurt."

I nodded slowly, taking that in.

"And are they also threatening you? Because I could see about getting you moved again."

He shook his head. "I got it calmed down now, I think. It's under control. And isn't there something about keeping your friends close, but your enemies closer?"

"Uh-huh," I said. "Yeah, there is. But look, you change your mind, you call me collect right away. Anytime."

He nodded. Then he took a deep breath. It was a lot to deal with—for anyone, much less a kid his age. To get off the subject, I guess, he gestured to my notebook and said, "You still got some scribbling to read me? You never asked your question."

"Oh, yeah." My question, unfortunately, was not going to cheer him up. "Uh, so, your mom told me she overheard you on the phone with

Karl, yelling at him to tell Pete to stay away from 'her.' Just wondering, how'd you know Pete Dupree?"

His face answered for him. Not the details, but enough for me to know that was indeed the Pete he meant.

When he didn't answer, I continued. "Pete's a big guy. You trying to keep him away from your mom?"

"Nobody comes near my mom. Not if I can help it."

"Uh-huh. Well, you did well. Nobody's come near her. She's okay."

He gave a quick nod that I read as thanks for letting him know.

"If you have something you can tell me about Pete Dupree," I said, "I'd appreciate it." To soothe the fear in his face, I added, "Nothing you tell me will come out at trial unless you tell me it can. His name does not have to come up. I just want to understand what's going on."

Another quick nod. He didn't often tell me things, I'd noticed, right when I asked. He preferred to think them through first. I was starting to think he had more forethought than most teenage boys, and certainly more than I'd given him credit for.

As I walked to my car, I found myself thinking that Jackson's hiding his jacket and lying about his whereabouts on the night Karl died might be encouraging signs, in a way. He may not have considered the consequences before committing arson, but even after what had to be a bad night's sleep—a filthy bait shack could not have been restful—he'd had the sense to know he might get in trouble, so he'd done what he could to hide the evidence. Then he hid it some more by lying all summer about where he'd slept. If he'd told anyone where he'd really spent that night, the cops would've searched the place and found the jacket. And with no time of death for Karl, that would've just added an arson charge on top of the murder.

With my lawyer hat on, I had to disapprove of hiding evidence. But in my father hat, looking at a teenage boy, I at least preferred some ability to anticipate consequences over a total disregard for them. It meant he had the capacity to steer back onto the straight and narrow. If I could get him out of jail, he might be able to make himself a pretty good life.

On the way to Broad Street, my phone rang. It was a blocked number. As a prosecutor, I always took blocked calls; tipsters and witnesses sometimes liked to hide their tracks.

"Hello, Leland Munroe speaking."

For a second, silence. Then a woman's voice: "Mr. Munroe? This is— you saw me at the restaurant."

Kitty. Katie. "Yes, hello!" I said. I took her cue and didn't say her name back. "Up in Charleston! Good to hear from you."

"I don't want you in there again."

"I hear you. I was never going to make a scene or do anything to get you in trouble."

"It's not about that. I just mean, Dunk warned me I wasn't safe in Basking Rock, so you can forget about me coming back there, or seeing you, or ever getting up on any witness stand."

"Okay," I agreed. Dunk had told her to leave? That was more than interesting. To keep the flow going, I reassured her, "Most of the witnesses I talk to never set foot in court. They just help me get a step or two closer to the truth."

"Okay." I could hear her breathing. After a second, she said, "He wouldn't want to see his boy spend his life in jail. And nothing I say can hurt him now. So it won't matter to him if I tell you he was selling

242

something—he used to say fencing, like, fencing stolen goods, but I never seen no goods. It's not like he had TVs sitting around in boxes."

"Uh-huh," I said. "Well, that's good to know. I'm doing my best to get that boy out of jail, and that helps."

"Oh, my goodness," she said. "He's still in there? Don't people get out on bail?"

"They don't usually grant bail for murder charges."

"But I can't believe he even—I mean, I always thought he was a little *scared* of his daddy. I don't mean in a bad way, maybe more just respectful. I mean, angry too, but that's teenagers, ain't it."

"It sure is." I sighed. "Yeah, I don't think he did it either. That's why I'm his lawyer." I got to Broad Street and swung around the block instead of parking. I wasn't about to interrupt this conversation.

"Well, I'm sure his daddy would appreciate that."

"I hope so. Hey, can I ask you, did you ever know his daddy to do heroin?"

"Oh my goodness, no. I dated a user once. Never again."

"What I'm trying to figure out," I said, going around another corner, "is why there was heroin on his boat. I don't know if you heard, but they found some."

After a second, she said, "Well, like I said, he told me he was dealing in stolen goods. That's what he called them, but I never saw anything, so them goods must've been small. Oh, and he was cocky about it, like he was getting something over on someone."

"Uh-huh. I hear what you're saying."

"Oh," she said. I heard something urgent in her voice. "I got to go," she said, and hung up.

I swore at my phone. Then I imagined my phone telling me I was an ingrate, because she'd already told me so much.

I swung around another corner, parked, and got out. Broad Street was two blocks long and derelict. Three boarded-up stores stood in a row, with wild grass and weeds between them that reached past my knees. I went around back to the tumbledown shack. Most of the paint was gone, and the door was unlatched. I knew that didn't mean I could legally go in. I also knew that I had to see the jacket myself before I could let anyone else know it existed. The last thing I needed was a pocket full of drugs, or a bloodstain, or no jacket at all, nothing to show Jackson had ever been there.

I glanced around, then stepped inside. The smell of mold hit me, and something else, a filth that made me think of rats. It was dark. I switched on my phone light. There were a few pallets lying around, like Jackson had said. I didn't see a jacket. There was an old trash can lid under one pallet, so I carefully lifted both items up.

And there it was, a light-blue denim jacket. It had black burn marks on one arm, and all over it were little holes that mice might've chewed. I set the pallet and trash lid carefully against the wall and spread the jacket out. The pockets were empty—another sign of fore-thought on Jackson's part, maybe—and aside from the burn marks, there was nothing else on it. Not a drop of anybody's blood.

I did not want this kid to spend another day in jail. I did not want to plead him down and see him stuck there for a year. He didn't deserve it. He was telling the truth.

30

THURSDAY, NOVEMBER 21, AFTERNOON

Thanksgiving was coming. I hoped the theme of the holiday, plus the prospect of enjoying a great spread at home with his kids, had put Ruiz in a charitable mood. I was driving over to talk with him. I'd told him today worked best for me, without explaining that the reason it worked best was that it was the only time he'd suggested when his boss wouldn't be available. I wanted Ruiz's candid take on the case, not what he felt comfortable saying in front of Ludlow.

I parked near the coffee shop, got his latte and my regular, and walked over to his office. He said hi like I was a friend, thanked me for the drink, and said, "Want a cookie? My wife made them. They're cinnamon, but those ones have powdered sugar too."

Two Tupperware containers were sitting on his windowsill, about half-full of thick, diamond-shaped cookies. I took a brown one and sat down. He grabbed a white one—or another white one, I supposed, since there were already specks of what looked like powdered sugar next to his keyboard.

"Good timing," he said, raising his coffee cup.

I raised mine back. "And happy Thanksgiving."

We chatted a bit. His holiday plans, which included fourteen visiting relatives, chorizo in the stuffing, and a couple of dishes his wife was preparing from plants she'd grown in their yard, sounded like the Mex-American version of a Hallmark movie. Mine just sounded sad: Noah and me eating rotisserie chicken, with pie out of a box for dessert. I'd invited Mazie, but she'd already signed up for double shifts that day. She'd said, "It keeps my mind off things."

It didn't make for a fun anecdote, so I moved on to business.

"I'm not here with the silver bullet that breaks the whole case wide open," I said. "But I want to give you a heads-up about where this is going and see what you think." For a little suspense, I paused to sip my coffee. "Oh, and we got time of death narrowed down." I told him about the photo and the Charleston wedding planner, who had relented and was willing to get on the stand.

"Okay, hang on," he said. He pulled open a drawer, got a legal pad, and started writing.

I also mentioned the selfie of Jackson, but not the arson defense yet. I didn't want to put the kid on the hook for a felony unless I was sure we would get something out of it.

He finished scribbling and looked up.

I set my cup on his desk and said, "That heroin on Karl's boat got me thinking. Because, you know, the whole town knew Karl was a drunk, but I never heard word one about him using hard drugs or having druggie friends. Drunks hang out with drunks, and he was no exception."

Ruiz was nodding. We were both immersed in the same small-town gossip. As long as we'd lived here, it had kept us informed as to who had what problems.

"So I asked around," I said. "I've got a lot of free time, as a consequence of starting out in my new line of work. I've talked to folks all over town, gone up to Charleston, dug through everything I could. And I keep hearing the same story: that Karl had started selling drugs."

"That how he managed to afford the Mustang?"

"Yeah, exactly." I was glad that hadn't escaped his attention. "And that car has disappeared off the face of the earth. You know he paid cash for it?"

Ruiz laughed and took a bite of his cookie. "These people, my God," he said, shaking his head. "I mean, a bright red sports car that you can't possibly afford. You know how hard my job would be if criminals were smart? If they even tried to be discreet?"

I laughed. "I had a case five or six years ago where, I swear to you, when I had the victim on the stand and asked him if the man who'd robbed his store was in the courtroom—"

He started cracking up. "No! Don't tell me! Did the defendant—"

"He raised his goddamn hand!"

He shot backward in his chair, laughing so hard I could see his molars. When he sat straight up again, he said, "My God. It doesn't happen often enough, but sometimes I love this job."

"Yeah, I'm with you on that."

He sighed, quieting down, and scribbled something on his legal pad. "Okay, so, Mustang bought in cash. You got a witness for that?"

"Local business owner. We can get his records of the transaction too."

Ruiz took a sip of his coffee. "Okay. For the drug dealing, you got witnesses?"

"One who I had to track down. Scared to testify. And another who will testify." I meant Mazie and her story of Karl being suddenly flush with cash.

"Okay, so…" He drew a line across his pad halfway down the page, wrote Mazie's name above it, and something else below it. A note about my scared witness, most likely.

"The other thing," I said, "is that he was screwing somebody over. It seems he was stealing drugs from someone else—skimming off the top, maybe, and selling on the side."

He nodded and said, "There's no shortage of crooks dumb enough to do things like that. They mostly end up shot. You got a witness for that?"

"At this point, just my scared one."

He looked at his legal pad and sighed. "You got any idea who he might've been stealing from?"

It was still just a guess, but I said, "You familiar with a Pete Dupree?"

He gave a big nod with his eyebrows raised. "Nothing I can get into right now, but yes indeed. Let's just say he is on our radar." He took a sip of coffee. "But back to Karl, what do you have to tie the two of them together?"

"Well, that's why I said this isn't a silver bullet. Not yet, anyway."

He wrote Pete's name under the line on his pad, then shook his head. "Okay, the thing is, I have no trouble believing Karl was dealing. And I can see him thinking he's putting one over on a bigger dealer and getting himself killed. You ask me who from our high school might do something that stupid, and he'd for sure be on my list. But I have no *evidence* tying any of that to the night he died." He looked at me. "I mean, up in Charleston, would you have dropped charges based on this? Or even reduced? When you got a witness placing your guy near the scene, with a motive and a weapon in hand?"

He had me there, and he knew it, even if he didn't enjoy it.

"I mean, I hear you," he said. "And with the dealing, and the photos and narrowing down the time of death, I can see how you got a much better chance of convincing the jury that there's reasonable doubt. But if I put that on one side of the scale, and the state's evidence on the other…"

He shook his head, a little regretfully, I thought. I had the feeling if Jackson got convicted, this case might trouble him a long time. For whatever that was worth.

"When I look at it that way," he said, "and I don't know any better way to look at it, I think we just got to let the jury do their job."

I'd arranged for Mazie and Terri to come to my office that evening, to prep Mazie for going on the witness stand, so I headed back there. I felt like things were so close with Ruiz. If I could get him any solid evidence, I'd have a shot at not putting the next thirty years of Jackson's life in the hands of a dozen strangers. Jury selection was three weeks away.

As I drove, out of desperation I called Garrett Cardozo, my drug-prosecutor friend in Charleston. It went to voicemail, and I left a sociable hello, plus a quick message that there were some local drug issues I'd like to speak about. I thought about calling Tony Rosa, thinking that heroin bust might've given him some intel that could help, but I'd never had his cell number.

At the office, I sent Rosa an email and then started setting up Roy's foyer like the courtroom. Tables for the prosecution and defense, a chair facing them to be the witness stand. When it was all set, I looked at my notes and psyched myself up to grill Mazie like I thought Ruiz might. A mother who had helpfully accompanied the cops to the police station when they were first investigating her son, without even asking them if she had to go with them at all, needed as much practice as she could get.

A few minutes later they arrived, dressed for court, as I'd instructed them: Terri in her pantsuit and Mazie in her dress. After showing them the setup and getting them some water, I told Mazie, "Okay, from here on out, forgive me, but I'm not going to act like a good host. I'm going to try and make this as realistic as I can."

Mazie looked worried. Terri put her laptop on the table and sat up straight, just like in court.

A good prosecutor wouldn't start by asking Mazie about the night Karl died. Ruiz didn't need her to establish that there'd been a fight; he had the neighbors for that. He'd start with Karl's abuse, to establish motive.

"Isn't it true, Ms. Grant," I said, "that Karl hardly ever paid child support?"

"Yes, that's true."

"So you must have struggled a lot?"

"I did the best I could," she said. "We never went hungry."

"I'm sorry, could you answer the question?" I pushed her politely. Juries never liked to see you bully somebody's nice mom, and Ruiz was no fool. "Didn't Jackson see you struggling to get by, working double shifts as a waitress? Never able to spend the time with him that you wanted to?"

She ducked her head down for a second like she might cry.

"I'm sorry, could you answer?"

"Yes. He did."

"And isn't it true that when Jackson was fifteen, Karl beat him so bad he broke his arm? Put him in the hospital?"

She started crying. I passed her some Kleenex and exchanged looks with Terri. Ruiz was going to have no trouble establishing motive. Watching this pretty mother weep as she remembered years of suffering and abuse would probably make some of the jurors want to kill Karl themselves.

And I couldn't tell her not to tell the truth, or not to cry. The jury had to see her as genuine from the get-go if I wanted them to believe what she said when it was my turn to ask the questions.

Between sobs, she said, "Leland, this is all my fault." She grabbed more Kleenex. "My son wouldn't be in jail if I'd left Karl sooner, if I hadn't let him come around—"

Before I could answer, Terri said, "Mazie, you did the best you could. And better than a lot of women I've known who were in your shoes."

She blew her nose. "I wanted my son to have a father."

"Course you did," Terri said. "All those boyfriends your mom had, and that stepdad, that's not what you wanted for him."

Mazie looked at her and said, almost dreamily, "You remember that?"

She nodded. "Even Karl was better than that, wasn't he."

After a long pause, during which she didn't blink once, Mazie whispered, "Yeah."

"So you did better," Terri said. "You got dealt a terrible hand, but you rose above that and did better by your son."

A light came on in Mazie's eyes. Not a strong one, but a new one.

What they were saying was news to me. All I recalled from high school was that Mazie and her stepdad at the time didn't get along.

"I've seen so many women," Terri said, "dive into drink and drugs to forget things like what you've been through. I've seen women who love their children fall apart and lose them to the state. You never did that. You raised your boy up right, and you were strong."

Mazie had a look on her face that I'd never seen. It was like she was thinking, for the first time, that she might've accomplished something or might be worthwhile.

"And you know your son is innocent," Terri said. "You saw him walk out of your house in clean clothes, and you washed those same clothes yourself the next morning before your breakfast shift."

"Yes, I did," Mazie said. Her chin was high. "He'd left his jacket somewhere, but he had on that same white T-shirt I gave him, and his light-colored jeans. I washed them on hot because there was not one drop of anything that could've been blood."

I'd seen mothers desperately begging a jury to believe their son was innocent. I'd seen mothers in denial claim that their son's personality made him incapable of committing the crime. But I'd never seen one testify like Mazie. If she spoke like that on the witness stand, like God's own truth was on her and she knew it from what she had seen, I thought that might give some jurors reasonable doubt all by itself.

And it only took one juror to set Jackson free.

31

MONDAY, DECEMBER 16, MORNING

I t was eight thirty a.m., and the courtroom was crowded. Ruiz and his assistant, me and Terri, and fifty citizens filling the jury box and half the spectator seats, waiting to be whittled down to twelve jurors and one alternate. To win, I needed to convince all thirteen that Jackson was innocent. In a conservative county, with a cop on the stand, evidence of motive and opportunity, and a defendant from the wrong side of the tracks, that wasn't much more likely than a lottery win.

So my goal was to get at least a few jurors who seemed like they might distrust the cops. If they did, and if even one of them was stubborn enough to hold out against the tough-on-crime types, we'd get a deadlock and a mistrial. Jackson would go free, for a while at least. Ludlow could still decide to try him again, but the more jurors I could get to vote against conviction, the less likely that was. And if he didn't, it would be over. Jackson would be free.

To the assembled citizens, Judge Chambliss delivered high-minded remarks about justice and impartiality. Then he asked the usual questions: Had they heard about the case? Did they or a close friend or relative know the victim or the defendant, or Ruiz, or me? His court rules didn't let us address the jurors directly at this stage. Each side submitted questions to him, and he asked them. While he talked to the jurors, excusing several for social or family connections to the case, Terri and I texted back and forth on our laptops about their responses and their body language.

Excuse #16, she said. *2 cop sons, wld love Blount.*

Number 16, a good-looking woman around fifty years old, was sitting in the alternate's box. I peeked at the questionnaire she'd filled out; she was a high-school teacher. That, plus her chunky necklace and purple cardigan, made me think she was less likely than average to take what cops said on faith.

I typed back, *You sure?*

Yes. Saw her arrive. Fraternal Order of Police bumper sticker.

I wrote back, *I stand corrected.* It occurred to me that I could save a fair amount of time by just not questioning anything Terri thought we should do.

We have ten peremptory challenges, to excuse jurors without having to explain why. After striking the ones we agreed on, out of respect for her abilities I used the last three to strike some who'd seemed fine to me but she didn't like.

By eleven a.m. the jury was seated. Mostly older, three Black, nine White. Chambliss explained their duties and the schedule: opening statements, lunch, and then the state's first witness.

Ruiz, as the prosecutor, went first.

"Ladies and gentlemen of the jury," he said, "I want to thank you for your service and acknowledge that it is a sacrifice. The Commonwealth of South Carolina would not ask this of you if it weren't important. And the case you will be asked to decide upon is about the most important thing there is: human life. A man was murdered. And I will show you, step by step through the evidence, that the defendant, his son Jackson Warton, committed that crime."

He paused while his assistant pressed some keys to bring up a photo of Karl on a large screen on the wall. Karl was on his boat, smiling, holding up a hooked fish.

"This is Karl Warton," Ruiz said. "On June 6 of this year, he was brutally murdered on board that very boat. Now, over the course of this trial, you're going to find out that, just like any of us, Karl was not perfect. Matter of fact, he had many flaws. He drank. He sinned. And I will even tell you right up-front that he neglected and abused Jackson, his only child."

A few jurors shook their heads like that was a damn shame.

"But we have not called you here," Ruiz said, "to sit in judgment on Karl Warton. We are not here to talk about his good acts or his bad ones. We're here to carry out our duty under the law: to affirm that murder is wrong—it is a sin and a crime—and to convict his killer of that crime."

Ruiz went on in that vein for twenty minutes. In his telling, Jackson was a child brutalized for years, powerless to protect himself or his mother. His story was compelling. I could see the jury rising and falling on his words, and I felt it myself: the anger, the childhood suffering. Ruiz told us that "when Jackson reached manhood, when at last he was strong enough to rise against his father," he decided to take revenge.

"And we know this," Ruiz said, "because on the night of the murder, a police officer saw Jackson walking toward the marina where Karl moored his boat, on a road that led nowhere else, holding a crowbar. And the officer testified to that, under oath, five weeks *before*—ladies and gentlemen, *before*—the autopsy came back showing that the murder weapon most likely was exactly that: a crowbar."

Ruiz spoke of bloodshed, betrayal, Cain and Abel. He knew his audience; the flags-and-Bibles approach worked well around here.

I knew Ruiz had to do his job. But I couldn't help but think that in a case where, I knew, he himself had some doubts, he was under no obligation to do it that well.

When he sat down, it was my turn. I wasn't used to going second, and I could feel the disadvantage. The story had already been told, and now I had to change it.

I thanked the jury and apologized for interrupting their Christmas plans with this trial. "But as the government told you," I said, pointing to Ruiz, "you have been called here on a matter of the highest importance." I planned to frequently refer to Ruiz and the police that way, since along with flags-and-Bibles, distrust of the government was a cherished value in these parts.

"A man was killed," I said, "at night, out on the water on his boat, and then he either fell or was pushed overboard. We're not sure what happened, or exactly where, because there were no witnesses to the crime, no fingerprints, and no murder weapon ever found. There's no security-camera footage, no cell phone records, no confession, no DNA left by the killer, no bullet casings to analyze. Nothing." I let that sink in for a second. "And, as I'm sure you folks can understand, a crime like that is very hard to solve. I don't envy the police force tasked with solving that."

Three of the jurors nodded.

"It's a hard task," I said, "when it's done *right*. It leaves no stone unturned. You've got to interview everyone who knew the victim. You've got to figure out if he had shady business dealings or, God forbid, criminal activities. You've got to see if he was using drugs, or gambling, or sleeping with another man's wife. And you don't do that to sully his good name, of course not. You do that because it's the only way to figure out who the people in his life were, and which of them might have been angry at him or wanted something that was his."

I looked at each juror before continuing. I had their attention.

"But the government didn't do that here," I said. "They did not investigate. It seems to me, and I think by the time you hear all the evidence it'll also seem to you, that they just decided that since Karl was a man who beat his son, it had to be his son who killed him. His son, Jackson."

I gestured to him at the table. He was wearing my old suit and looking a little overwhelmed.

"Now, Mr. Ruiz has said a witness saw Jackson walking near the marina on the night. When you hear that witness on the stand, I think you'll agree that he was mistaken." I couldn't say anything specific about Blount's testimony, since he hadn't given it yet.

"Jackson is a high-school graduate, and at the time all this occurred, he had a steady job at Barrett's Hardware here in Basking Rock. But according to the government, this hundred-and-fifty-pound kid somehow managed to overpower his hundred-and-eighty-pound father, on the deck of Karl's motorboat, and beat him to death. That's what they're going to ask you to believe, on faith, without any physical evidence—no footprints from Jackson on the boat, no DNA, no nothing."

One juror, a gray-haired Black man, had the look on his face that I wanted to see: a skeptical squint that I read as, "That can't be right."

"The government wants you to think," I said, "that this boy, who has no history of aggression, suddenly turned into a murderer. Now, child abuse is a terrible thing, but I think we all know that the vast majority of abused children don't turn around and kill their parents. That almost never happens, and it didn't happen here. Matter of fact, one more thing the government is not going to tell you, but you will hear it from our witnesses, is that six months before Karl was killed, Jackson actually stepped forward and *saved* his life." I paused, looked from juror to juror, and said, "The government will be telling you that Jackson wanted his father dead. But last Christmas, at a family dinner, when Karl swallowed something wrong and started choking, Jackson sprang into action, gave him the Heimlich maneuver, and saved... his... *life*."

They were listening closely. This mattered to them.

"A man lost his life here," I said, "and that is a terrible thing. And now his son, this nineteen-year-old boy, might lose his freedom. He's facing thirty or more years in prison for supposedly killing the man whose life he saved just a few months earlier. Does that make sense to you?"

After a pause, I said, "This is America. And in this country, we have a presumption of innocence. You must, under the law, presume that Jackson did not commit the terrible crime he's accused of. That is how we protect our *liberty*. We cannot let the government put this boy in prison unless they show us evidence proving, beyond any reasonable doubt, that he committed the crime. Proving that Karl abused Jackson isn't enough—that would truly be visiting the sins of the fathers upon the children. And proving that Jackson was sometimes angry at Karl for that abuse is not enough. Of course he was. Anyone would be. But anger isn't murder."

I let that phrase hang in the air. I hoped one of them would repeat it in the jury room.

"What the government has to prove," I said, "beyond any reasonable doubt in your minds, beyond any troubled conscience with the Lord, is that on the night of June 6, a boy with no history of aggression whatsoever got on his father's boat, rode out with him somewhere on the water, physically overpowered him even though Karl was larger, and beat him until he was dead.

"But there just isn't any evidence of that. And you have been called, as jurors, as Americans, to decide whether the government can prove to you that this boy is a murderer and that his freedom should be taken away. I think, once you've heard the state's evidence, your answer will be no."

I looked at them all again, gave them a nod, and said, "Thank you, and God bless."

I felt good walking back to the table, and I could see on Terri's and Jackson's faces that they liked what I'd done.

There was nowhere to go but down.

32

MONDAY, DECEMBER 16, AFTERNOON

R uiz was not a flashy lawyer. Once we were past setting the stage with our opening statements, he got down to work. A documentary about accounting methods would have been more interesting to watch, but I soon realized what he was up to.

I'd expected him to call the medical examiner first, to discuss Karl's autopsy. That was the usual order of a murder case: start with the hideous crime, the innocent victim and the violence done to them, the gruesome pictures that would shock the jury into understanding how real this was. The blood and emotion would make them realize, on a level they hadn't before, that a person was dead. That would make them care, so they'd pay attention to the mind-numbing technical evidence coming later.

But Ruiz had heard my point about the investigation not being thorough. His first witness seemed designed to show the jury that wasn't the case at all. He called the crime-scene investigator who'd examined Karl's boat and written the report listing every species of tree leaf and each kind of dirt found on board. The man was about as charismatic as I would expect a dirt analyst to be. Ruiz had him walk the jury through the entire process of examining the boat, with photographs: the rubber-gloved hands using plastic tongs to pick up bits of debris and slide them into numbered plastic bags, the chemicals used to find hidden bloodstains, and the exact measurements of each stain. Ruiz made sure to ask how long each step took and how long it had taken to do each lab test and write the report. A very long time was the message: this was a solid investigation.

At one point Ruiz stood at his table leafing through the report—looking for something, he said. Since he was not the type to improvise at trial, and I could see from all the Post-Its that he knew how to mark a page, I figured he was just letting the jury see how long the report was. It was the dullest start to a murder trial I had ever seen, but it was a one-two punch: my argument that the investigation wasn't thorough seemed pretty flimsy now, and I looked foolish for having painted with such a broad brush. Now I would have to make the distinction between the forensic investigation, which was solid, and the police's search for suspects, which had stopped at Jackson and gone no further.

When Ruiz finished his direct, I did one of the shortest cross-examinations of my career. In about sixty seconds, we established that Karl must've lost at least a liter of blood, based on the size of the stains. To translate the investigator's metric system into something our jury could understand, I said, "So that's a whole wine bottle's worth of blood and then some, correct?"

"I believe a standard wine bottle is 750 milliliters."

"So a wine bottle plus a can of Coke?"

He looked at me like I was a member of some different, and less intelligent, species. "If you prefer to think of it in terms of beverages," he said, "it would be a wine bottle plus three-quarters of a can of Coke. And that's just what was on the boat, not what went into the water."

"Thank you."

I took another minute to establish that one of his techs had found heroin on Karl's boat and that they'd handled the sample correctly and had a clear chain of custody for it. Then we got to the evidence I wanted: the fact that, unlike typical street-level heroin, which had a median purity of just 13 percent—"The other 87 percent," he said, "can be anything from baking soda to rat poison"—this sample was 91 percent pure.

"And where do you more typically see that level of purity? What level of the drug trade?" The answer wasn't in his report, but I knew it from prosecuting drug cases up in Charleston.

"Well... I'm hesitating," he said, "only because in my lab we have no direct knowledge of drug distribution hierarchies. We're informed by police investigators and others with direct knowledge."

"And what do they inform you?"

"That those numbers would more typically be seen at a higher level of the hierarchy."

"Higher-level dealers, in other words," I said. "Correct? Before the little guys cut it to increase their profits, and the littler guys cut it again, and so on down the line?"

"That would be my understanding, yes."

"Thank you. I have no further questions."

I walked back to the defense table. Their own witness had just provided a link between the murder scene and the drug-dealing evidence I wanted to introduce later. Without that, Ruiz would've objected to my evidence, and the judge might've tossed it.

On my laptop, I sent a quick text to Garrett. He'd left a voicemail, but I wanted to cut out the phone tag and talk to him before I put the drug evidence on.

Ruiz called the medical examiner to the stand, and the gruesome part began. I'd stipulated to everything I could—the number and size of the wounds on Karl's body, the fact there was postmortem predation by fish—so he would have no cause to show the most hideous photos to the jury. The fewer the better, since images like that tended to make juries want to punish the defendant.

The medical examiner, unfortunately, had a colorful way with language. He described Karl's injuries so vividly that every gory photo I'd kept out with stipulations might as well have been emailed directly to the jurors. Then Ruiz added to the horror by putting a photo I hadn't been able to keep out, a close-up of Karl's swollen face and slashed neck, up on the screen. Several jurors looked nauseated, and the rest looked angry.

"That neck wound," the witness said, "nearly severed Mr. Warton's jugular vein, resulting in massive blood loss that in my medical opinion was the immediate cause of death."

"So, to clarify," Ruiz said, "when you mentioned earlier that the assailant inflicted head injuries using the boat's railing, what was the order of events?"

"Well, I would say that first the assailant pounded Mr. Warton's head against the railing—brutally and repeatedly, given the amount of tissue and blood that my colleague found there in his examination of the boat. And then, since the largest bloodstain was located just under five feet away, either Mr. Warton tried to escape or the assailant dragged him that distance. That's where the assailant swung the crow-bar, causing a hacking type of wound, as you can see there in the photo."

"So at what point did Mr. Warton die?"

"Shortly after that hacking injury."

"And, in your medical opinion, did Mr. Warton suffer pain?"

"Oh, most certainly. Extreme pain."

I glanced at the clock. It was nearly five, so my cross-examination would have to wait until morning. Trial day one would end on this note, with the jurors ruminating on blood, gore, and suffering.

Ruiz had done well.

My phone rang as we were heading down the courthouse steps.

"Garrett!" I said. "It's been a while!" I gestured to Mazie and Terri to go on without me. He and I spent a minute catching up, and then he said, "Hey, reason I called back so quick is I'm heading out of town tomorrow and won't be back until just before New Year's. But I've got nothing on the agenda for dinner—the wife and kids already left town—so if you can make it up here, we could talk tonight."

I pulled into Garrett's driveway outside Charleston at a little past seven. Our topic wasn't something to discuss in public, so he'd ordered Chinese food and I'd swung by to pick it up.

Inside, we got our meal set up on the coffee table. He flicked the TV on to the shopping network and ignored it. I said, "Making it harder to eavesdrop? I do that too."

He laughed. "My in-laws wanted to give my oldest girl one of those smart-speaker things for Christmas. I said, 'I am not bugging my own home.' I don't know what folks are thinking these days."

We were partway through the egg rolls when he said, "So, it's not just to help you out that I wanted to talk. If we can establish a link, connecting your murder to my drug cartel could put my guys away for that much longer. So, fire away. What's your story?"

I laid the whole thing out for him. What happened to Karl, what had led me to believe he'd gotten into drug dealing, and why I thought he'd found himself caught up in something bigger than he realized.

About Pete Dupree, he said, scooping out some more kung pao chicken, "Just speaking in generalities here, doesn't waste hauling strike you as a good way to smuggle just about anything?"

Generalities meant he was talking about a case whose details he couldn't share.

"It certainly does," I said.

"And if you were moving drugs, would you rather do it in some vehicle that any traffic cop can pull over, or run a good part of the trip on board some high-end tourist boat?"

"Yeah. I think he may very well have infiltrated our local yacht charter for that reason. But he stopped working for them last spring, so I don't know where that leaves us."

"Infiltrated is an interesting word." He didn't look at me; he was getting more fried rice.

I took that to mean, *The wrong word, but I can't tell you why*.

"Anyway," he said, sitting back on the couch, "who's got the waste contract now?"

That was a good question. I hadn't seen anything about that in Blue Seas' files. We had what seemed like every other contract Henry had ever signed. I said, "I'll find out."

265

We were on our third servings when I brought up Blount. I still had no information on what he'd wanted the Warton brothers to testify to, and no way of proving Blount wasn't where he said he was on the night Karl was killed. "And above all," I said, "if he's lying, *why?*"

"Oh," Garrett said, "you know there's only ever two reasons. Either the liar's getting paid or he's getting blackmailed."

"Well, his truck's nearly ten years old," I said. "And there's nothing fancy about his house."

He broke open a fortune cookie and tossed half of it in his mouth. "Without getting into details, I can tell you that we've recovered dozens of hours of surveillance footage, going back years, from a business down by you. And not security stuff like watching the cashiers and the doors. They were watching their customers."

I was puzzled for a second, picturing customers doing the usual things in some restaurant or store. Then Dunk's strip club came to mind. His customers might well not want folks to see what they got up to in that dark and windowless place.

"Oh," I said. "Jesus, blackmailing their customers?"

He shrugged and ate the other half of the cookie.

"So if by chance," I said, "any of that footage showed customers breaking the law, are you guys offering immunity? I mean, if the customers know something that could help you out?"

"That's on the table. In cooperation with state prosecutors, for the state crimes."

"Witness protection, maybe? Is your cartel dangerous enough to need that?"

He nodded. "If you can get your people to talk," he said, "it's all on the table."

I could see from his crossed arms and steady gaze that he couldn't tell me more. But he'd said enough: there were people, plural, involved in Jackson's case that he had reason to believe could testify against his drug cartel.

I just had to figure out who. And get them to talk.

33

TUESDAY, DECEMBER 17, MORNING

It was time for me to cross-examine the medical examiner. The vivid pictures he'd painted the day before were still going to inflame the jury—there was no way around that—but I hoped if I could get the evidence from him that I needed, his style would help the jury remember it.

"So, Dr. Turner," I said, "you've testified that Karl died of massive blood loss, and your colleague Dr. Armstrong told us that he'd lost at least a liter of blood. That's a lot, correct?"

"It sure is. For a man Karl's size, just the amount Dr. Armstrong observed on the boat could put him in hypovolemic shock. And that's invariably fatal, unless you're in a hospital when it happens."

"Okay. And I apologize for this graphic detail, but based on your medical knowledge, if a man's jugular vein is cut, how would the blood exit the body?" He looked confused. "I mean, and again I apologize, but would you describe it as, for instance, trickling out?"

"Oh, I see what you mean. No, not at all. You have to understand, this was a living man, and his blood would've been under pressure, just like yours or mine." He was gesturing with both hands, getting far too enthusiastic for the topic at hand. "So when the hacking wound I spoke of was inflicted, the blood would've exited the artery under pressure, at speed."

"Is there a plain-English word you might use to describe that? Spray, perhaps?"

"I might use the term 'spurt,' myself, but your word works too."

Two members of the jury recoiled as if the blood he was describing had just sprayed them. I sent them a silent apology, but it couldn't be helped. This information was a puzzle piece that I needed to put in place before presenting the defense evidence.

"And, Dr. Turner, I believe in your report you indicated that this wound was inflicted from the front. In other words, the assailant would've been standing in front of Karl. Is that correct?"

"Yes. I can't speak to whether he was directly in front or off a little to one side—"

"But in any case, to the front?"

"Yes."

"Okay. And wouldn't that be the same direction the blood would, as you put it, spurt?"

"So the laws of physics would suggest."

"In other words, yes? The blood would spray forward?"

"Yes."

"So you would expect, wouldn't you, that the assailant would—well, he'd get a lot of blood on him, wouldn't he."

"Well, that depends how far away he was."

"But—remind me, Dr. Turner, how big was this boat?"

"Oh. Yes, in this particular case, there was only so far apart that they could be."

"I believe, based on your colleague's report, with the location of this bloodstain, they can't have been more than about two or three feet apart, correct?"

"I believe that's accurate, yes." My gory question seemed to have inspired him, since he came back to it without any prompting: "So, yes, I would expect the assailant to have a significant amount of blood on him."

"A significant amount of blood. Okay. And I understand, Dr. Turner, that you also performed tests on all the samples that the police provided you from their search of my client, Jackson Warton? Finger-nail scrapings, clothing, hair and so forth?"

"I did, yes."

"And can you confirm you didn't find any of Karl Warton's blood on him? Or anybody's blood?"

He paused a moment. "That's correct, but—"

"No blood. Thank you. And I understand you also performed drug tests on Jackson after his arrest, correct?"

"Yes."

"The usual urine and blood tests, and even hair?"

"All three, yes."

"Because some drugs last longer in the hair, correct?"

"Yes."

"About how long after heroin use would you be able to get a positive test on hair?"

"It can vary. Anything from one to three months."

"And did Jackson's hair test, or any of those tests, come back positive for heroin?"

"They did not."

"So you found no sign that Jackson had used any heroin. Correct?"

"That's correct."

"Thank you. I have no further questions."

I went back to the table satisfied. The puzzle was partly assembled, and when I added my pieces—Jackson's jacket, Mazie's testimony about the laundry, and the question of how the heck nobody noticed a blood-covered Jackson walking all the way home the next morning—hopefully the jury would see there was reasonable doubt.

Ruiz called Blount next. As the lead detective—and also a timeline witness, given what he was going to say about seeing Jackson—he would probably be on the stand for a good three or four hours.

Blount was, it seemed, the best piece of evidence the prosecution had. I had one shot at weakening that evidence. And I was taking that shot today.

I spent lunchtime with Jackson and Terri in the tiny conference room that the court left empty for criminal defense teams. Over sandwiches from the courthouse vending machine, we discussed what I'd learned from Garrett and how to work it into my cross of Blount. The plan was to establish what I could about Blount's tendency to cut corners and go a little extrajudicial on people he thought were crooks. If that line of questioning alone didn't make him angry, we had a few others that we thought would get him there. Once it looked like he was about to lose his composure on the witness stand, I would hit him between the eyes with, "Detective Blount, have you ever been threatened with blackmail?"

Anger could make a man say more than he ought to, but Blount was not stupid. What I hoped was that his face would give him away, at least to the handful of jurors who were open to the possibility that cops can lie.

If that question didn't do the trick—if he thought I was bluffing—I was ready to ask him if it was Dunk McDonough who'd blackmailed him. And then I was ready to get strung up by Ruiz and Judge Chambliss, because I had nothing to back up those questions, no evidence I could introduce at all. This whole strategy was desperate. But so were we.

Just before Chambliss was about to call the jury back in, his bailiff came in the main doors, walked over to Ruiz, and handed him an envelope. Ruiz ripped it open. Whatever it said seemed to surprise him.

He stood up and said, "Excuse me, Your Honor. May we approach?"

He gestured to me, and we went to the bench. Chambliss said, "Something come up, Mr. Ruiz?"

"Yes, Your Honor. My superior, Mr. Ludlow, is down at the county jail, and he sent this over." He held up the envelope. "He couldn't call, since they don't allow cell phones at the jail, so—"

"Please get to the point, Mr. Ruiz."

"We have a jailhouse informant prepared to testify that Mr. Munroe's client confessed."

I looked at him. "You have got to be kidding me."

Judge Chambliss sighed like someone had just told him he needed a couple of root canals. "And I suppose, Mr. Ruiz, you're going to need a continuance?"

"Yes. I apologize, Your Honor. This comes totally out of the blue for me, but—"

"Mr. Ludlow presumably had a little more notice. Does his note state when this alleged confession occurred?"

Ruiz looked at it. "Uh, well, it says they were housed together until October. The informant and—"

"That was two months ago, Mr. Ruiz."

"I'm aware, Your Honor, but—"

"You can have your continuance. It runs until tomorrow afternoon. Mr. Munroe, can I assume you're going to want to argue we shouldn't hear this witness, or his testimony should be limited somehow?"

I nodded.

"Okay. We'll do that at noon. The jury will be back here, seated and ready to go at one p.m."

That was a spanking if ever I saw one. Ruiz thanked him for it.

"Your Honor," I said, "I think, in fairness, we're going to want full disclosure on what this informant may be getting from the solicitor's office."

Chambliss nodded. "Mr. Ruiz, that defense request is granted."

"I'd also like to know," I said, "if the informant is down at the jail awaiting trial, versus already serving out a sentence." Ruiz knew what I meant: could Ludlow have offered him a plea deal?

"I can't speak to that. I was only just advised."

Chambliss said, "You're going to need to find out, pronto. You two get going. I'll inform the jury."

I turned back toward the defense table, spotted Terri, and changed course to follow Ruiz. I needed everything he had on this jailhouse snitch so I could pass it on to her.

All Ruiz had was the name, age, and what charges he was in on. He let me snap a photo of the witness statement.

I came back, slapped my hands down on the table, and told Jackson, "Hey! We have a short vacation. It won't be fun." More quietly, I said, "Terri, he and I need to talk, and in the meantime I have someone for you to look up." I handed her what I'd scribbled down from Ruiz. She started typing it in while I was still talking. I said, "Work your magic like never before. There is nothing I don't want to know. The color of his daddy's boxer shorts, what made his granny turn alcoholic, anything you can find. This is a jailhouse snitch, and we need to take him down."

At the words 'jailhouse snitch,' Jackson just looked confused.

I grabbed my bag and files, then whispered to Terri, "I want Ludlow too. If you have time."

In our little conference room, I emailed myself the witness statement so Jackson could read it on my laptop screen. When he saw the guy's name, he said, "Oh. Oh, shit."

"Jackson, did you tell this guy you did it?"

"I let him think I did," he said. "To scare him. He—oh, God." He sprawled against the back of his chair, head hanging over the back, and covered his face with his hands.

I could feel the second hand ticking down. The twenty-four-hour window Chambliss had given us to figure this out was shrinking, but something in the way Jackson was sitting told me to keep my mouth shut.

Elise used to do deep-breathing exercises to relax. I tried some. Then I realized tightly clenched teeth probably were not part of the exercise and tried again.

When he finally sat back up, he looked haunted. He said quietly, "Can anyone hear us?"

"No. I checked with Terri."

He nodded.

"If I tell you something," he said, "will you keep it secret? Not say it in court?"

"I'm trying to get you out of jail. I do that by saying things in court. But I give you my word, I won't say any of this unless you tell me I can."

He set his forearms on the table, clasped his hands together, and shut his eyes. I didn't know if I was about to witness a confession or a prayer.

"My dad," he said, "was dealing drugs. Serious drugs. He was making bank and tried to bring me in, but I said no. I didn't want to go to jail." He laughed at the irony of that. His eyes were still closed. "He stashed them on his boat and at that ice cream stand. And he had this friend we used to go see at the Broke Spoke, Pete Dupree. Pete knew Dunk real well. He seemed okay, but after a while he got scary. He said my dad was ripping him off, and he was going to—he said my mom was going to pay." His praying hands clenched into one big fist.

"Jackson," I said, gently, "why didn't you tell me this before?"

"Pete's still out there," he said. "And he's got friends in here. In jail, I mean."

I asked, "That how your jaw got broken?"

He nodded. Then he looked at me and said, "Mr. Munroe, I got no evidence of this, but I think Pete killed my dad. But I would rather take the fall and stay in jail for thirty years than give him any cause to hurt my mom."

34

TUESDAY, DECEMBER 17, AFTERNOON

After they took Jackson back to jail, I drove to my office. I needed a quiet place to think. Roy was golfing, and Laura never intruded.

Jackson had made it clear he didn't want me to put in one word of evidence that Karl was a dealer. Even if I named no other names and never mentioned any cartel, it still got too close to Pete. And if I had any doubt left that Jackson was a smart kid, he erased it when he said, "Anybody can come watch the trial, right? You said it's public. If one day they hear you saying my dad was dealing heroin, how do they know that tomorrow you're not going to start talking about Pete?"

I went over what Garrett had told me, or allowed me to understand. If Blount was being blackmailed, that explained a lot, but there wasn't much I could do with it. It was impossible to call up the lead detective in my current murder trial and tell him, "Hey, if it so happens you committed a crime that some cartel is blackmailing you about, I have a friend willing to offer immunity, but please call him before you testify any more against my client." If he didn't embrace that offer with open arms, I'd get kicked off the case for witness tampering.

Jackson would be shunted off to some public defender with a hundred other clients, while I tried to convince the ethics board not to revoke my law license.

Garrett had suggested that more than one person connected to my case might be interested in his immunity deal. And he'd paused on one word I said: infiltrated.

I got on my computer and started searching the Blue Seas files. In twenty minutes I pulled up over a hundred contracts. Carpet cleaning, silverware, laundry. No waste contract.

I had pictured Dupree going after that contract in order to use Blue Seas as a cover. But if I was reading Garrett's hint right, Blue Seas wasn't tricked. They were in on it.

I remembered Henry at the shrimp fest, standing there and taking all the ridicule Dunk was dishing out. If Dunk was our local blackmailer, that made sense. On the other hand, Dunk's remark about Henry's wife—what was it? "My strip club is the least of her worries"? That sounded more like what Dunk had on him was adultery. I had no trouble seeing Henry as a cheating husband. That was far more likely than him being involved in some drug cartel.

But small-town adultery was of zero interest to Garrett. That was not what he'd been talking about.

I picked up my phone.

"Leland!" Henry said. "You win your murder case already? I wasn't expecting you to call in the middle of the day."

I laughed. Henry was a nice guy. Or he had social skills. I wasn't sure which.

"Not quite there yet," I said. "We got a recess, though. And I dropped by the office because a Blue Seas issue was nagging at me. It's a little delicate. I was thinking maybe you could come in for a quick chat?"

"Oh my. Uh, today is a mess—any chance you could come here?"

"This is actually something we might want to insulate," I said. "Make sure nobody overhears."

"My goodness." He thought for a second. "And I'm in Charleston tomorrow. But I could stop in on my way. Maybe seven a.m.? Before court?"

"See you then."

Terri texted to say she had something on the snitch. I asked if she could come to the office. Then I went to the door, leaned out, and let Laura know if she wanted, she could leave early, do some Christmas shopping or whatever. She said thanks, grabbed her purse, and headed out.

When Terri arrived, she looked serious. Her normal big smile was just a flicker when I said hello.

"You have bad news?"

She looked around the office. "Are you by yourself?"

"Yeah, I sent Laura home."

"Okay. I have … kind of scary news."

She walked past me into my office, sat where a client would, and set her laptop on the desk. I got us both coffees while she was starting it up.

When I came back, she had a document on her screen that started with a mug shot. It was a kid, maybe twenty years old. "This is our snitch," she said. "He's awaiting trial for vandalism."

"He's been in the county jail for two-plus months on vandalism charges?"

"He was pro se," she said, meaning he didn't have a lawyer at his arraignment, "and he couldn't make bail."

I set her coffee down. "What's the scary part?"

"His license and all the papers for this case have a local address," she said. "But when I searched for previous addresses, look what came up."

I peered at her screen. "Holy shit. Isn't that Pete Dupree's old house? Who is this kid?"

"Well, his name's not Dupree. But that's where his driver's license said he lived before he came here. And he only came here this summer." She was shaking her head at her screen, like she couldn't quite believe it. "And what would you say if I told you the arresting officer and sole witness to the vandalism was Blount?"

"Jesus. Do you think Blount arrested him just to get him in with Jackson? On orders from Pete?"

"It's a hell of a coincidence if he didn't." She took a deep breath, like she was trying to stay calm. "I tried to think of another explanation. I'm *still* trying. And I keep thinking, you know, Karl was just trying to make a buck, but it went too far. He got himself into something a whole lot bigger and more dangerous than he realized." She looked up at me—I was still standing beside her—and said, "Leland, so did we. So did we."

35

WEDNESDAY, DECEMBER 18, MORNING

I arrived at the office before dawn and put the coffee on. About twenty minutes later, Henry's silver Mercedes swooped into the parking lot. I went to meet him at the door. I didn't know if I was imagining it, but behind his usual confident smile, I thought I caught a hint of nervousness.

"Morning, Leland." He glanced over his shoulder at the sky, which was still more gray than blue. "Or maybe I shouldn't say that until the sun's actually up."

"Close enough," I said, letting him in and heading for the coffee maker. "I just made a fresh pot. Want some?"

"No, thanks. Already had a triple espresso to keep awake on the drive to Charleston." He looked around the office. "Leland," he said. "Are we alone here?"

"Yes, we are." I was watching him out of the corner of my eye as I poured a cup. "Roy is not a seven a.m. guy."

He nodded and gave a deep exhale, like he was psyching himself up for something.

"That's my office there," I said. "Let's step on in."

He went in but didn't sit down. "Pretty decent view," he said, looking out my window at the palm tree. "Better than staring at the parking lot."

"Yep." I walked around him to my desk and sat. "So, Henry, I'm sorry to mess with your schedule, but something came up that I thought you'd want to know."

"Yeah," he said. "Little disconcerting, the whole not-being-overheard thing, but I appreciate the discretion." He turned and took a seat.

"Confidentiality is something you can count on in me."

"Well, thanks."

"I know you got a busy day," I said, "so I'll get right to the point. I have it on good authority that it at least *appears* a contractor of yours may have used Blue Seas as a cover for drug dealing."

It took part of a second for his face to assume a surprised expression.

I continued, "And I've been informed that anyone at Blue Seas who can provide good information on that could be given immunity." Accusing him of being involved was not my way, even if I'd been sure he was. Which I wasn't.

"Uh, wow," he said. He nodded slowly, eyes wide, like he needed a second to process this.

"Immunity or even, if it comes to that, witness protection."

"Huh," he said. "You mean like on TV and whatnot? Moving a whole family out of harm's way?"

"Yep," I said. "Exactly."

He leaned back in the chair, laced his fingers together across his belly, and tilted his head like he was appraising me. He was quiet long enough that I noticed the ticking of the clock on my office wall.

Finally, he said, "Leland, you ever done something you're ashamed of?"

"Of course." I smiled a little. "But I doubt we got time to get into that, since Roy gets in around nine."

It was a quarter past seven. He smiled back.

He moved his clasped hands to the back of his head, stuck his elbows out, and shut his eyes. "So I want you to picture," he said, "if you'd been doing something wrong, for some other people, and then you manned up and told them that was it, no more. But then you came downstairs real early one morning to get some work stuff wrapped up, and one of them was sitting on your couch, right in your goddamn living room. Got through your burglar alarm somehow. And he had a Glock in his hand. And he smiled at you and said, 'How you doing? Family still good?'"

I said, "Doesn't seem like you'd have much choice."

He nodded, brought his hands back to his lap, and leaned forward. "Leland," he said, "I need to get my family out of here. There is nothing I will not do to achieve that. You just tell me who to call."

"Federal prosecutor friend of mine. I'll send you his number." I took out my phone. As I sent it, the first ray of sun hit my desk, filtered through the palm fronds outside. I was skeptical of signs, but that seemed like it might qualify as a good one.

His phone pinged. He looked at it and said, "Up in Charleston, huh? Shoot, maybe I'll call him on the way."

"I'm sure he'd like to hear from you."

He nodded, slapped his hands on the desk, and stood up. I stood too, to shake his hand and say, "You have yourself a good trip, now."

"Thanks. And I mean it." He went to the door, stopped, and looked back at me. "One thing I've wished I could've told you," he said, "but I had to think of my family first, is that Mazie's son did not kill Karl."

In my poker voice, I said, "Uh-huh. I didn't think so. You happen to know who did?"

He hesitated. "It'll be safer," he said, "for everyone, if I just tell your friend. And anyway, this might be better going through the feds than the local police." He held up one hand in a wave goodbye and walked out.

I sighed and sat back down. There was nothing to do but compartmentalize and get back to dealing with the trial. In a few hours, I had to be back in court trying to give Chambliss a solid legal reason to keep Ruiz's jailhouse snitch from testifying. And to keep us safe, I needed an argument that had nothing to do with Pete Dupree or any drug cartel.

My phone dinged while I was starting up my computer. I looked over, hoping Henry had had a change of heart and was texting me the name of the murderer.

On my screen was a photo of some park or green space. The message was from a number I didn't recognize. I touched the photo to make it bigger.

It was the park where I walked Squatter, but from high up, like it was taken from a nearby roof or upper story. In the distance, a person was crouching down. I zoomed in. The person, squatting to adjust a little dog's leash, was Noah.

A text bubble popped up. *Nice family.* Then another photo. The park was a blur of green in the background. In the foreground, in sharp focus, was the black barrel of a rifle resting on a windowsill.

I nearly vomited on my desk.

Then I took a breath and forced myself to think. What were my options? Text Noah to get out of there? No. Short of a trapdoor in the grass, he couldn't get out of range in time. And what if he looked around and this sniper realized I'd warned him?

Call the cops? Which ones could I trust? And they'd take too long anyway.

Buy time.

I wrote back, *Who is this?*

We have a proposition.

Ok.

After a second, an address came through. Then, *Come talk.*

I answered, *If you keep sending pix. Need to know he's ok.*

If u bring cops/anyone, the response said, *he dies.*

I stood up to leave, then sat back down to scribble a note. If I didn't get out of this, I was at least going to leave some evidence. I wrote the address down. Then, "If I'm killed, cartel did it, Jackson innocent of Karl, call Garrett Cardozo," and his number. Then I folded it up, hid it under my keyboard—I didn't want anyone finding it and coming after me while Noah was still in danger—and left.

The address was in a rougher part of town. Compared to any big city it was nothing, but to us it was the rough side of the Black neighborhood. At every stop sign, I checked my phone. Two more photos of Noah came through.

The house was small and run-down, but someone had kept it neat. Trimmed grass, faded curtains. I parked, ran across the street and up the porch steps, and knocked. Nobody answered. I heard nothing from inside.

A text pinged: *Back door.*

I looked around. A few cars were parked on the street. It was a sunny morning. Palm trees bent over the gray roof of the shotgun shack next door. If I walked around to the back, I might get invited inside and shot in the head. A proposition could be discussed on the front porch.

I wrote back, *Talk out front?*

The answer came. Two photos. Noah sitting on a bench with Squatter asleep on his lap. Then the windowsill, with a long, brass-colored bullet sitting on it.

Then a word: *Hollowpoint.*

The kind of bullet that expanded, or exploded, inside the victim. Maximum lethality.

I answered, *Going around back now.*

I went down the steps. When I got to the walkway, a thought stopped me: They must know Noah and Jackson were friends.

To buy a second to think, I crouched down and took off my shoe, pretending I felt a rock in it. I knocked it on the cracked cement.

They might think Jackson had told him something, or even that I had. Once Noah had served his purpose by getting me to this house, why would they let him go? What reason did I have to trust them?

I put my shoe back on and stood up. As I walked around the corner of the house and down the side, Ruiz came to mind. He was the law; he had resources. He was a father and a good man. I scrolled back to the first photos of Noah and the rifle and sent them to him. *My son in danger,* I wrote. *Be discreet please! Where would sniper be if this view of park?*

I didn't even know if Ruiz was up yet. I stopped for a second, closed my eyes, and prayed to the only being I ever prayed to: Elise. The prayer was two words long: *Save him. Save him.*

Then I went around to the back of the house. This side was lower than the front, a half basement. The door was slightly ajar. I knocked. It swung open.

At the far end of the room, Terri was standing with her hands up. When she saw me, she yelled, "Run! Just go!"

A deep male voice said, as relaxed as if this were a social engagement, "No, please, come in."

His voice was familiar. I said, "Morning," pushed the door the rest of the way open, and stepped inside.

Tony Rosa was holding Terri at gunpoint from about four feet away. In an armchair to the right, Collin Porter sat with one leg crossed over the other, smoking a cigarette.

"Morning, Leland," he said. "Thank you for joining us. I know you and Tony already know one another, and I took the liberty of inviting your friend along too."

"You can let her go," I said, walking over. "If you've got a proposition for me, she doesn't need to hear it."

He chuckled. "Let her go," he said, almost to himself, and chuckled again.

Tony said, "Don't be a fucking idiot, Leland."

Porter reached into his blazer, and I flinched, expecting a gun. His hand came back out with a pack of cigarettes. He lit one off his own and offered it to me. As I leaned over to take it, a dark shape on the floor behind his chair caught my eye. Terri's dog. A pool of blood. I thought I saw Buster's chest rise and fall, just a bit, but he'd clearly been taken down for the count.

"So, the proposition," Porter said, "has changed. Anthony, why don't you explain?"

"Me, sir?"

Porter nodded.

"Okay."

I looked in Tony's direction. He kept his eyes and his gun on Terri. I flicked my glance her way. We didn't need words to know this was it.

Tony said, "Mr. Porter just didn't see a role for you guys. I mean, a way that you could be useful if we brought you in. So he came up with a different idea, which is that the two of you were lovers—"

I said, "Oh, but we aren't. We've just been friends since—"

Tony glared at me and said, "Shut up, Leland!" Then he resumed his shooting stance, looking at Terri. "So the story is, you two were lovers, but then things went wrong. You got jealous."

I locked eyes with her and saw terror there, but fury too. She hadn't given up.

Porter picked up where Tony left off. "And that's why you lured her here this morning—"

I gave Terri a nod, then lunged and punched Porter in the jaw. It was a crappy punch from a bad angle, but it made Tony swing around. I got a glimpse of Terri launching herself at him, and then Porter hit my gut with the hardest punch I'd ever taken.

As I doubled over, he burst out of his chair and shoved me toward the nearest wall. I hit it, turned around, and saw Terri and Tony struggling on the floor. His gun went off as Porter stalked toward me, pulling his own gun from his belt. It was pointing at my face when one of his feet slipped on Buster's blood. He flailed to get his balance, and I ducked, pushed off the wall, and rammed him with my shoulder. A gun fired again, and Terri started screaming like a Valkyrie. I grappled with Porter, trying to push him out of the way so I could see if she'd been hit.

She was still screaming, one hand clamped on Tony's wrist, her elbow locked to keep him from pointing the gun at her. The blast horn of her voice in his face was pure rage, pure power, a thing she needed to find the strength to hold him off.

Then another sound came from outside: the whoop of a police siren. I felt Porter's muscles freeze. The siren shrilled again. He shoved me away and ran out the back door.

I yelled Tony's name. He looked up, then looked around. His arm slackened as he realized his boss was gone. Terri stopped yelling and tried to catch her breath.

I walked over, took Tony's gun, and kicked him hard in the ribs.

Outside, some cop's voice on a bullhorn said, "Police. Police. We have you surrounded. Drop your weapons and come out with your hands up."

Terri got to her feet and held her hand out for the gun. She popped the clip out, gave it to me, and racked the slide to get rid of the last bullet. Then she tossed the gun toward the door, walked over to Buster, and squatted down.

"I'm so sorry," she said, stroking his fur. "Buster, baby, I'm so sorry they hurt you." He whined weakly as she struggled to try to pick him up, and I eased her aside and gathered him up in my arms.

Then, together, we walked to the door.

36

TUESDAY, DECEMBER 24, MORNING

J ackson was released just before lunch on Christmas Eve. After the FBI made several arrests and Garrett spoke with Ruiz's boss, after charges were formally dropped and all the paperwork was completed, the only thing left to do was go get him. I drove, because Mazie said, "I can't look at the road. I'll cause an accident. I just want to look at him."

We went in, and I waited a little while in the jail's waiting room, letting them have a moment together. When they came out, Jackson was wearing the freshly laundered clothes Mazie had brought: jeans, death metal T-shirt, black fleece. He was so skinny that they hung on him. Apart from that, he was himself again. Or not exactly. He was himself, but stronger.

I stood up, shook his hand, and clapped him on the shoulder.

He clapped my shoulder back and said, "Thank you, Mr. Munroe. I can't wait to get home."

. . .

That night, we all gathered at my house for dinner. The two of them, me and Noah, Terri, and even Ruiz, who brought a gift-wrapped box of his wife's cookies to add to our grocery-store Christmas dinner. We passed them around, and everyone toasted Jackson for coming home a free man.

I hadn't been up to explaining to Noah or anybody else what all had gone down—whenever I tried, I felt that gut punch that Porter had landed on me—so Ruiz filled them in. The sniper, he said, had been Dunk, who was now in jail in Charleston. Detective Blount had had the pleasure of arresting him and handing him over to the FBI.

Garrett had told me Blount and Henry were turning state's evidence, although since the case against the cartel was still ongoing, he wasn't at liberty to say what information they'd provided. I still didn't know what Blount had done to get blackmailed in the first place, and I wondered if I ever would.

Garrett had also shared what he'd told the solicitor's office that got them to drop all charges against Jackson. Karl's killer, he told me, was Dunk.

I'd asked him if Pete had ordered Karl's death—I wanted Jackson to know the whole truth, and if his hunch that Pete had killed his dad was right, I wanted him to know that too. But that wasn't something Garrett was free to say.

From the other end of the table, Jackson asked, "Mr. Munroe, would you mind passing the salt?"

As I handed it down, I noticed Terri sneaking a bit of her chicken to Buster. He was still healing, but his appetite was back to normal, and the vet had said things looked good for a full recovery. Terri lived six blocks from the house where we'd been terrorized, and she'd walked Buster by there every morning, practicing his off-leash skills. We thought Rosa and Porter must have dragged a scent trail through the grass, to lure Buster down back. When Terri went after him, they got them both. I'd told her it wasn't her fault, but she still winced every time he whimpered, and he appeared to be eating better than Terri was these days.

"Here," I said, handing her the bag of Squatter's treats I always carried in my pocket. "They'll probably be like after-dinner mints to him, but I bet he'll like them."

She smiled and fed him one. "This is real nice," she said, "but I'll feel better when they catch Porter."

"Yeah," Ruiz said. "Or whatever his real name is. Maybe Rosa will flip and help them track him down."

"And Pete," Mazie said.

"Garrett thinks they both left the state," I told her. "And maybe the country. Not much point sticking around when your whole network collapses."

"I hope he's right."

Terri asked Ruiz, "One thing I still don't understand is how the cops found us. Leland didn't have time to tell you where we were, did he?"

"No," I said. "I just told him where Noah was."

Ruiz laughed and took a sip of Coke. "Leland," he said, "you live in a small town. On his way to the park, I had Blount radio every cop on patrol looking for that Malibu you drive. Most of them called their friends too, so half the town was looking for you. And then on top of that, I mean, picture this: A middle-aged White guy in that part of town, before eight in the morning? Wearing a suit, and *running*?" He shrugged. "People notice. One of the neighbors called his son, who's a police officer, to tell him something strange was going on. That plus the radio call, and the son put two and two together."

"Wow," said Noah. "That's so cool."

Terri smiled at him. "Yeah, you like detective work, don't you. Figuring stuff out. I remember."

Later that night, when Ruiz had left and things were winding down, I was loading the dishwasher while Mazie and Terri chatted on the couch. It hadn't occurred to me that they would get along so well, but they did. Squatter was napping on Terri's lap, while Buster slept at her feet.

Back in Noah's room, where he and Jackson had gone to play video games, I kept hearing them crack up.

My house felt alive again. It felt like a home.

In my head, to Elise, I said thank you. *I guess we did it*, I told her. *We're going to be okay.*

END OF DEFENDING INNOCENCE
SMALL TOWN LAWYER BOOK 1

Do you enjoy compelling thrillers? Then keep reading for exclusive extracts from *Influencing Justice* and Ethan Reed's *Lethal Justice (Ion Frost Book One)*.

To be notified of Peter's next book release please sign up to his mailing list, at www.relaypub.com/peter-kirkland-email-sign-up.

ABOUT PETER KIRKLAND

Peter Kirkland grew up in Beaufort, South Carolina. As a kid, Peter loved history and learning about his area. One year in school, he was given a project to research a few South Carolina law cases and the precedents they set and their effect on people's lives. This research project lit the flame for his passion for law and creating a more equal justice system since. Soon after this, Peter began reading legal thrillers voraciously and enjoyed the legal maneuvering and justice found within. As an adult he has continued researching the law and understanding the system and its effects on individuals. A few years ago, he decided to try writing his own legal thriller.

Now a full-time writer, he uses his research, passion for justice, and real case studies to bring together courtroom dramas with deep, rich characters, and gripping twists and turns. New to the industry, Peter would love to hear from readers and other authors and invites you to connect with him through:

facebook.com/AuthorPeterKirkland

amazon.com/Peter-Kirkland/e/B0942NYRL9

bookbub.com/authors/authorpeterkirkland

goodreads.com/peterkirkland

PETER KIRKLAND

INFLUENCING JUSTICE

SMALL TOWN LAWYER - BOOK TWO

BLURB

A small-town murder hides a dark secret.

When social media influencer Simone Baker asks Leland Munroe to
defend her on charges stemming from another influencer's death, the
former prosecutor initially says no. He wants a quiet life practicing
business law and continuing to rebuild his relationship with his son,
Noah. But with bills to pay and no other clients coming through his
door, Leland takes the case.

At first, he figures the prosecution's weak evidence should make for a simple defense. But Simone's situation isn't as straightforward as it seems, and she weaves a tale of evidence tampering by local police, missing young women, and online manipulation.

As Leland and his PI friend Terri Washington investigate, they realize the case goes far beyond a single murder. Innocent women may be entangled in a criminal organization Leland hoped was gone from Basking Rock for good. And as the jury's verdict looms closer, it's not just Simone's freedom that hangs in the balance...

Leland's and Noah's lives are on the line as well.

Grab your copy of Influencing Justice
www.relaypub.com/blog/authors/peter-kirkland

EXCERPT

Prologue:

Easter Sunday, April 12, 2020

I'd come up to Charleston alone, to the graveyard, to talk to my wife. I parked around the corner, grabbed the little box I'd brought off the passenger seat, and walked to the entrance on the old side of the cemetery, because it had always been her favorite part. The trees were draped with Spanish moss, and the gravestones tilted at weird angles, with moss and lichen growing over the names and dates. Weeds grew between the broken flagstones I walked along. Even in the bright sunlight of Easter morning, the place was spooky, but Elise thought it was romantic. We never thought she'd end up here so soon.

It took a few minutes to get to her spot, in the new part. The stones here were upright and shiny. Pink granite, white marble. But there was nothing on her grave yet besides grass—a little overgrown—and a flat plaque with her name. They'd advised me to wait six months or a year for the earth to settle before placing a stone. Fifteen months had come and gone, and I still couldn't afford what she deserved.

Nobody was around. It was time for folks to be in church. I looked down at the ground she was under and tried to say, "Happy Easter." The words stuck in my throat, so I tried again.

A breeze made the grass flutter.

"Brought you a piece of king cake," I said, opening the box. Elise was born in New Orleans, and her traditions had become mine and Noah's. I hadn't made it up to Charleston for the Feast of the Epiphany, so this cake was the Easter version, frosted pink. I took it out and set it on the grass.

"I hope you're watching," I said. "I hope you can, because you'd see Noah's doing better." I smiled and shook my head. "Those binoculars you gave him when he was, what, seven years old? That he used to spy on the old man across the street? I think you were on to something. If you were here, you'd see—he actually *wants* to go to school now, because it has a purpose. Says he wants to be a detective, and I think he means it."

She'd understand why I was spending what little I had on his physical therapy and his community college tuition. She'd say that's exactly what I should do, not put that money into some hunk of stone for a woman who wasn't here anymore. But the fact I couldn't do both made me feel lower than dirt.

"Not detective," I said, correcting myself. "He says 'private eye' instead. I guess it's more romantic. He got that from you."

No breeze came. The grass didn't flutter.

I dropped my head. I didn't know why part of me still expected a response.

Grab your copy of Influencing Justice
www.relaypub.com/blog/authors/peter-kirkland

BOOK ONE IN THE
ION FROST THRILLER
SERIES

LETHAL
JUSTICE

ETHAN REED

BLURB

Justice has never been so cold.

Former Special Forces Operative Ion Frost has one job left before he vanishes off the grid for good: deliver his dead comrade's dog tags to a boy named Lincoln. It should have been a quick, easy stop.

But for wanderer Ion Frost, things have a way of getting complicated…

Upon meeting Lincoln, Ion learns that his older sister, Taya, has been missing for over a week.

Ion's plans to disappear get put on hold.

Then an assassin takes out Lincoln in a brutally efficient murder. With Lincoln dead and the dog tags missing, Ion is sure of one thing… There's a dark side to this sleepy, small town.

Now Ion is in the thick of it. He's determined to find Lincoln's killer, and deliver his own personal brand of justice. But the harder he searches, the more questions he finds. Who wanted Lincoln dead? Where is Taya?

And how long before his own brutal past catches up with him?

Grab your copy of *Lethal Justice* (Ion Frost Book One)
Available August 25th, 2021
www.relaypub.com/books/lethal-justice

———

EXCERPT

A great shadow crept across the desert road, methodically swallowing cracked asphalt as it prowled forward. The form casting it drifted, steady and measured, approaching an abandoned vehicle parked sideways on the roadway. The car was a mid-nineties Corolla, rusted and sun-bleached, its driver-side door left open. The whistling wind chased sand across the asphalt. The shoal water of the Dori River beyond passed silently beneath the narrow one-lane bridge.

The eclipsing form approached on two armor-weighted legs. Eyes peering out behind a blast-resistant visor squinted past the harsh sunlight at the landscape before him. Scattershot poppy fields to the west provided the only color beyond the pale cloudless sky and tawny desert earth, their flowering violet blooms and green stems standing out against the lifeless terrain. The man looked closely at the poppies, surveying his environment. He noticed the pods had been scored. The opium would be collected tomorrow.

EOD Specialist Frost, United States Army ordnance disposal specialist, stalked to the rear passenger side of the car and tilted his head to get a better look. Wedged under the wheel well, set directly beside the fuel tank, crouched a magnetized copper box with a few wire leads hanging from its side.

Frost turned to look back at the rest of his team, twisting at his waist in his suit. The three men stood two hundred feet back, behind concrete Jersey barriers left behind by a previous regiment. They were dressed near-identically in Special Forces ACU gear: bulky interceptor body armor, black T-shirts, UCP camouflage trousers, and black mountain combat boots. All three held M4 carbines in gloved hands. Two wore twin turtle shell ballistic helmets, and the other enjoyed the shade of a wide-brimmed boonie.

They were just outside Zangabad, Afghanistan, a small village in the Panjwai district of Kandahar province. It was a chart-topper for IED deaths in the country, with the Taliban seeking to carve gradually away at the NATO forces until they could reclaim the region they considered their true homeland. During that time, they'd secretly rigged up numerous homes, mud compounds, and vehicles across the district with improvised bombs and killed any villagers who refused them or ratted them out.

"What is it?" Sergeant First Class Anderson, Frost's commanding officer, asked over comms. His voice snapped with humorless impatience in Frost's ear.

Frost turned back and looked again at the Corolla and the sticky bomb under the wheel well. The wires suggested the package contained a DTMF spider receiver. It could be remotely detonated from anywhere, so long as the triggerman held the paired transmitter.

Frost glanced around the flat landscape, searching for spots he might hide if he were the triggerman. Fields of poppies and grapes stretching to the west. Sprawling desert beyond the bridge to the south. The village of a dozen or so mud homes behind his team in the north. To the east, only sand and sky.

"We shouldn't be here," Frost said into his throat mic.

"You've done this a thousand times," SFC Anderson replied. "Let's get on with it and go."

"Has the village been secured? Swept for electronics?" Frost asked.

"Swept this morning, Cap says. There's nothing."

"All they'd need is a phone," Frost said.

"Heat got you shook or what, Frost?" asked Frost's squadmate, Sergeant Peña.

"Maybe they gave you that crab premature," Specialist Dean chimed, pushing up the brim of his boonie hat from his cover two hundred feet back.

The Senior Explosive Ordnance Disposal badge, or crab, was awarded to an EOD specialist after five years of in-field experience. Frost had thought the resemblance to a crab was only passing, but he took pride in his badge regardless.

"Weren't you were supposed to be the cool one?" Peña asked. "Or were you named Frost prematurely, too?"

Frost looked back at the team. It was possible they were needling him to get him past his worry. But the unusual deployment, Anderson's haste, and what he knew now about his fireteam... Frost couldn't shake the feeling that—as they stayed safe behind the Jersey barriers while he stared down a live explosive—they were reminding him of how powerless he was.

A week ago, Dean had gotten drunk and loud. He'd decided to brag to Anderson and Peña about what he planned to do with the massive amount of cash they had earned by secretly providing security for the local warlord Hamid Zahir. Evidently, they'd been protecting Zahir's heroin shipments from ambush by rival Taliban forces for some time and earned a king's ransom for their services. Dean or Peña might have later guessed that Frost had overheard—they'd acted strangely toward him ever since. Frost, in turn, had wondered how far up the chain of command he had to go to keep himself safe if he reported them.

Frost glanced again at the scored pods of the poppy field to the west. Maybe it was one of Zahir's fields, and the team was simply roping Frost into disarming a bomb on behalf of the warlord. A bomb the Taliban had left for Zahir's men and not for coalition forces.

Frost turned his attention once more to the wheel well and the dented copper box that'd been stuck to it. Maybe there wasn't even anything in it. Maybe. But he'd be surprised if he was that lucky.

"Is there a problem with the device, Specialist Frost?"

Frost stared at the IED.

"No, there's just—something's wrong here."

"Yeah, I'd say so," Peña said. "We're in the middle of Zangaboom with our pricks hanging out waiting for you to finish stalling."

"If we'd come with some support—"

"The village was cleared of T-Men two days ago, Frost," Anderson said. "Support's just a waste of manpower. Now, are there any other operational issues you'd like to discuss, or can we get on with it?"

"Yeah, come on, man," Dean said. "Let's just do this. I got a cooler of Millers waiting for me back at base."

Frost ignored Dean, addressing Anderson. "Well, *some* T-Man rigged up the bomb I'm staring at, right?"

"Can you do this, Frost?" Anderson said, terse and acidic. "Or do I have to get one of them green EOD fuck-ups to come in here and botch this?"

"Poor kid'll probably blow his damn legs off," Dean said.

"Mm-hmm. EOD fuck-ups are a dime a dozen around here, you ask me," Peña said.

"Of course I can do this," Frost said.

"Then do it," Anderson said. "Because right now, you're one excuse away from disobeying a direct order."

Frost glanced back at his fireteam. The three looked like apparitions drifting through the heat haze, ghostly shadows waiting to ferry him to the other side.

Something moved in the mud homes behind the team, where two village elders had emerged. The men were in their sixties, perhaps, but spry and animated. They hurled curses at the team as they approached, but Frost thought they might specifically be addressing him.

"Watch your six," Frost said.

The team members looked back and saw the approaching elders. Peña turned and started towards them to try to calm them down.

"Watch their hands for a cell," Frost said.

"There ain't no cell, Frost," Anderson said.

Peña spoke to the elders in Pashto, holding his free hand out in a placating gesture. But the two men weren't interested in him. They continued to angrily shout and point at Frost, brushing past Peña and continuing down the road.

"I didn't get your answer, Specialist Frost. Can you do it?" Anderson asked again.

"What're they saying, Peña?" Frost said.

"They want you to get away from their fuckin' poppy fields," Peña said. "The hell you think they're saying?"

"Frost?" Anderson growled.

Frost looked at Anderson and turned back to the IED. Something was twisting his gut, but he couldn't be sure what. The whole scene was wrong. Just what did he think would happen here? Would a Taliban triggerman leap out of the poppy fields? Or maybe Anderson would be the one to flip the switch, tying up Frost as a loose end. Pushing him to make a decision with the knowledge that he was ignoring a direct order and risking his military career if nothing really was wrong. All of it hinged on one thing: how much did his team think he knew?

Frost took a deep breath and knelt beside the car.

"I'm preparing to examine the device," he said.

A small cyclone of dust kicked up in front of Frost. His eyes stung with sweat, his clothes soaked through beneath his suit. He reached out and grabbed the copper box with both hands, gently pulling it towards him. The magnetic hold broke free from the wheel well, and Frost carefully set the box down on the dust and gravel in front of him. He felt the underlip of the lid with his fingertips. There didn't seem to be any adhesive holding it shut. There weren't any booby traps that he could make out, just a single bolt latch without a lock.

Frost exhaled, taking a moment to gauge his luck. He sucked in one quick breath, then slid the bolt open and lifted the latch in two swift moves. Nothing happened. He breathed out again.

Inside the box nestled a DTMF receiver attached to blasting caps, the caps set inside a dozen modified M112 demolition blocks. Loose nails and screws lay all around the charges in a metal nest of shrapnel.

Frost glanced back down the road and was surprised to see that the village elders were heading straight for him, a hundred feet out now, still screaming and gesticulating.

"Hey, what the fuck?" Frost said. He rose to his feet. "Peña, Dean, restrain these guys!"

The two elders marched faster. Spittle flew from their mouths as they cursed him in Pashto. They pointed at the field and at Frost.

"Where the fuck are you guys?!" Frost said.

Pop. Pop. Blood sprayed across the front of Frost's helmet, and it took him a second to realize it wasn't his. The two elders lay crumpled on the concrete.

An eerie quiet fell over the scene. Nothing but the high whistling of the wind now. Frost looked at the dead men. Blood spilled over the desert moondust that powdered the road.

He looked back at his team. Peña and Dean lowered their carbines, still standing behind the Jersey barriers. Anderson held a cell phone.

Frost tore away from the car as fast as he could, running clumsily in his bulky bomb suit. The bomb went off. A shock wave threw Frost through the air as if he'd been hit by a semitrailer. Nails and screws ripped through the protective Nomex-Kevlar of his bomb suit. Chunks of the old Corolla shot into the air—whole fragments of the chassis, the roof, and the hood. A mushroom cloud of black smoke rose into the day, trailing flame beneath it.

Frost slammed into the ground. He gasped for air and rolled onto his back to stare up into the sky. A bell rang in his ears. He glanced down at himself. His entire left side was blackened. Most of his ABS suit had been torn away. Several large chunks of shrapnel had cut into his legs, his arms, and his torso. Smaller pieces sat embedded in his exposed skin, like cancerous diamonds burning into his flesh. His blood baked in the heat of the sun and the wreckage. He groaned loudly, the tinnitus now overtaken by the white noise of radio static coming through his earpiece.

Frost looked back to the pale sky a final time. A piece of heavy metal sheeting was plummeting back to earth. Heading straight for him. He shut his eyes and resigned himself. Soon, all was lifeless again upon that desolate terrain.

Grab your copy of *Lethal Justice* (Ion Frost Book One)
Available August 25th, 2021
www.relaypub.com/books/lethal-justice

Printed in Great Britain
by Amazon

38966073R00178